alone
at night

also by KJ Erickson

The Last Witness
The Dead Survivors
Third Person Singular

For

June Gorntizka
Carol Beglau
Dee Henehan
Helen Lifson

The four best mothers

acknowledgments

Thanks to Rachel Ekstrom, Carly Einstein, and Kenneth J. Silver for keeping all the balls in the air, and to Steve Townsend and Keith Hersey for counsel on sniper rifles and ammunition.

2003

CHAPTER

1

A door with height charts running either side of the frame is a door you should think twice about walking through.

Not that anybody does.

The last thing people going into a convenience store think about is that they've just got up close and personal with the possibility of real trouble. The kind of trouble their car alarms and home-security systems aren't going to help them avoid.

Marshall Bahr thought about trouble every time he went into a convenience store. He knew what every law enforcement officer knew: anytime a guy walked into a convenience store with a gun, anybody else in that store was one wrong move away from injury if you were lucky or death if you weren't.

Mars did more than think about trouble when he went into a convenience store. He thought about how lousy convenience-store security systems were. Not enough security cameras. Crummy video quality. Inadequate lighting. No hidden panic systems wired to police dispatchers. No security cages for employees.

And his personal favorite. A convenience-store clerk working alone at night.

Just the thought of a convenience-store clerk working alone at night made Mars grind his teeth, made bile rise in his throat.

He was counting on that bile in his throat to give him the energy he needed to be an effective cold case investigator. Energy that had been missing since he'd left his job as a special detective in the Minneapolis Police Department and joined the State of Minnesota's Cold Case Unit.

After all, it had been a convenience-store murder his first day on the job as a uniformed patrol officer that had begun his career and that had confirmed for him that law enforcement was a job worth doing.

He thought about that for a minute. About how it had felt years ago to solve that case. It hadn't just been about solving the case.

Just as much, it had been about Hannah Johnson.

Three hours and forty-three minutes into his shift on his first day as a sworn officer, he'd gotten a call to a convenience store. Robbery in progress.

What he remembered about that call was until that moment, there'd never been a time in his life when he'd been more conscious of his body. Of how hard his heart was pumping, of how hyperalert his senses were. Most surprising, how unafraid he'd been.

It was obvious when he'd pulled the squad car to an abrupt stop in the convenience store's parking lot that the robbery in progress was now an after-the-fact event. A half-dozen people, some crying, milled around outside the store. One heavyset woman came at the squad car like a banshee.

"She been shot, you hear me? You get in there, now!"

The convenience-store clerk's body was behind the counter. Mars could hear the ambulance sirens behind him as he knelt next to the woman. He'd put his hand at her neck, knowing before his fingers touched the skin he'd find no life. He lifted his gaze and found himself looking level into the eyes of a little girl.

Hannah Johnson was, in her own words, eight years and three days old. The convenience-store clerk was her babysitter and had taken Hannah with her while she worked what turned out to be her last shift as a SuperStore clerk.

Never mind that the shift was from eleven o'clock at night until seven the next morning. This was not the time to start making judgments about the way people lived their lives, especially about the way kids got tangled up in the way adults lived their lives.

Hannah Johnson had been sitting on a box behind the counter, reading a book, when the shooter had entered the store. Sitting on that box, where she'd been unseen, had probably saved her life.

Mars called Child Protection for somebody to come out until they could locate Hannah's family. He asked a woman who'd come into the store to sit with Hannah until Child Protection showed up, then he'd gotten Hannah an Orange Crush out of the cooler.

Department policy prohibited interviewing a minor without a guardian present, so before Homicide arrived and as the Crime Scene Unit collected evidence, photographed and measured the scene, Mars had started to interview other witnesses.

This did not go well. He wasn't getting any consistent stories or useful descriptions.

All the while, he could feel Hannah's eyes on him.

As a child protection worker took Hannah by the hand, Hannah and Mars made eye contact again. Mars hesitated. It made sense to leave talking to Hannah to the Homicide suits. Probably tomorrow instead of tonight.

"Just a minute," Mars had said, acting against the grain of what made sense.

He'd walked over to Hannah, putting a hand on her shoulder. "Hannah, can you tell me what you saw?"

The Child Protection worker had pulled Hannah closer to her.

"Not now, Officer. This has been traumatic. Give us a call in the morning . . ."

Hannah said, "I know. I can tell . . ."

Mars looked at the Child Protection worker, who looked down at Hannah.

"You don't have to, honey. Not now. You can talk to the policeman later."

Hannah said again, "I know. I can tell . . ."

She could and she did. She described the shooter's height relative to a marketing display next to the cash register. She described the part of the gun that had been visible over the countertop. She described a tattoo on the shooter's wrist.

"When he ran out," she said, "I went to the front door and looked. It was a tan car that had a big dent on the trunk. The numbers on the car were FXL six-one-three. I couldn't see which state."

Hannah Johnson had gotten a second can of Orange Crush for the road. She'd earned it. Everything Hannah Johnson told Mars held. They arrested the shooter in less than twenty-four hours.

All these years later, his first day on the job stood as the most satisfying, gratifying twenty-four hours in Mars's professional life.

Mars had stayed in touch with Hannah Johnson, always feeling hopeful about the human condition after he'd seen her or talked to her. Hannah's mother was available on an unpredictable basis and Hannah's uncle, with whom she'd lived when Mars had met her, had problems of his own. Hannah spent a substantial part of her life after Mars had met her moving from one relative to another, with occasional pit stops in foster care.

Mars kept track of Hannah through Child Protection Services, and when those checks revealed that she'd moved to another shirttail relation or a new foster home, he'd call her at the new home. And he always, *always,* sent her birthday cards. Mars wanted to be sure that wherever Hannah Johnson was, she knew that there was one adult in her life who stayed constant and who thought she was a special kid.

Later, when Mars began working partners with Nettie Frisch, Nettie had asked him who he was writing the birthday card to. So he'd told Nettie the story about his first day on the job.

"How do you know when her birthday is?" Nettie had asked.

"Because," Mars said, "it was three days before my first day on the job. When I asked her how old she was, she said, 'Eight years and three days.' Easy to remember."

Every once in a while, Nettie would ask him, "How's that kid— Hannah Johnson? How's she doing last you talked to her?"

The answer was that the circumstances of Hannah's life went up and down. Mostly down. None of which had prevented Hannah from graduating from high school with honors.

Hannah Johnson had been a great start to a career in law enforcement.

* * *

What Mars needed now was a great start to his cold case career.

It served both their purposes that he and Nettie decided on investigating the unsolved murders of convenience-store employees as their first major cold case initiative.

Mars wanted to bring back the bile to his professional life.

Nettie wanted to use the investigation to test the five-state criminal database she was building.

Their first pass at defining the scope of the investigation failed. They'd run cases involving the murders of convenience-store employees in the five-state region through Nettie's pilot database.

What had come out of that effort was too many cases with too few logical connections. They considered narrowing the time period, but felt narrowing the time frame ran a risk of eliminating related cases.

It had been Nettie, running the data backward and forward against a variety of criteria, who'd suggested looking at abductions of convenience-store workers. She'd given Mars three cases based on that criteria, two involving the abduction and murder of a convenience-store employee, and one that involved an abduction where no body had been found.

The perpetrators' method of operation in the three cases was similar from one case to the other. All the convenience stores were located within 150 miles of each other. All the stores were located near an interstate highway.

And all three involved a female convenience-store employee working alone at night.

A circumstance guaranteed to raise bile in Mars Bahr's throat.

They'd begun with the two cases where the abduction victims' bodies had been found.

But after two months of rereading case files, reinterviewing families, friends, and suspects—after two months of running sexual predator files to identify possible connections to the areas or the victims, after two months of retesting, reexamining forensic evidence—they knew no more than when they'd started.

"So, what do we do next?" Nettie said.

"We go with what we've got left," Mars said. "Andrea Bergstad.

7

1984. Redstone Township, Minnesota. Working on an October night at the Redstone One-Stop, never to be seen again, dead or alive."

"You're going down to Redstone?"

"I've called the guy who was chief of police in Redstone in 1984. I'm taking Chris to the airport tomorrow morning, and I'll leave from there."

"Big plans for Chris's last night at home?"

"The interment, Nettie. Tonight's the interment."

"How could I forget?"

CHAPTER
2

They carried the Styrofoam cooler between them. Mars carried a spade in his free hand. Chris Bahr carried a potted plant with his free hand.

They walked slowly across the lawn, the difference in their heights making their passage unsteady. This was the backyard of the house Mars had lived in all his married life, the house Chris had been born to, the house Mars and his ex-wife had sold four months earlier. It was the backyard where, during a deep freeze the previous January, Mars and Chris had attempted to bury Chris's cat.

The burial had failed in its stated purpose, but had achieved a higher goal. It was after the failed burial that Chris's mother, Denise, had decided to give Mars custody of Chris.

Denise had also granted Mars custody of the unburied cat.

Neither Mars nor Chris felt equal to another dead-of-winter burial, so the cat had taken up residence in the freezer in Mars's apartment. Sarge, wrapped in the same towel they'd taken him home from the vet in, had been interred in a Tupperware container. Chris had taken great care to "burp" the container, assuring Mars that doing so would remove all air and further retard decay.

"The other thing is," Chris said, "there shouldn't be any smell at all."

They had looked at each other after he'd said this, each seeing the lack of confidence in this assurance on the other's face.

The first time Chris used ice cubes from the freezer, he'd walked over to the sink and spat the cube into the drain.

"The ice cubes taste funny," Chris said.

Whether the ice cubes actually *did* taste funny was a matter of conjecture. But on a point like this, if you *thought* something tasted funny, it did. It wasn't like scientific evidence to the contrary was going to change your mind.

Within another week, Mars and Chris agreed everything they put in the refrigerator tasted funny. This included cans of Coca-Cola—probably pretty solid evidence that how things from the refrigerator tasted was a function of their imaginations. Knowing that didn't keep the Coke from tasting funny.

So, since January, the only thing in the refrigerator at Mars's apartment—and, when they moved to the condo in April, the only thing in the refrigerator at their condo—was a Tupperware container in the freezer.

It had been their plan to bury Sarge as soon as the ground had thawed in the backyard of the house Mars and Denise had bought after they were married. But then all their personal plans had accelerated. Buyers came forward for the house with a substantial cash bonus offer if they were able to take possession by April 15. Mars had a chance to buy a condo from a colleague in the police department who'd give Mars a deal if they didn't have to use a realtor. And Chris pointed out that if Denise moved during his spring break, he'd be able to go to Cleveland with her and "help her get settled."

Mars understood the subtext of Chris's suggestion and was touched. Leaving Chris was going to be wrenching for Denise. Having him make the move with her—even if it meant Chris spent only a week in Cleveland, then a couple days with Denise at Disney World before he flew back to Minneapolis—would go a long way toward making the good-byes easier.

The musical chairs dance—the house being sold, Denise moving to Cleveland, and Chris and Mars moving into their downtown condo—had begun in April, long before the ground was thawed. Now, on a hot and humid June evening, the night of the last day of school and the eve of Chris's departure for his summer visit to his mother, the two of them were in the backyard of a house they no longer owned nor lived in.

10

The new owners of the house had turned the backyard lights on and waved, but they left Mars and Chris to their business.

"Do they know what we're doing?" Chris asked. He kept his voice low.

"I had it put in the purchase agreement," Mars said. Then he recited the language he'd written himself. *"Purchasers agree that sellers may, by prior arrangement, install a planting for memorial purposes at a mutually agreed site within six months of sale date. Purchasers will have final approval of plant choice."*

"What is it, anyway?" Chris said, still whispering.

"It's what they said they wanted. A northern lights rhododendron. Whatever that is."

"Is this the right time to plant a rhododendron?" Chris said. It was the kind of thing he thought about and that Mars never did.

"Beats me," Mars said. "If it isn't, *they*"—he tipped his head toward the house—"don't know any more about rhododendrons than I do."

Chris shook his head. "I don't think this is the right time."

"Oh, *really?*" Mars said. His patience for giving Sarge a proper burial was wearing thin. "Think about it this way. What we lack in timing, we more than compensate for by the high quality of fertilizer we're putting in."

"Dad!" Chris said. But even in the fading light, Mars could tell Chris was working hard not to grin.

They dug for maybe twenty minutes before Chris took the Tupperware container out of the ice chest and removed the towel-clad body, lying it gently at the bottom of its new grave. He held his hand against the towel for moments before starting to scoop dirt on top of the towel with his hands. When there was a six-inch layer of dirt covering Sarge, Mars and Chris started shoveling dirt into the hole. Then they placed the northern lights rhododendron in the hole and finished packing dirt around the plant.

They stood for a while, looking at the plant, without saying anything. Then Chris said, "There were all kinds of things I was going to say in January. Now I can't think of anything. Except to tell Sarge that I loved him."

Mars swatted at the escalating swarm of mosquitoes that were gathering around them.

"Can't do better than that," Mars said, bending to pick up the spade. "C'mon. The bugs are getting bad. And we've got to be up early to get you to the airport and me out to Redstone Township by early afternoon."

As they drove, Mars said, "Anything you need to pick up before we get home?"

"Let's just go home," Chris said. "I want to make ice cubes."

CHAPTER

3

An hour and a half after leaving Chris at the Minneapolis-St. Paul International Airport, Mars pulled his car under a gas-station canopy, went through the motions of paying at the pump, then, as his tank gulped unleaded regular, headed into the station store.

It was just before 11:00 A.M. He had two and a half hours to drive the remaining seventy-five miles to Redstone Township to make his meeting with Sigvald Sampson, the former chief of police in Redstone.

Two and a half hours to drive seventy-five miles on a road where he'd maybe see ten cars between here and Redstone. Two and a half hours to drive seventy-five miles on a road where if you'd been able to lock your steering wheel in place, you could have read a book while you drove. Two and a half hours to drive seventy-five miles on a summer day where the biggest weather issue was a thermometer that was reading eighty-six degrees before noon.

Bottom line, he could have gone into the office for at least an hour before leaving for Redstone Township.

There were reasons he hadn't done that. None of them particularly logical, all of them specific to Mars Bahr's character and the increasing dissatisfaction he'd been feeling on the CCU as the convenience-store abduction cases failed to jell.

The truth was, spinning out the road trip to Redstone felt only marginally less dishonest to Mars than not going into the office before he left.

This moral parsing of work ethics was new to Mars, and he wasn't much good at it. Mars had to acknowledge that what drove his anxiety about what was or wasn't an honest day's work was part of a much bigger problem than the workday clock.

For most people, having a job where you had regular hours and didn't work weekends would have been an advantage. For Mars, it symbolized everything that was wrong with the job. No surprises, nothing urgent, no fresh blood that made the hairs rise on the back of your neck.

He liked and respected other members of the Cold Case Unit he'd met—maybe especially respected their ability to work doggedly, with their own brand of passion, without the urgency of a still-warm body and the chaos of raw grief. Whatever it was that allowed them to bring dedication to case facts that had long ago gone stale was a mystery Mars had not begun to solve.

"Can I help you?"

The guy behind the counter asked the question in a pointed way. He'd noticed Mars looking the place over.

Mars held his can of Coke up as he headed toward the door. "No, but thanks for asking." He meant it. How many convenience-store security tapes had he seen where a perp had been in the store looking things over in advance of actually pulling the job?

He left the convenience store, a little shocked by the flat, hard slap of heat that hit him after the store's icy interior. Back in the car, the car's air-conditioning fan blowing full blast, Mars thought through what he knew about Andrea Bergstad's 1984 disappearance.

There had never been a body. For that matter, there was no hard evidence that Andrea Bergstad had been abducted. She was working at the store, on the phone with a friend, when she said she had to go. Someone was coming in. The store's surveillance tape showed Andrea moving toward the door, talking to someone, then she was gone.

The Redstone Township's case records indicated that periodic checks had been made in public records to see if Andrea Bergstad had resurfaced. After five years those checks—or at least a record of the checks—had stopped.

Could you be sure after five years that someone was dead? Was it possible for no part of a body to surface in five years?

The answer to the first question was maybe. The answer to the second question had always been yes. And now, as Mars drove down the empty rural road toward Redstone, surrounded by thousands of acres of fields that had not been trampled by a human foot for maybe twenty years, by marshes that had grown more clogged with undergrowth each year, what seemed remarkable was that they *ever* found missing bodies.

So it hadn't bothered Mars that in one of the three cases there was no conclusive proof that an abduction or a homicide *had* taken place.

What did bother him was the absence of productive emotion. The Cold Case Unit's policy was to take cases that had been unsolved for ten years or more. After ten years, grief transformed itself into a protective emotional barrier. Families were afraid to hope. They'd told and retold their loved ones' stories so many times that the stories they told were more real to them than the long-dead victim. Mars was reminded of a movie he'd seen about a woman who'd developed an obsessive love. Years after the relationship had ended, still obsessed with the idea of the love, the woman had passed the man on the street without recognizing him. Mars couldn't stop himself from wondering if these families were to pass their loved one now, ten years or more later, there would be no recognition.

Coming to that conclusion filled Mars with guilt. These were real people, who'd suffered real losses, and those losses were greater, not less, because the murder had never been solved.

Mars was used to dealing with people who were hysterical with emotional pain, whose lives had been slammed to a halt—and often into chaos—by the horror of murder. He felt deep frustration that cold case survivors revealed nothing in their words, their expressions, their silences, that led him to a subtle understanding of the victim and the circumstances that had led to the victim's death.

At an intellectual level, he knew this was his problem. It was not the survivors' fault that time had changed their loss. His colleagues in the Cold Case Unit were not to be faulted because they *could* find meaning and purpose in the abstractions of death. It was a weakness in his own character that made fresh murder necessary for him to do his job. He didn't take any pride in that. It made him feel ashamed.

Six miles out of Redstone he followed a directional sign from the county road he'd been driving to the interstate. He wanted to take the exit from the interstate to the One-Stop Station that had been the scene of the 1984 abduction. He knew from reading case reports that in 1984 the One-Stop had been almost a mile off the freeway and that there had been no other buildings within three miles.

This area of the state had been in economic decline over the past two decades, moving downward in tandem with the farm economy. So what Mars expected as he approached the Redstone exit was that things would be pretty much unchanged from what they'd been in 1984.

He was wrong. Taking the Redstone exit, Mars drove by a Dairy Queen, the Redstone Industrial Office Park, a Country Inn, and a Kmart before he saw the One-Stop. Maybe a quarter mile beyond the One-Stop was a small cluster of tract houses.

Go figure. Every other rural community in this area of the state was dying on the vine, and the outskirts of Redstone were sprouting new life.

The development that surrounded the One-Stop meant Mars had to use his imagination to envision what the One-Stop would have looked like in 1984, just off the interstate, a couple miles from town, nothing else around, on a black October night.

"Like a shit magnet," he said out loud as he pulled into the One-Stop parking lot. The thought of seventeen-year-old Andrea Bergstad being alone inside the isolated One-Stop in the middle of the night brought the bile back.

For a moment Mars felt that exposing that risk was something worth doing. For a moment Mars felt a little of the old fire in the belly.

Mars knew the inside of the 1984 One-Stop by heart. He'd examined the police diagrams based on the surveillance video and watched the videotape four times before driving down to Redstone.

What he found now looked pretty much unchanged. The key locations within the store—the rest rooms, the aisle where Andrea

Bergstad was last visible, the checkout counter—were just where they'd been in 1984. One thing had changed. There was no wall phone back by the refrigerated cases, next to the corridor leading to the rest rooms. Very few convenience stores had indoor phones anymore. *Too convenient for the wrong kind of customer.* Cell phones had made a big difference. If you doubted that, just try to find a pay phone these days. They were going the way of typewriters and carbon paper.

The other thing that appeared unchanged were the security systems. It had been obvious coming in through the front door that the outside cameras weren't functioning; they looked like they'd been there since 1984 and out of commission for most of the time since then. Only one of the two monitors behind the counter was live.

"I'm starting to obsess on this subject," Mars muttered to himself.

The fact was, no amount of security or surveillance would have put him back here in 1984. And that's where he wanted to be. He wanted this cold case to be hot. He wanted to be the one who'd gotten the call.

He wanted to be Sigvald Sampson in 1984.

1984

CHAPTER

4

A phone that rang after midnight always meant one of two things to Sigvald Sampson.

A car accident or a domestic.

Sampson threw back the bedcovers, propelled by the inevitable rush of adrenaline that hits when a ringing phone interrupts sleep.

"Sorry to bother you," Averill Hess said, sounding uncertain, "but a couple things have come up. You may have to come out here."

Averill Hess was the most senior of the three deputies who rotated dog shift coverage on the Redstone Township Police Department. Senior or not, if you had a real problem between 11:00 P.M. and 7:00 A.M., Averill was not the guy you'd want on the job.

"What couple of things, Averill? And come out where?" Sigvald Sampson said, reaching for his pants on the chair beside the bed even before Averill Hess answered him.

"Dispatch got a call just before midnight," Averill said, breathing in short, shallow gulps. They stood inside the One-Stop service station and convenience store. Two state patrol officers had come in before Sig, and Andrea Bergstad's dad had just pulled up out front in a pickup.

"A customer called to say the store was wide-open, but there wasn't a clerk around. The dispatcher patched me through." He stopped, his eyes shifting nervously. "This deal on the call didn't sound like a problem to me. I figured Andrea was in back or whatever . . ."

"How'd you know it was Andrea working tonight, Ave?"

Sig said it flat, the question carrying more weight than the words deserved.

Averill's eyes darted faster. "I always make a drive by the One-Stop. Just to check everything's okay. Tonight I'd come by maybe, I don't know—half hour before the call came in? It was Andrea, working, alone. Everything was fine . . ."

"*Damn,*" Sig said, just under his breath. There was no excuse anyone working alone out here at night. Especially a young woman working alone at night. He'd told Tom Fiske, the store manager, there was no excuse scheduling a clerk to work alone at night.

They get shift differential pay, is what Fiske had said, like that made it all right.

Bob Bergstad came in through the front door, his hair uncombed, looking like he had a pajama top under his parka.

"What's going on, Sig?" Bergstad's eyes were bright for someone who'd gotten called from his bed in the middle of the night.

"Probably nothing." It was a reasonable answer, given what they knew right now. But it already felt soft to Sig.

"A customer called in saying the store was open, no clerk was around." Sig tipped his head toward Averill. "Ave saw Andrea here a half hour or so before we got the call saying the store was empty. Everything was fine . . ."

"That's her car out there," Bob said, tension building in his voice.

Sig nodded. "I thought so. I'm thinking a friend called, said they'd pick her up after her shift . . ."

"She was on the phone when I stopped," Averill said, sounding satisfied to back up Sig's guess.

Sig turned to Averill. "The guy who called. The customer who found the store empty. Where's he now?"

Averill tightened his mouth, then let it go loose again. He shifted from one foot to the other. "He was gone by the time I got here . . ."

Sig stared at Averill. "You asked him to stay and he left? You get his name, any ID?"

Averill wasn't meeting Sig's stare. "I didn't think it was a big deal. And I was just out here, anyways. I figured it was nothing. Like you said."

22

"Is that a no?" Sig said, not taking his eyes off Averill.

Averill swallowed hard enough that Sig saw him do it.

"No what?"

"*No* you didn't get his name and *no* you didn't get any ID on him."

"In my professional judgment it wasn't necessary," Averill said, starting to sound defensive along with nervous.

Sig changed the subject to avoid showing his anger in front of the state patrol guys and Bob Bergstad.

"Bob? Who should we be calling? Someone Andrea might have gone out with after work . . ."

Bergstad shook his head. "You know Andrea, Sig. No way she's gonna walk out of here and leave the place open. And it's a school night. She knows she'd be in trouble with me going out after she's worked a late shift . . ."

Sig said, "You never know what a kid's going to do. Even a good kid like Andrea. Right now it's more likely Andrea did something out of character than . . ." He stopped. Putting words to the alternative didn't serve any purpose at this point.

In the momentary silence, Bergstad said, "Erin Moser might know something. Mike Krause would be the other one, if he was in town. But he called just before Andrea left for work. Long distance, from school. He wasn't planning on being back until the week before Christmas. He was trying to talk Andrea into going down to the college and driving back with him then."

"Bob, you head on back home. Call everyone you can think of that Andrea might have gone with. First off, I want you to give Erin a call. I'd call her myself, but I'd probably scare her senseless if she hears my voice on the phone in the middle of the night. Then call Mike and see if Andrea said anything to him when they talked on the phone tonight that gives us an idea about where she might have gone . . ."

Bergstad nodded and started out. Then he stopped, coming back toward the cash register. "I want to check one thing," he said, going behind the counter, where he ducked down. When he straightened up, he was holding a purse.

"She never went anywhere without her purse," Bob said.

* * *

23

After Bob and the state patrol guys left, Sig turned to Averill.

"Let's take a look at the surveillance cameras. See if we can get the tapes out."

Averill found a ladder in the storeroom. They were zero for three on the first three cameras, none of which appeared to be live. The fourth camera, focused on the area in front of the cashier counter, had a lock on the cassette case. After checking out the area around the cash register without finding anything that looked like a key for the cassette case, Sig gave up.

Standing under the camera, hands on his hips, looking up, Sig shook his head in frustration. "We can't risk damaging the tape by fooling around with it now. The first thing you've got to do is get hold of Tom Fiske and get him out here to retrieve the tape. Then get the tape back to the station." He looked at Averill, who didn't give any indication of having heard what Sig had just said.

"Averill. Heads up. I've got four things I need you to do, and I want you to write them down, so we've got half a chance at you doing them right."

Color rose up Averill's neck, but he took a notebook out of his jacket pocket and flipped it open.

"Number one, I want the whole place taped off as a crime scene. The building, out to the pumps, including Andrea's car on the side of the building. Then, when you call Tom Fiske, tell him he's closed until further notice. When you talk to him, tell him we need his help in retrieving the surveillance tapes from the video system. After you talk to Fiske, I want you to sit down and write out everything—I mean everything—that was said between you and the guy who called in. You got that, Averill?"

Averill stared at his notebook. Then, with the tip of his pen, he counted down what he'd written. "You said four things, but I count only three things . . ." He looked down at his notebook again. "Unless you're counting the call to Fiske as two things. I mean, counting telling him he's closed as one thing and asking him about the surveillance tapes as another thing . . ."

Sig closed his eyes, and kept them closed. "What's important,

Averill, is that you do everything I told you to do. Count them any way you want, but do them." Then Sig opened his eyes and looked directly at Averill.

"I'm only going to ask you this next thing once, Averill."

Averill lifted his notebook again, prepared to write. Sig put his hand on the notebook, pushing it down.

"Eye contact, Averill. I want you to look me in the eye when I ask and when you answer."

Averill looked at Sig, then his eyes darted sideways before they returned to Sig's face.

"When you stopped by out here, Averill. Did you do anything—anything—that upset Andrea?"

Averill looked like he was having a hard time getting Sig's point, then he looked mad.

"Hell, no. It was just what I said. I stopped by like I always do on rounds, just to see everything was all right. I didn't even know it would be Andrea working. I didn't talk to her or nothing. She was on the phone, didn't even hang up while I was here. So I left. That was it. Jeez . . ."

"This isn't going to be hard to check, Averill. So if you have anything else to say, now is the time to say it."

"Check all you want," Averill said. "What I told you is what happened."

"I have to ask, Averill. You're still under written notice for what happened with the Sasser girl."

Averill began another denial, but Sig stopped him. "Enough already. You've said nothing happened, I'm going to take you at your word." Sig zipped up his parka and started pulling on his gloves as he walked toward the front door.

Without turning around to look at Averill, he said, "Now get started on that list of things I asked you to do."

The bad feeling that had begun with being wakened by the ringing phone stayed with Sig as he headed back to the station. Based on what he knew so far, it was way early and all kinds of facts shy of being

25

worth worrying about. But early and shy of facts don't hold up against a bad feeling in your gut. Which was exactly what Sig had. A bad feeling in his gut.

Not that he had all that much experience with serious crime. He'd been on the Redstone police force for thirty-one years, the last eleven years as chief. The only homicide he'd had in all of that time had been a domestic. A husband slamming his wife's head against a wall. She was unconscious when Sig showed up, never came to, and Sig had arrested her husband on the spot. He'd gotten a full confession from the husband within an hour of the arrest, and the husband took up residence at Stillwater State Prison within ninety days of the murder. An investigation like that, a fellow doesn't need to waste time and energy worrying about how his gut feels.

Nothing like what his gut told him he was up against starting tonight.

CHAPTER

5

Erin Moser had forgotten her gloves, so she drove toward the township police station with her sweater sleeves pulled out from under her jacket, down over the heels of her hands. The wool against the steering wheel gave her no grip and the wheel kept sliding away from her, keeping her on edge, where she'd been since getting the call from Andrea's dad.

It wasn't just the call from Andrea's dad, coming in the dark, an hour after Erin had fallen into a thin, anxious sleep, that had put her on edge. It was that the call hadn't surprised her.

"Andrea!" she'd said as soon as the call woke her. Even in the fuzzy instant between sleep and consciousness, Erin knew the call was about Andrea. She knew the call was about Andrea because she'd been on the phone with Andrea only hours before, and the way the call ended had been wrong. The way the call ended had left Erin with a knot in her stomach. The way the call ended had left Erin half expecting a call in the middle of the night.

As Erin drove, she replayed every word of the call in her mind.

"So, are you going to tell me what's going on?"

"Not now, Erin. Not on the phone. Maybe tomorrow. We could drive out to the quarry after school and talk."

"Andrea! Come on. You're making me nuts. Is it about you and Mike?"

Andrea made a noise that was almost, but not quite, a laugh. "Not about Mike. Definitely not about Mike."

Erin pushed. "Okay, if it's not about Mike, is it about . . ."

"Don't say it. Not on the phone."

"Andrea, I can't stand this. You've got to give me a hint."

A pause. "Oh, shit. It's that dumb dick Averill."

"Ignore him. I heard the Sassers are gonna sue the township over what happened to Kim. Can you believe him pulling her over and doing a pat down?"

"Believe that Averill would do something dumb? How hard is that?"

A voice in the background, then Andrea said, "Thank God. He's gone—hang on—you know that old Mel Carter song we like, 'Hold Me, Thrill Me, Kiss Me'? . . . it's coming on KZ, I'm gonna turn the sound up."

"The song you liked," Erin said to nobody.

"Can you hear it?" Andrea asked when she came back on the line.

"God, you must have maxed the volume, it's like I'm there."

Andrea sang along, sounding like she used to sound, happy and full of energy.

"I can't believe how retro this song is," Erin said. "I remember when you started liking this song. It never was about Mike, was it?"

Andrea stopped singing.

"You know what else? Just now, while you were singing? It's the first time you've sounded happy, sounded like yourself since . . ."

"Don't say it, Erin."

"You said you were going to give me a hint about what's going on. Before Averill showed up."

"You asked me to give you a hint."

"You can tell me something."

A long silence, then, "Erin, this is really serious. Anything I tell you, you've got to promise—you've got to swear—that you'll never, not ever tell anyone. And if you do, I'll say you're lying and I'll never talk to you again. I mean it, Erin . . ."

"You don't even have to ask. You know I'd never say anything . . ."

"Okay, all I'll say right now is that I've made a big decision. I mean a really big decision. Oh, wait . . ."

"What?"

"Somebody's here. I've gotta go."

"A customer? Did Averill come back? I'll stay on the line until he goes. I hate it, you being out there all by yourself."

"Not a customer. Not Averill. I wish it was a customer—even Averill. But it's not. Gotta go. I'll talk to you tomorrow."

And then, a dial tone.

And now, hardly three hours later, Erin Moser was on her way to the Redstone Township Police Department, churning in her mind what she should say about Andrea. She knew what she couldn't say—couldn't say because Andrea wouldn't want her to and couldn't say because . . . because, in fact, Erin didn't know anything. Not for sure. Somebody else might have talked about what they thought was going on, what they'd suspected since summer. But Erin wouldn't do that. She wouldn't do that because it might not be true. And if it was true, it could be bad for Andrea.

"But what if," Erin said out loud, "Andrea's really in trouble?"

Erin's imagination failed her then. She couldn't imagine how telling would help Andrea. But she could imagine how telling would hurt—hurt Andrea and a lot of other people, besides.

She couldn't risk that, not without knowing for sure that telling would help.

CHAPTER

6

Walking into the quiet station, past the dispatcher, Sig Sampson's gut felt worse, not better. There was something in the air with this situation, something that told him what he was up against would likely get a whole lot worse before it got better.

Opening the door to his office, his worst fears solidified. Erin Moser sat in a corner chair, huddled in her parka. Sig's best hope before he'd walked into his office was that Andrea was with Erin. Erin's presence put that hope in an early grave.

More than her presence, it was how Erin looked that worried Sig. How you'd expect Erin would look in a deal like this was scared. Scared and something else you'd see with teenagers when they got involved in something more dramatic than what their daily lives offered. They'd be a little wired to be at the center of something big. Wired until the drama got real and pain set in.

How Erin looked wasn't like that. How Erin looked was defensive, tight.

He sat down in the chair behind his desk without taking his jacket off. So it was the two of them, sitting there in heavy winter coats at two o'clock in the morning.

Erin caught Sig's look, then started slowly pulling the zipper up and down on her jacket.

"Averill said Andrea was on the phone when he did a security check around eleven-thirty. You talked to Andrea tonight, Erin?"

Erin didn't stop pulling on the zipper, but she nodded. "It was me on the phone when Averill was at the One-Stop."

His throat tightened. "Andrea said Averill was there?"

"What Andrea said was, 'Oh, shit. It's that dumb dick Averill.'"

Sig let it pass. "That's all? You didn't hear them talk to each other?"

"I said to Andrea, 'Ignore him.' Then I heard someone talking in the background. All Andrea said after that was, 'Thank God. He's gone.'"

He could imagine the scene. Andrea on the store phone next to the pop coolers on the back wall. Averill coming in through the front door, asking Andrea if everything was all right. Andrea not even taking the phone away from her ear, just waving Averill off.

For the first time since the ringing phone had wakened him, Sig drew an easier breath.

"We're trying to figure out where Andrea might have gone, Erin. She say anything to you that helps us out here?"

Erin took time, then shook her head. Not looking at Sig.

"She didn't say anything that made you think she had plans after work?"

Erin didn't say anything, but she looked like she was thinking about Sig's question. He gave her time, watching her mind work by keeping his eyes on her face. After what must have been a minute, he repeated the question, his voice soft but with more emphasis.

"Erin, did Andrea say anything about where she might have gone?"

Erin sat up straighter and stopped playing with her zipper. She was a smart kid and she knew that Sig Sampson thought she was holding back. She had to say something. Something, but not too much. Nothing about the person coming in not being a customer. She tells Sig that, and everybody Andrea ever knew goes on the rack.

"Right before she hung up, a couple of minutes after Averill was there, she said someone was coming in, she had to go."

"Did she say if it was Averill coming back?"

Erin shook her head. "I asked if it was Averill coming back, and she said no. Then she hung up."

"Erin. Do you remember the exact time Andrea said someone was coming in, when she said she had to go?"

Erin thought back. Remembering the radio. "I could hear the radio at the One-Stop. KZLT. There was a song, a Mel Carter song, 'Hold Me, Thrill Me, Kiss Me,' I think the title is. That was on just before Andrea hung up. You could check their play list."

"You could hear that, on the phone?"

"Andrea loved that song. It came on while we were talking, and she turned the volume way up. And she was singing along . . ."

"That was what—within five minutes of when Averill left?"

"Maybe less. Maybe a minute or two."

Sig nodded. He could match Averill's patrol log against KZLT's play list to get a handle on when Andrea had said someone was coming in to the One-Stop. Having Erin provide a time meant Averill had a backup to his account, giving Sig a bit more peace of mind about Averill.

"That's helpful. Did she say anything about where she might be going after work—I mean, maybe not saying anything specific, but just something that now, when you think about it, might mean she didn't plan on going home tonight?"

Erin weighed a response. "The one thing she said was that she'd see me tomorrow—I mean, today. Before that, we talked about going for a ride out to the quarry after school."

Sig kept his eyes on Erin's face. He'd seen Erin Moser around town since she'd been a toddler. A smart kid from the first, getting smarter by the minute. Andrea, she was a bright kid, a beauty, but Erin had something else. A seriousness, a cynicism behind a big brain that meant she was a force to be reckoned with, even at seventeen.

Sig didn't have any reason to doubt what Erin had told him. What he felt certain of, his eyes still on her face, was that she wasn't telling him anywhere near everything she knew.

"That's it? Nothing that made you think maybe she had plans after work?"

Erin didn't hesitate before she said, "No. Nothing about going anywhere after work. Just about after school today."

Sig noted how quickly Erin had answered the question. A pattern

32

was emerging. What Sig thought was happening with Erin was that she hesitated answering when she was holding back.

"How'd Andrea seem to you, Erin? Anything bothering her? I don't mean just what she said tonight. I mean lately. Any problems that might be bothering her?"

Another hesitation. This time longer than before.

Erin shrugged, but she didn't look at Sig. "I don't know. She was tired. She's been working way too much. Plus school, dance line, stuff like that." She shrugged again, but didn't say anything more.

So, Sig thought, *something was bothering Andrea.* He considered pushing, but didn't think pushing would work with a kid like Erin. What he thought was the best way to handle Erin was to let her decide when she wanted to talk.

"Sometimes, Erin, you think of things when you don't expect to. You leave here, you're driving home, and you think of something, you call me. Anytime, day or night, you think of something, you call."

Erin nodded, then started to play with the zipper on her jacket again. "That's it? I can go now?"

Sig stood, giving Erin a slap on her back. "That's it for now. We're both tired. Go home and get some sleep. Just remember. You think of something, you call. Okay?"

Sig stood stock-still for minutes after Erin left. Considering whether to press on until morning or go home and try to get some sleep. At one point, he started to pull his jacket off. Then the dispatcher stuck her head in the office and gave him a message from Averill. Tom Fiske wouldn't be available until tomorrow morning. So there was no chance of their having the surveillance tape before then.

That pretty much decided Sig. He pulled his jacket back on. When he'd need energy was in another four, five hours. After daylight, when people were around that needed to be talked to. There wasn't all that much he could do now, and it wouldn't do anybody any good if he was pooped when he needed to be in high gear.

So he left the station, giving a wave to the dispatcher, saying he'd be back at seven, and headed home.

CHAPTER
7

Home. There was an idea for you. It hadn't been home since his wife had died three years earlier. He never really settled in there anymore, and sleep on a normal night could be tough to come by. Tonight was going to be tricky. Sig figured he'd take his shoes off, turn on the TV in the den, and crank the recliner back. The strategy was to convince his brain he didn't want to sleep. Then he'd have a shot at drifting off.

It happened just like that. Except after being asleep for less than an hour, two words pierced his consciousness and woke him with a start. He pushed the recliner lever and sat straight up.

Case Theory.

The words rattled in his brain, like a pinball spinning crazily through a maze. Sig stood, shaking his leg, which had gone numb in his sleep.

Case Theory.

Sig walked from the den, lit only by the light of the TV screen, toward the kitchen to make coffee. His leg and his memory started to come back to life as he walked. The words began to come into focus, taking him back through the years to a dreary hotel conference room in St. Paul.

What he remembered was sitting at a table, alongside maybe thirty other law enforcers from all over Minnesota, facing a lectern. A three-ring binder open in front of him to a tab divider labeled "Techniques of Criminal Investigation."

At the lectern, a deadly dull guy in a blue suit read each of the

34

words under the topic in the three-ring binder. An overhead projector replicated the binder's words behind the lectern.

What Sig remembered thinking in that St. Paul conference room was that nothing he'd been told in the two-day, in-service training session had anything to do with law enforcement in Redstone Township. Looking around him at the other attendees, most of them from rural Minnesota communities, he'd guessed they felt pretty much the same. Several were sleeping, a couple were doodling, all of them from time to time exchanged glances that expressed indifference or disdain.

But now, those two words, spoken by the guy in the blue suit, on the page in the three-ring binder, and projected on the screen behind the lectern, came back to Sig with force.

Case Theory.

The words had force because Sig knew case theory was what he hadn't been paying attention to since getting Averill Hess's call hours earlier. And not having a case theory was part of what was keeping Sig's gut tight.

While the coffee perked, Sig sat down at the kitchen table. He picked up a pen that sat in a jar along with a bottle opener, a six-inch ruler, and God knew what else in the bottom of the jar. Then he turned over a utility bill envelope and started to consider all the options about what might have happened to Andrea Bergstad.

The theories that came to mind began with a benign statement of possibility. Like, *somebody Andrea knew.* In seconds, Sig's imagination took him from benign to malignant. A prank gone wrong. A carload of teenage boys—drunk?—driving by the One-Stop, seeing Andrea inside, illuminated, alone.

Hey, it's Andrea Bergstad . . .

She alone?

The car stops, idling while they watch the station from the road.

Man, wouldn't you like to . . .

Let's get her!

Laughter. Someone socks the kid who says it on his arm.

Just take her for a ride, the kid says, sounding more serious.

Put her in the backseat, another kid says.

Take turns with her in the backseat, someone else says . . .

Sig shook his head hard and rubbed his face to wipe the image from his mind. If it was a prank, it had to have gone wrong in the same way Sig imagined it. Because if it hadn't gone wrong, Andrea would be home by now.

Sig got up from the kitchen table and walked over to the wall phone.

"I'm guessing you're not asleep," he said when Bob Bergstad picked up. "You hear from Andrea yet?"

He got the answer he expected. "And Mike," Sig said. "You reach him?"

It would have to be checked, of course, but what Bob told Sig pretty much put Mike in the clear. First off, Bob reached Mike at his college dorm, which was a good six-hour drive from Redstone. If phone records verified that Mike had called Andrea before she left for work, from his dorm, there was no way Mike could have driven to Redstone and back to his dorm between the time he'd called Andrea and the time Bob reached him at the dorm. Even without the phone records, Mike said he'd played cards with three guys at the dorm from the time he'd gotten off the phone with Andrea until an hour before Bob called. That would be easy to check.

The answer Bob gave to Sig's next question was also what Sig was expecting.

"She didn't say anything to Mike about going somewhere after work," Bob said. "Mike said he'd call her again after her shift, and she told him not to. Said she was really tired and wanted to get to bed as soon as she was off work. That was it."

Bob gave Sig a quick rundown on others he'd reached. Nobody had any idea where Andrea might be. "Everybody's as sure as I am she wouldn't have just walked off, leaving the station wide open."

Sig heard a tremble in Bob's last words. The impossible was starting to look like a probable. Circumstances were starting to justify the way Sig had felt about this situation from the first.

It didn't make any sense to share his pessimism with Bob. "Get to bed," Sig said. "I'm developing some angles that we can follow in the morning. I'll need you bright-eyed and bushy-tailed first thing."

He stood at the phone for a while after hanging up.

Then he said, "Shit," and pushed himself away from the wall and back toward the table.

The second case theory that came to mind gave him no more comfort: *Andrea had been taken by a stranger.*

Why that would have happened was something tailor-made to tighten your gut. There was only one reason to take Andrea, and a couple ways it could have happened with a stranger. Somebody came by the One-Stop planning to get gas, a candy bar, to clean out the cash register—whatever—and decided when they saw Andrea that she was what they wanted. A small but somehow more ominous variation on the same theory was that a stranger came to the One-Stop planning to take Andrea. Sig had no firsthand experience with the type of person who'd do that, but what he did know, secondhand, made him light-headed with fear.

"I'm not up to this," he said out loud, dropping his pen on the table. The sense of purpose that writing down case theories had given him had been dissipated by the reality of what might have happened.

"I need to call the BCA," he said, a small surge of hope reasserting itself. The State Bureau of Criminal Apprehension had technical and staff resources that could support a rural police department with limited experience handling a major criminal investigation.

A major criminal investigation? Is that what he was dealing with? He heard himself on the phone to the BCA, saying that a seventeen-year-old girl had left her job at a gas station convenience store and he was concerned she'd been kidnapped or worse. No, there was no evidence of violence at the scene. Any reason to suspect the missing girl might be troubled about something? Erin Moser's hesitation when Sig had asked her the same question about Andrea came back to him, fresh and disturbing. Hearing Erin's response, Sig had felt certain something had been troubling Andrea. Sig tells the BCA that, and they're going to give him the old, take-two-aspirin-and-call-me-in-forty-eight-hours response. And he wouldn't blame them if they did.

Still. It wouldn't hurt to call the BCA first thing in the morning. Get it on record that this one felt wrong, had felt wrong, from the first. And who knew. Maybe they wouldn't blow him off. Maybe somebody at the BCA had a gut as sensitive as Sig's.

He used the three simple theories of the case to make out a list of the things that needed to get done first. Top of the list was to view the One-Stop's security tapes. Check with Averill about any carloads of boys he might have run into while he was on patrol last night. Check with school counselors about any guys that had been hassling Andrea. Sig thought about the last thing. Give Erin a call about that, as well. She'd know as much as the school counselors, and it would give Erin another chance to talk about whatever it was she hadn't been saying.

And call the BCA. Give it a shot. If nothing else, he could ask for help in identifying any sexual predators in the area who used an MO that involved abducting young women from workplaces.

The back-of-the-envelope list made Sig feel some better. He considered trying to sleep, then decided on a shower instead.

He was back at the station before the sun was up.

CHAPTER

8

Shortly before 10:00 A.M. Sig sat in a dark conference room facing a TV screen. Dark was necessary, because the tape quality in normal light was shit. Tape quality in the dark was also shit, but in a dark room, images that in daylight were at best impressionistic blurs became vaguely recognizable abstractions.

Sig ground his teeth as he watched the screen. "This is the best quality you can buy, Tom? Damn near worthless from where I'm sitting."

Tom Fiske fiddled with the VCR, timing it to begin from the time Andrea's shift had begun at the One-Stop. "I don't make any decisions about the security equipment," he said, backing away from the monitor. "Corporate sends us the equipment, gives us installation specs, ships out new tapes on a schedule."

Fiske stood in front of the monitor for a moment, holding the remote in his right hand, fast-forwarding the gray fuzz until the tape clock reached 17:55:38. Then he clicked PLAY on the remote.

"Okay," he said. "Andrea's shift started at 6:30 P.M. You see her coming into camera range four minutes and twenty-two seconds ahead of that. She goes over to the register and talks to Jen—oh, I forget her last name—who worked the shift just before Andrea."

"Hold it for a minute," Sig said. "This angle we're looking at. This is from the camera in the corner at the back of the store, back by the pop coolers? Looks like it's aimed at the cash register. The other cameras you've got—two outside facing the parking lot and another

39

one inside the store at the front, catty-corner from the camera that's giving us the angle we're getting now—together those four cameras are going to give us full coverage of the store?"

It was too dark for Sig to tell what was happening with Tom Fiske's face in response to Sig's question, but the silence that followed was not encouraging.

His voice low, just a bit more than a mumble, Fiske said, "What we figured we needed was coverage on the cash register. We're gonna get robbed, that's where the action'll be."

Sig said, "What you're saying is the other three cameras aren't going to give us anything? You didn't have the other three cameras filming last night?"

"You have any idea how much maintenance there'd be on four cameras? The two outside cameras, especially. We had those going when we opened the One-Stop three months ago, but they never did us any good. We've had some problems with no-pays at the pumps. Nothing we got off the cameras was any help. You know that, Sig. We sent those tapes over to the station, and you guys told us they weren't any good."

"What we said when you sent the tapes over on the no-pays was that cameras mounted on the building weren't going to do anything for you at the pumps. We told you to mount cameras under the pump canopy. All of which is beside the point. No-pays at the pumps aren't what we're talking about here, Tom. For the problem we've got with Andrea Bergstad, I want to see somebody walking in through the front door at the One-Stop. If you'd had the outside cameras working last night, we'd have got something on that. Or from the camera over in the front corner. This angle, at best, we're going to get a profile of anyone who took Andrea last night."

"Don't jump to conclusions," Fiske said. "Let's run it and see what we've got before you start bitching about the tapes."

What they had was worse than Sig's lowest expectations. Even Fiske knew it was bad.

When Andrea was behind the counter, right next to the cash register, you'd maybe recognize her. Maybe. If you *knew* her, *maybe* you'd recognize her.

40

Problem was, the only time Andrea was behind the counter, next to the cash register, was when a customer came in to pay for gas or buy something. Then Andrea would appear from wherever she'd been in the store—in the bathroom, stocking shelves, sweeping floors—and ring up the purchase.

What you'd see of the customers was usually the back of their heads. Every once in a while a customer would come to the counter from just the right angle, and you'd get a bit of profile. But the profile wasn't sharp. The best you could get was male or female and a rough sense of height, dark or light hair. Sometimes not that.

Sig pulled his chair closer when the tape clock approached the time Averill had said he'd stopped by the One-Stop. There was no sign of Andrea on the tape except for a brief moment when a hand flashed out from the bottom corner of the picture frame.

"Back to the hand in the lower left corner," Sig said. "Then freeze it."

The hand hung suspended in the air. A girl's hand? Could have been. What Sig thought was that the position of the hand was consistent with Andrea being on the phone, back by the pop coolers, talking to Erin. Then Averill had come in—the time was right for that—and Andrea waved him off, her hand flashing into the camera's range.

So far, this was the most useful bit of information that had come from the tapes. It didn't tell Sig anything he didn't already know, but it confirmed the facts that he did know based on what Erin and Averill had told him.

The tape rolled on for maybe another minute when, suddenly, Andrea came out of the corner of the frame and walked, fast, toward the cash register. She went behind the counter, reaching up for something. What she was reaching for you couldn't tell from the tape. Then she turned around and came back in the direction of the phone, disappearing once again into the frame's lower right corner. Every now and again you'd see her hand for a moment. Once, her elbow popped out, as if she'd lifted her arm and put her hand on her head.

Moments passed with nothing but the empty store—one row of shelves, one end of an aisle, the counter—visible on the monitor. The only movement on the monitor was the rapid flicker of the clock on the screen's lower right corner, tracking seconds, minutes, and hours as they passed.

And then, abruptly, Andrea came into view again. Moving hesitantly toward the cash register, but with her eyes in the direction of where the front entrance would be. Was she talking to someone? Impossible to say. For the briefest moment, she glanced to her right, like she was checking the shelf, her head disappearing, as if she'd bent down.

The last image of Andrea was as she moved out of the camera's range. She could have been going toward the door—or not.

They rewound the tape, watching the last images of Andrea over and over. Not knowing any more after the fifth rerun than they'd known the first time.

"Pick up from where we see her for the last time," Sig said. "I want to see who comes into the store after this."

Again, minutes passed when all to be seen was the narrow view of the store's interior. Until, exactly twelve minutes and thirty-nine seconds after their last view of Andrea, a woman came into the frame. She'd been moving quickly, but stopped as if pulled back on a short leash. She looked around, her mouth moving, then she waited, as if for a response, looked down, then turned heel and left.

In seconds she was back, followed by a man. They both walked toward the camera, the top of the man's head staying at the bottom of the frame after the woman disappeared. He must have been five, six inches taller than Andrea—just enough taller to keep the top of his head in the frame.

"He's on the phone," Sig said. "He's calling the station to say there's no one in the store."

Less than two minutes passed before the woman came back into the frame, and the two of them left, the man ahead, the woman behind, the woman looking back over her shoulder, dipping out of sight for a moment, and then she was gone.

They watched the tape until Averill came into the One-Stop, looking pie-eyed and confused. He walked aimlessly around the store, ducking out of sight, moving out of camera range, looking straight up at the camera every now and then.

When Sig saw his own image enter, he told Fiske to stop the tape. He stood and stretched, shaking his head in frustration. "Damn it, Tom. There's no excuse not having full video coverage on the store. What we've got here is good for pretty much nothing. At best I'm going to be able to pull some images to help us find the couple that came into the store and phoned in. *Maybe* the images will be good enough for that . . ."

Fiske tried hard to look like the injured party. "For what we get out of those cameras there's just no way that it pays to have four running. A deal like this comes along how often? We're supposed to do a couple hours' maintenance every day on a surveillance system because once in a blue moon some teenager is going to go missing?"

Sig's frustration turned to anger. "You guys have a formula for how many hours of maintenance you are willing to do per human being at risk? The cameras aren't all of it. I told you that when we were doing security planning before you opened. I said no one working alone at night. Especially no woman working alone at night. You have a woman working alone and you just add one more motive for some lowlife to commit a crime. The other thing I said was a silent alarm with a direct connection to our station. That and a bulletproof security cage for your clerks . . ." Sig held up both hands as Fiske started to interrupt him. "Okay. I know that isn't foolproof. But it's something. I told you, you put in a security cage, we'll provide shift change coverage for you. Anything I asked you to do you could have paid for by selling milk for an extra ten cents a gallon. People picking up stuff at the One-Stop, they could care less what they're paying. They're at the One-Stop because it's convenient. They're at One-Stop because they can get the milk when they pay for their gas, not because it's the cheapest place to buy milk." Fixing his eyes on Fiske, he said, "It's why it's called a convenience store, right?"

Fiske met Sig's stare. "Something else you said. You said you'd have your patrol cars out at the One-Stop at least twice a night. And that you'd make sure they came on an irregular schedule, so anyone watching the place wouldn't know what to expect. Averill Hess always came the same time. Just before a shift change, so he could hit on whoever was working."

43

Sig stood, silent. *Damn Averill. Damn himself for letting the situation with Averill go on as long as it had.*

"I hadn't known that. If it's true, I'll see it changes."

Fiske sensed he'd gained some ground, and he moved fast to take the advantage. "You've had me closed down since after midnight. That's costing me plenty. When are you going to let us get back in business?"

As Sig left the room he said, "As soon as you've got all four security cameras up and running."

Sig took time to cool down before he called the BCA. The last thing he wanted to sound like when he called was some off-the-wall maniac.

He'd given careful consideration to his approach. He figured he'd start with the request for assistance in identifying sexual predators who might be suspects in a case like this. If he got a sympathetic response on that, he'd level with the BCA, tell them while he didn't have a lot of facts to support his concerns, all his instincts were flashing red. Would it be possible to get some technical and staff assistance to make sure Redstone was doing everything that should be done on a case like this?

The call went better than expected, even if the BCA didn't offer to send a team down to Redstone right off. They promised to fax him a sexual predators list before close of business and reviewed on the phone everything Sig had done to date.

"Sounds like you're on track," the fellow said. "Guess it feels a little to me like the kid did a runner. That she'll turn up in a day or two. I know what you're saying about her being a good kid and all, but teenagers . . ."

"Well, I suppose that's what my head says, too. Just that my gut feels real different."

The fellow at the BCA hesitated. "I'd never tell a police officer to disregard his gut. That's for sure. But if we sent a team out every time an officer in the state twitched, we'd blow our budget in a week."

He hesitated again. "What you can do that might help us both out. The kid that's gone missing. Andrea. She a good-looking kid?"

44

"A beauty," Sig said. "And smart. National Honor Society last year."

"Photogenic is what counts," the fellow from the BCA said.

"Like I said, a beauty."

"Okay. You need to do this anyway. Wire us the best photograph you've got on her. If there are home videos, send those up by messenger. Send us all the case details as you've got them. Any personal details that'll suck the media in, be sure to include that. I'll have our public information folks put a media alert together. We'll handle it as a missing persons case and see the information gets posted across the state. If it's a slow news day and this kid is as good-looking as you say, we'll get some media interest. That's the way it works. If she really has been taken, you need to use everything you've got."

Sig nodded as he wrote down what he needed to do.

"One other thing. Does the kid's family have any connections to elected officials?"

The question came at Sig from left field, so he had trouble focusing on an answer.

"The reason I ask. A call from her family to your state legislator might help. Might motivate someone over at the capitol to give us a call. We get a call from a state legislator, it makes a difference. Same with media coverage. Media picks this up, makes it easier for us to put some resources in. It shouldn't, but that's the way the world works."

After Sig hung up with the BCA he called Bob Bergstad. He brought Bob up-to-date on what they were doing, then asked a question.

"Am I right remembering you were Redstone County Republican chairman a few years back?"

"You bet," Bob said. "Still on the party's statewide steering committee." His voice was energized by the opportunity to give a positive answer to Sig's question, by the prospect of a distraction from the void of Andrea's absence. He said he'd call the state party chairman as well as a couple state legislators he knew as soon as he was off the phone with Sig. "Hell," he said, "I've organized fund-raisers for all the state's Republican office holders. Our current congressman included. Some of them even met Andrea at one point or another. She helped out on a lot of door knocks and literature drops. Got some of her friends to help, too. I'll call all of them."

When Sig hung up he felt like some of the weight of the case had been lifted from his shoulders.

It was just his gut that still felt tight.

CHAPTER

9

The first evidence that the BCA's media strategy had worked came a day later when a reporter from Channel Six in the Twin Cities showed up. In hours, a crew from another station arrived, and by late afternoon Sig had had calls from the *St. Paul Pioneer Press* and the *Minneapolis Star-Tribune*.

It was disconcerting to Sig to have the Twin Cities reporters right in front of him, in the flesh. Redstone got its television news from stations in Sioux Falls, South Dakota, and the Twin Cities. Sioux Falls was closer by seventy-five miles, but Redstone being in Minnesota, most people watched Twin Cities television. So the reporters turning up were all familiar faces.

Their involvement in the case felt like a point of no return to Sig. For one dreamlike, irrational moment, it felt to him like he'd made a decision that changed what had happened. It felt like if they'd never got the media involved, the case would be less real. But with television crews camping out in the station, with the phone ringing constantly in response to what people were seeing on the news, reading in their daily newspaper, there was no denying that Andrea's disappearance was anything less than real. The *Minneapolis Star Tribune* carried an article on the front page of the Metro-State section on the fourth day of the investigation. It was short, with no jump to a back page, but it included Andrea's photo and sketches of the two individuals believed to have phoned the police from the One-Stop the night of Andrea's disappearance. The *Strib* article was the first media source to publicize

47

an offer from the district's congressman for a $25,000 reward for information leading to Andrea's safe return.

The reward offer annoyed Sig on three counts. Mostly because it was a grandstand gesture offered by a pol who aspired to be the next junior senator from Minnesota. Sig saw it as a crass, self-interested move to use a tragedy for political gain. Then there was the fact that Sig had been a lifelong Democratic Farmer-Labor voter and the congressman in question was a right wing Independent Republican.

Sig's subjective judgments about the reward offer aside, a more practical complaint was that the reward increased the number of nutcase calls, but didn't produce anything substantial.

All they got that was even worth following up on was an elderly couple who said they'd seen a young woman running across a field a quarter of a mile from the One-Stop around the time Andrea had gone missing. Two people swore they'd seen Mike Krause's car in town the night of the disappearance. A guy who'd been at the One-Stop early in Andrea's shift called because there'd been a car sitting outside the One-Stop when he'd gone in and the car was still there when he left—even though he hadn't seen any other customers in the One-Stop.

None of these reports could be verified and under questioning, all of the witness reports had serious gaps. Only the wife had seen a figure running near the One-Stop and the wife, who was seventy-seven, had cataracts and couldn't give any specific details about the figure she thought she'd seen running. And neither the husband nor the wife were sure about the time they'd seen someone running.

As it happened, Mike Krause hadn't taken his car back to school with him. Part of why he'd wanted Andrea to drive up to his college before Christmas vacation was to bring the car and drive him back. And Mike's alibi had checked out, solid as steel.

The fellow who'd been suspicious about the car parked at the One-Stop couldn't give a detailed description of the vehicle. When Sig questioned him about Andrea's car, the witness didn't rule out that that was the vehicle he'd seen.

Most frustrating to Sig was that neither the media coverage nor the reward had gotten them closer to the couple who'd come into the One-Stop and made the call to the station. That made Sig nervous. Why would someone take the time and trouble to call in and then not respond to efforts to question them? The only reason Sig could come up with was that there was a reason they didn't want to be connected to Andrea's disappearance.

Sig would have given a lot to know what that reason was.

For the next week Sig slept only when not getting sleep interfered with his ability to think. He personally interviewed every student in Andrea Bergstad's class, every teacher she'd had since junior high, and all the employees at the One-Stop. Nothing he found out in the process gave him anything substantial to follow up.

He had spent the first days of the investigation dreading calls and visits from Bob Bergstad. The effort it took to be encouraging and supportive—without giving false hope—drained Sig. Now, well into the second week of the investigation, Sig suddenly realized he hadn't heard from the Bergstads since they'd talked about Bob making contacts with elected officials.

Bob and Ruth Bergstad were naturally reserved people who had little interest in sharing their problems with the public. They had cooperated with the media during the investigation because they knew it was their best chance to find Andrea. But it had been hard for them.

For anybody who'd known them, how hard it had been showed on their faces, in how they stood, in their voices. Some folks thought the Bergstads were cold people. Sig thought they were—always had been—people who didn't know how to show emotion to each other, much less people they'd never met.

People who'd known the Bergstads for years also knew that Andrea's disappearance was not their first piece of bad luck. They had gone, in the space of a couple of years, from being an influential family who'd been active participants in the community's civic and political life into a family that had been stripped of material well-being and social position.

Bob had been a farmer, a cautious man who hadn't been seduced by the temptation of expensive new equipment that had buried many farmers under a crushing burden of debt. But *land* was a siren song that proved irresistible. Land was more than a necessary component to his life's occupation. Land, and the possession of land, was spiritual, it went to the root of why Bob Bergstad was a farmer.

When two sections of land adjacent to Bob's property had come onto the market, Bob had taken on a heavy debt load to finance the purchase. He'd had no trouble getting a loan. Those were the days of asset-based lending, and asset-based lending had been fueled by soaring land prices.

When land prices took a precipitous fall, anyone who'd borrowed based on the value of their land fell, too. Including Bob Bergstad. He'd had to sell the two sections he'd borrowed to buy and almost half of the property he'd owned outright. What was left was not enough to support his family. He'd taken on odd jobs in town and he'd helped out on other farms during planting and harvest seasons. There were many others who'd suffered losses of both money and dignity in this far-spread decline of the farm economy, but none in Redstone Township who'd fallen as far as Bob Bergstad.

People became uncomfortable around him, not because of anything he said or did, but because he had become a doppelganger of bad luck. A ghostly reminder that good fortune and present blessings were not to be taken for granted, not to be trusted. He and Ruth became increasingly isolated, more and more separate from the life of the community at whose center they had once lived.

Ruth Bergstad's problems went even deeper. She'd had several miscarriages before Andrea had been born. After the birth she had veered into religious fanaticism. In another time, in another place, her problems might have been recognized as postpartum depression. In a rural community in the early 1980s, she was left alone.

Her fanaticism intensified, governed by a mystical sort of fundamentalism that was recognizable only to her, ruled by a God only she knew. During the years that Bob had been active in Republican politics, she'd organized a group of fellow Right to Life supporters to lobby at the state legislature in St. Paul. But even with a shared purpose, the group fell apart under the impossible pressure of Ruth's rigid view of morality. For a time she traveled to Sioux Falls or to Omaha to meet with groups there. The result was always the same. Within months she would leave the group in anger at their lack of true understanding, or the group would begin to distance itself from Ruth, recognizing that her commitment was tainted by something beyond what any of the group felt or shared.

During the years when Bob and Ruth were prosperous farmers and leaders of the community, Ruth was viewed as eccentric. Independence and strongly held views were familiar rural traits. After their fall from good fortune, people continued to feel a distant sympathy for Bob, but their tolerance for Ruth evaporated. She was disliked. The words "insane" and "crazy" began to be used to describe her. No one wanted to think about what the Bergstads' life was like on their remote farmstead.

That Andrea had been a golden child from birth had left Ruth unchanged. At first people said the child was a reward for what the Bergstads had suffered trying to have children. Even after their financial fall, Andrea had seemed to be both a compensation for what had been lost and a promise for a brighter future.

And now this. Their golden child was gone and what remained was two isolated adults who gave every appearance of being ill-suited to consoling one another. It seemed to everybody who knew them that their destruction was complete.

What had remained unspoken between Sig and Bob had been that they both knew that Andrea working at the One-Stop—Andrea working alone at night at the One-Stop—wouldn't have happened if the Bergstads hadn't fallen on hard times. Anything Andrea had by way of clothes or even buying gas for the old junker of a car that she drove, she paid for herself out of what she earned working at the One-Stop. What she didn't spend on necessities, she saved for college, because if she wanted to go to college, there was no question finding the money would be up to her.

The Bergstad family's history was on Sig's mind as he considered calling to bring them up-to-date on the case. He sat with his hand on the phone, even lifted the receiver before he thought better of it. It troubled him that Bob hadn't called. Sig felt he needed to see both the Bergstads to assure himself that things were in order. It wasn't something he looked forward to doing, but it felt necessary.

It took him fifteen minutes from the station to the Bergstads' driveway. He hadn't been out this way for a long time, so the condition of the fence, the appearance of the house as he drove up, surprised him. The Bergstads' place had always been a showplace. Lawns mowed way out to the road, white fence posts straight and looking freshly painted.

Out on the open prairie, it only took a winter or two of neglect, a couple of summers of blazing heat and thunderstorms, to make a place look shabby. What Sig found today was evidence that there had been at least a couple of years of neglect. There were weeds all the way along the driveway from the road to the house, and parts of the wood fence had been replaced with makeshift baling wire.

The house was no better. The last time Sig had been out here all the house shades were partially lowered to the same level; awnings were sharp and trim. Today, shades were either all the way down or at random angles. The awnings were frayed, one hanging loose on the second story of the house.

Sig now understood why Bob had been adamant that he'd come into town to meet with the media and to talk to Sig about the case. He'd said he hadn't wanted the media to upset Ruth, which was believable. He'd said he wanted Sig to spend his time working the case, not driving back and forth between town and their place, which had made sense.

But seeing the property as it was now made Sig sick at heart. He'd heard people say the Bergstads' place was looking run-down, but seeing it for himself brought home the change that this family had suffered. This wasn't a home, it wasn't a place lived in by people with limited money. It was a place where people lived who had given up hope.

Sig's next emotions were embarrassment and guilt. He was embarrassed for Bob's sake. He doubted Ruth would care much, one way or another, but he knew Bob would mind Sig seeing the state of things. And he felt guilty that he'd paid so little attention to what had happened to the Bergstads since they'd sold most of their land several years ago.

He weighed these emotions against whether he should return to town or go on up to the house. The concern he'd felt on realizing he hadn't heard from Bob came to mind and decided him. He continued, slowly, down the driveway, hoping the Bergstads would see him coming and have a chance to prepare themselves for a surprise visitor.

Bob came out on the porch before Sig opened the car door.

"What's happened?" he asked.

Sig closed his eyes. Something else he hadn't bothered to consider. What a damn fool he was. Of *course* his coming out here when he'd never come before would make the Bergstads think something important had happened. Probably something bad, or he would have called.

He shook his head as he got out of the car, then he lied. "No, no," he said, holding up both hands and making a gesture of dismissal. "I was just driving out this way, realized we hadn't talked lately, so thought I'd stop by. Nothing to be concerned about. Thought maybe Ruth would pour me a cup of coffee."

Sig had braced himself to find the interior of the house as decayed as the exterior. While it wasn't as bad as he'd expected, it felt sad and airless. Surfaces were dusty. Where shades were open, light shafted through the room without adding brightness. Sig had felt his house was bleak after his wife's death, but compared to what he found here, his place was downright homey.

It was Bob who made the coffee. Sig sat at the kitchen table, picking up a newspaper that had been lying on the table, folded to the crossword. It had pleased Sig that one of the Bergstads did crosswords. He liked to think of them being able to take their minds off Andrea. Being able to take their minds off each other, for that matter. Then he noticed that only three or four of the open boxes had been filled in and that the newspaper was a week old. He pushed it aside, saddened by how much the old newspaper, the empty crossword, told him about the Bergstads' lives.

To fill the silence as Bob puttered with the coffee, Sig said, "Like I was saying, there isn't much new. But we haven't been in touch for a while . . ."

Bob walked back to the table with two steaming mugs of coffee. He sighed as he sat down at the table. Then he held his mug in both hands, as if he were cold. It was something Sig had noticed years back, a way of distinguishing a man who worked with his hands from a man who didn't. A man who worked with his hands could hold a scorching hot cup in his hands without flinching. That was Bob. A fellow like Sig had to let it sit awhile.

Bob still didn't say anything. Sig tried again. "One problem we've got is that media coverage has tapered off. A case like this, we need the coverage to get new leads. I plan on calling the BCA later today and seeing what they suggest. They're good at this media game—you and Ruth up to going through another round with the press?"

Bob shrugged. "Whatever." He drank from the mug. It seemed to Sig like Bob drank the coffee to avoid having to say more.

"How's Ruth holding up?"

"She's managing. We're both managing."

Bob turned the hot cup in his hands, his lower lip extending, his eyes cast down into the cup.

Sig looked around the kitchen. "Maybe being out here isn't the best place to be right now. I mean, the two of you, alone. Especially now with winter setting in. You won't have much work out here until March, most of your work will be in town through the winter, won't it?"

Bob didn't answer. Sig realized Bob might be thinking about the cost of renting a place in town. That thought gave Sig an idea.

"Maynard and Aline Iverson will be heading down to Arizona in another week or so. They stopped by the station to arrange security at their house while they're gone. Said they wished they could find someone to stay in the house while they were gone. Why don't I give them a call, see if they'd be open to you and Ruth staying for a few weeks . . ."

Bob shook his head. "Ruth wouldn't have that. Living in another woman's house."

He hadn't bothered to thank Sig for the suggestion. Sig couldn't blame him for that, it had been a shot-in-the-dark kind of idea. Said more to make Sig feel as if he were doing something useful than having any real chance of being something the Bergstads would want to do.

Bob seemed to hear how abrupt his rejection had been. He looked up at Sig and gave him a weak smile. "That, and the Iversons being ELCA Lutherans. That would never do for Ruth."

Sig said, "Ruth here?"

Bob tipped his head in a vague direction away from the kitchen. "She's upstairs. She'd have come down, but . . ." He let the sentence hang, then said, "I'll tell her what you said about the media. But it might just be me this time. Ruth's feeling more and more like this whole thing is in God's hands. Like there isn't much we can do one way or another."

It was a response Sig took personally. It was a foolish thing for Ruth to say, but Sig could hardly blame her. After all, what had he accomplished in the investigation in the past couple of weeks?

For no reason Sig could figure, as he drove away from the Bergstads', down the narrow, derelict driveway, it was as if Andrea were with him in the car.

He drove for miles, unnerved by the sensation, until he spotted the Redstone water tower on the horizon. It was then that the meaning of the experience came to Sig.

He thought about Andrea Bergstad driving out that driveway every day to come in to town. To go to school, to go to work at the One-Stop. He thought about what Andrea left behind her when she headed toward town. A depressed father. A crazy mother. A house that was falling down around her. Driving down that driveway must have felt like an escape to her. Seeing the water tower coming up on the horizon must have felt like safety and sanity were within reach.

Even going to work at the One-Stop, alone at night, must have felt safer to Andrea than staying in that house.

What Sig thought was that Andrea's emotions driving down that driveway, day after day, had been so strong that the energy of her feelings had been ground indelibly into the space. What had happened back on the Bergstads' driveway was that Sig had crossed an electrical field charged with Andrea's emotions.

It hadn't been his imagination that she had been in the car with him, she *had been there*. What was left of her *had been there*.

"Hell," he said to himself, slapping the steering wheel. "Who's calling who crazy? I've got a ghost riding in the car and I think her mother's nuts?"

Rationally he could mock himself for having had the thought, but he couldn't shake the sensation. Something powerful, something as real to him as his own flesh had happened back there on the Bergstads' driveway.

The question that came to him next sent a chill down his spine.

A sensation that real—was that energy from the grave?

Or from a living spirit?

CHAPTER

10

"They say there's nothing new," the guy at the BCA said when Sig called to ask for the BCA's help in keeping media coverage going.

"That's my point," Sig said. "The best chance we've got for something new is if their coverage shakes something loose. Without coverage, this case is going to dry up and blow away."

"I hear you. But they're gonna cover the story only as long as it gives their viewers something fresh. Give them a new visual, Sig, and they'll cover it."

Sig sighed. These media angles were beyond him. He knew just enough to know that what the BCA was telling him was right. But a new visual? Like what?

"Sig?"

"Yeah."

"When we got the tip from the couple who thought they saw Andrea running near the One-Stop . . ."

"It turned out to be nothing."

"I know that, you know that. But a good visual might be volunteers—as long a line of volunteers as you can muster, hand in hand, shoulder to shoulder, walking across fields, looking for something, anything—could you get that together? We'll issue a release announcing the search. You might get some coverage on that."

Four days later, on a bright October Saturday, something less than a hundred townspeople held hands and strode across a broad, fallow field, their purpose belied by the fact that their eyes weren't on the ground, but looking ahead, focused on the camera crew that backed up in front of them, shooting and filming as the volunteers walked.

Everybody, that is, except Sig Sampson, who walked near the center of the line, his eyes fixed on the ground underfoot. His concentration was rewarded with a handful of empty shell casings any field in hunting country would yield. And one genuinely oddball artifact: an unfired .308 hard-point cartridge. It had a gratifying heft to it. He palmed the cartridge, liking the feel of it against his hand, not taking time to look at it closely for fear his curiosity would send up a false alarm of hope. He dropped it in his pocket and kept walking.

One television station carried less than ten seconds of coverage on the volunteer search, the announcer's tone perfunctory, regretfully dismissive. The best coverage came in the *Strib*'s Sunday edition, which ran an arty, four-column-wide black-and-white photo of the line of volunteers silhouetted against the horizon. There was no story with the photo, just a caption line.

FAMILY AND FRIENDS OF MISSING TEENAGER ANDREA BERGSTAD SEARCHED REDSTONE TOWNSHIP FIELDS ON SATURDAY. OFFICIALS SAY THERE ARE NO NEW LEADS IN THE CASE.

The photographer who took the shot must have been kneeling down, because the perspective on the line of volunteers was slightly distorted. The volunteers *loomed,* looking bigger than life.

Sig stared at the photo, the paper spread out on his kitchen table, his first cup of coffee of the day on top of the paper. He couldn't figure how it was that looking bigger somehow made the volunteers look hopeless. But that's how they looked, at least to Sig.

It was then he remembered the cartridge he'd picked up from the field. He shoved away from the table and walked into the hall, where he fumbled in the closet for the jacket he'd worn on the search. Finding it, he dug into the right pocket and pulled out the cartridge. He hefted it again, taking from it the same tactile pleasure he'd felt in the field when he'd caught its brass glint in the stubbled field, bending over and picking it up.

He walked back to the kitchen table, setting the bullet on its flat end on the table. It pleased him. He couldn't have said why, but it did. And he saw no reason not to take pleasure where he found it. There was, God knew, precious little to be had.

After the search there was no media coverage for another week. When more coverage did come, it was not welcome.

"Redstone Township Officer Under Investigation for Sexual Harassment Was Last Confirmed Person to See Missing Teenager."

Averill, Sig whispered under his breath as he read the story that had been faxed to him for comment by the *Strib.*

"No comment," is what he'd said when the reporter called for Sig's reaction.

"Chief Sampson," she said, "we have a source who claims that Erin Moser, Andrea Bergstad's best friend, has told Redstone Township police that the last individual who entered the One-Stop before Andrea disappeared was *not* Averill Hess. Can you at least give us a confirmation or denial on that?"

"I will not discuss specific details of the investigation," Sig said, surprising himself at how quickly the words came. "That Officer Hess is under investigation for an unrelated incident is a matter of public record."

Sig sat with his hand on the phone for moments after he'd hung up. *Damn.* He should have put Averill on administrative leave as soon as Andrea disappeared. Then he shook his head. He should have put Averill on administrative leave as soon as the incident report with Kim Sasser had been filed.

He hadn't because . . . ? At least a couple of good reasons. It was a he-said, she-said kind of deal and Kim's account of the event had changed significantly from her first complaint. The incident report she'd signed said Averill had ordered her to empty her jacket pockets, and when she'd refused, Averill had pulled the pockets inside out, leaving his hands in the pockets longer than necessary.

Averill's side of the story was that Kim had passed him, speeding, and he'd seen her take a drink from what appeared to be a beer can as she drove. He'd pulled her over for speeding, asked her to exit her vehicle, and when he'd not found a beverage container in the car, asked her to empty her pockets.

Where Sig thought Averill was on thin ice was with his claim that he believed Kim had been drinking beer as she drove. How do you tell if the driver of a car speeding by you at night is drinking beer or a can of pop? If Averill didn't have a solid reason for believing that Kim had been drinking beer while she drove, Averill didn't have any business ordering her to empty her pockets—with or without Averill's hands involved.

It was Sig's guess that Averill had, as Averill was apt to do, taken advantage of the situation to throw his weight around. That the car's driver was a teenage girl was probably part of the mix in terms of Averill's motivation.

Whatever. It just hadn't seemed to Sig, at the time, like the basis for a suspension.

Hindsight, of course, filled him with regret. Regret that questions about Averill would now cloud the investigation of Andrea's disappearance, taking it down blind alleys, diverting attention from the real issues in the case.

More fundamentally, Sig thought that if Averill had been on suspension, another officer taking the call about the One-Stop being empty wouldn't have let the couple at the One-Stop get away.

The first morning Sig walked into the Harvest Café on Main Street, the morning after the news coverage on Averill had run, the whole place went quiet as soon as he'd opened the front door.

Guess what they'd all been talking about.

Marlene, who'd been waiting tables at the Harvest for as long as the linoleum had been on the floor, gave Sig a look as she whipped by him with a coffee carafe in each hand.

"Need a shot of something in yours?" she said as she passed.

Sig headed to his regular table. The same table and the same tablemates he'd joined nearly every weekday morning since he'd been on the police force. Two of his tablemates had become township supervisors and one was Redstone's only attorney. A couple days out of the week the pastor from the Lutheran church was at their table, depending on if he had a funeral to run later in the day. Other tables at the Harvest were formed based on family ties, crops raised, cattle bred, whether you worked in town or on a farm—the organizing factors had changed over the years but which table you sat at rarely did.

The Harvest was the functional equivalent of Redstone's town square. Anything worth talking about was discussed between seven and nine in the morning at the Harvest and what you knew about what was going on in Redstone started at the Harvest and spread from there.

No one at Sig's table looked at him as he sat down.

Rube Gornitzka, the Lutheran pastor, said, "It sounds like your problems with Averill aren't behind you." He had a hand on the *Minneapolis Star-Tribune,* folded open to the story on Averill.

Rube's comment was unusual for a Harvest Café conversation in that it was a complete sentence, it was a sentence with more words than usually got used in any single utterance by a Harvest Café regular, and it was right to the point.

Sig figured that could be explained by Rube's being an ordained pastor. If it had been anyone else, the comment would have come out more on the order of "Read the paper yet?"—with a tap on the article for emphasis if a really significant point was being made.

In fact, words probably ranked third in importance as a means of communication at the Harvest. Silence was what really told you something and the looks that got exchanged when someone did say something counted for a lot more than what got said.

Sig responded in classic Harvest Café style, colored by his newly acquired media experience.

"No comment."

His response was met by his tablemates with eyebrows that moved, lips that twisted or got sucked in—a physical vocabulary that didn't translate to any other venue but had deep meaning on this morning at this table.

Hell, Sig thought as he walked out of the Harvest after eating a plate of scrambled eggs and cottage fries with a side of toasted white bread. *This business with Averill just screws everything up.*

CHAPTER

11

After the first news stories on Averill, Sig spent more time meeting with the Township's Board of Supervisors than he did investigating Andrea's disappearance. People stopped thinking about what happened to Andrea, and instead spent most of their time thinking about how Averill did it and how he'd covered his tracks.

For Sig, his last great hope in getting the case back on track continued to be Erin Moser, his memory of how she'd looked to him that first night at the station, and his firm conviction that night, and since, that Erin knew something that was worth knowing.

He'd called Erin three times to check statements made by other people, not because he thought she'd know, but because he hoped calling her might get her to talk more. On the first two calls, she was more silent than she'd been the first night. On the third call, he thought he detected hesitation in Erin's response. It seemed as if she were spinning the conversation out a bit, like she wanted to keep talking. What he thought was, with time passing, Erin was starting to believe that Andrea might not be back. And if Andrea wasn't coming back, maybe there wasn't any reason not to tell Sig everything she knew. But Erin didn't tell him anything on the third call.

Still. Something had seemed different.

Two days after the first media stories had run about Averill, Sig was leaving the station in a hurry, late for driving up to St. Paul for a case status meeting with the BCA and two state legislators who'd been helpful in lending support to the investigation.

He was getting into the car when Erin drove into the station parking lot. Sig had hesitated, cursing under his breath that now would be the time she'd show up. But, his gut again. His gut had told him from the first that Erin was important to the case and there wasn't any way he was going to drive away without finding out why she was here.

He walked over to her car, Erin rolling down the window as he approached.

"Hi, Erin. You here to see me?"

She looked away from him, then back.

"I guess. Just wondered what was going on."

That's what she said, but it felt like there was more to her being here than that.

Sig looked at his watch.

"I'm due up in St. Paul. Running a little late. But come on in. I can take a couple of minutes."

Erin continued to sit in the car. Then she shook her head.

"It's okay. I can come back tomorrow. I've gotta get to school, anyway."

"No," Sig said, putting his hand on the car door. "C'mon in. I can take the time."

Erin turned the key in the ignition, the engine revving. "It'll wait, Sig. I'll come over tomorrow."

Sig stood back, keeping his eyes on her. "First thing in the morning, Erin?"

She stopped the car, looking at him as directly as she ever had. Her expression startled Sig. She looked like she was about to cry.

Then she nodded, rolling up the window as she backed out.

The last time in the investigation of Andrea Bergstad's disappearance that a ringing phone wakened Sig Sampson was fourteen hours after he'd left Redstone for St. Paul.

He'd gotten back to the house from St. Paul after dark, so tired he'd fallen asleep in the den recliner.

Being wakened from a deep sleep had left him too disoriented to consider why the phone would be ringing at two-thirty in the morning. When the dispatcher told him there'd been an accident and he was wanted at the scene, he responded like an automaton, pulling on boots and a jacket and heading back out to the car.

The accident had occurred two miles out of town, on a narrow, winding road through an area of thick woods.

He knew as soon as he saw the body lying crumpled along the road's narrow shoulder. He recognized the dark green color of the jacket first. The same jacket he'd seen her wearing in the station parking lot. Then her hair, strawberry blond and curly, darkened by a clotted mass along one side of her head. One arm and both legs lying at angles that meant multiple fractures. Her left hand bloodied, but the ring finger undisturbed, the same ring he'd seen on her hand, on the steering wheel of her car hours before.

A young man stood in a clutch of emergency workers, a county deputy, and a Redstone officer. The fellow was crying, wrapped in a blanket.

"It was like she jumped at the car, I swear," he said, his voice swallowing half the words with emotion. "I mean, I came around the curve, right there . . ." He turned, one hand emerging from the blanket, a gloved finger pointing back at the sharp angle where the road turned from due north to west. "I wasn't even going all that fast. It was so dark, and then she just came at the car, I didn't have time . . ."

The Redstone officer approached Sig, pulling him aside, the county deputy officer just behind him. The county officer stopped, lighting a cigarette. This was not an easy thing to do. The wind was blowing relentlessly, first blowing out the lighter, then blowing the ash from the cigarette.

"The victim is . . ." the Redstone officer said.

"I know who it is," Sig said. "What I want to know is, what was she doing out here, alone at night?"

"Her car is about three-quarters of a mile back," he said, nodding in the opposite direction from the way Sig had come. "Flat tire. I'd guess she was walking to get help. Probably when she saw the car coming she was going to try to flag it down. Almost no shoulder here—she must not have realized how close she was to oncoming traffic. Night like tonight, she'd have a hard time changing the tire herself.

She didn't have gloves, no boots, no hat. She's what—two or three miles from home?"

"Farther than that," Sig said, "much farther than that."

His heart so heavy he could barely walk, Sig got himself to the spot where Erin Moser was lying. He looked down at the body. But he couldn't see anything but her face as it had looked that morning, staring back at him, filled with a deep sadness.

It was an image Sig would carry with him for years to come.

2003

CHAPTER

12

Mars looked at his watch. He still had forty-five minutes before he was due at Sigvald Sampson's place. He decided to give Redstone's Main Street a drive-by.

On his way into town he passed the high school, a newer-looking building that had a big sign out front announcing that it was the Tri-County Consolidated Secondary School. Another sign of the times. Rural communities no longer had a population base to support hometown high schools. The building made him think about the fact that there probably wasn't much of Redstone that Andrea Bergstad would recognize.

If the interstate area showed signs of prosperity, Redstone's Main Street was a testament to decline. The hanging plants that dangled from streetlights seemed a poor compensation for empty storefronts. That Redstone had survived was probably attributable to its being the site of the Tri-County school and to the coupon processing business that had moved into the office park out by the interstate. What was left on Redstone's Main Street was a bank branch, the Harvest Café, The Pump Bar, a storefront that had been converted into the Redstone Senior Citizen Center, and at one corner of the town's only intersection controlled by a stop sign, a squat red-brick building signed as the Redstone Township Police Department.

Mars idled at the stop sign. There were no cars behind him or to either side, so he had time to consider making a courtesy call at the police department. His first call had been to the current chief of police, who had to be reminded who Andrea Bergstad was. Then he'd suggested that Mars talk to Sigvald Sampson.

"The Bergstad case was on Sig's watch. We sent the case files into the BCA a couple years after Sig retired. But I'm sure he'd still be worth talking to."

Reopening cold cases was a sensitive matter. Especially if the Cold Case Unit initiated the new investigation. It was easier if the Cold Case Unit received a request from the original jurisdiction requesting a CCU review. But even then, there was always the possibility that by opening a cold case you'd uncover a serious error by the local investigators. You could ruin a career or destroy friendships by solving a case that a local jurisdiction had mishandled, leaving friends and families to suffer not just the pain of loss, but the added burden of uncertainty. The ultimate horror for the local jurisdiction was a mistake that resulted in more people dying.

Even with the substantial risk of negative exposure, many local jurisdictions referred cases to the CCU without getting a request. And most jurisdictions, upon getting a CCU request, accepted the request with gratitude for a chance to resolve a case. It didn't surprise anyone that it was the jurisdictions that reacted with hostility to a CCU request that inevitably had the most to lose by having someone take a second look.

The first local jurisdiction Mars called had taken personal offense at the suggestion there was anything to be found out about their case that they hadn't already considered.

Mars had responded by saying, "I've reviewed the case file and was impressed by your investigation."

This was the pitch regardless of the CCU's judgment about the quality of the original investigation. After that spoonful of sugar, you segued to whatever cause fit the case you were reopening, usually one of three things: new technology, new information, or a link to another case.

With the convenience-store crimes, Mars had genuinely been impressed with the quality of Redstone's investigation, particularly as he assumed that homicide investigations weren't part of the daily drill in Redstone Township in 1984. He didn't detect any resentment on the part of the police chief to having the CCU come in, but he didn't detect much interest, either. It was what the chief had said. The Bergstad case had happened on someone else's watch. This chief had a new agenda.

Sigvald Sampson, on the other hand, the guy who had the most to lose if the CCU turned over something new, had seemed overjoyed at the prospect of having the CCU come in on the Bergstad case.

Thinking back to the current police chief's response to Mars's initial inquiry and Sampson's response, Mars decided to pass on the courtesy visit at the police station. He'd be early getting to Sampson's, but Mars guessed early would be just fine.

It was.

They sat in Sig Sampson's den, a preternaturally dark room, refrigerated by a dripping window air conditioner. An empty two-pound coffee can sat under the window. Tinny *plinks* echoed from the can with distracting regularity.

Sig Sampson was not distracted by the dripping air conditioner. He had prepped himself for this meeting. This was a conversation he'd been wanting to have for a long time.

He started with an old envelope, on the back of which he'd written his theories of what had happened to Andrea Bergstad. Mars thought Sig's ideas pretty much covered the possibilities, starting with that Andrea had left by choice, that there was a reason she didn't want to be found. Sig's other ideas were that kids had taken Andrea as a prank and the prank had gone sour. The last two theories were one theory driven by two different motives. The first motive was robbery—someone had come into the station to commit a robbery and had decided to take Andrea instead.

"Good choice," Sig said. "She was a beautiful young girl." He shook his head. "But the possibility that really bothers me is that someone planned to take her. That they'd been watching the station, waiting for an opportunity. I thought from the first, someone like that would make sure we'd never find her."

"That's the one that sounds right to you?" Mars said.

Sig let himself sink back on his recliner. He took off his glasses and massaged his eye sockets with the fingers of one hand. Then he looked around the room as if an answer were there, if he just knew where to look.

"I'll tell you the truth. I never was on top of this case. I was in way, way over my head. That's what bothers me as much as anything. If this had happened somewhere else, where they had law officers with some experience, we wouldn't be sitting here nineteen years later scratching our heads."

"You're wrong about that," Mars said. "What you did holds up just fine. The only thing extra I can offer is tying this to a couple of other cold cases involving convenience-store abductions. My partner is developing an interstate database—Minnesota, the Dakotas, Iowa, and Wisconsin—that will allow us to look at case facts and suspects from all five states and see what pops out. We're using this investigation as a protocol case to test the database."

Sig looked at him. "How'd you pick this case to start with?"

Mars shrugged. "My turn to be honest. I've always had a bug up my ass about convenience-store crime. I figure the worse thing that could come out of this investigation is we could publicly embarrass the guys who let their employees hang out there, dangling like shark bait."

Sig slapped the arm of the recliner. "That's a cause I'll sign on to. You know, before the One-Stop got built out by the interstate, we had car theft, the occasional break-in—penny-ante stuff—domestics—one domestic that turned into a homicide—drunk and disorderlies. Nothing I didn't have figured out before we got to the scene. In the first year the One-Stop was open, we had three armed robberies."

He sat thinking about that for a minute before he said, "Damnedest thing is, the way things have changed, starting with the One-Stop, now with meth labs popping up and gambling turning everybody into a thief, drug dealers coming here from up your way and from Sioux Falls—well, if I had as much experience in my first thirty years on the job as I had in my last two years, I might have been up to the Andrea Bergstad investigation."

Mars said it again. "You don't have to make any apologies for that investigation. I mean that."

"I've thought of a hundred things I should have done different."

"So have we all," Mars said. "The best job I ever did, there were a hundred things I did wrong." He let that message hang in the air for a bit, then said, "I'd like to go back to your case theories. One by one. What you've got that supports or contradicts the possibilities. I've read the files, but I want to hear it from you. I want you to tell me what your gut told you—facts or no facts. I want you to tell me everything you can remember about the night Andrea Bergstad disappeared. Down to the smallest detail."

Sig nodded. "You've got time? Because I remember that night like yesterday. What I can't promise you is that what I remember—what I knew—is anything like the whole story."

"Like yesterday is what I want," Mars said.

They moved over to a desk, and Sig pulled black vinyl three-ring binders from a shelf over the desk as he talked. Sig Sampson had never stopped working the case, even after he'd retired. His thinking was sharp and analytically correct. He was careful never to overstate facts, careful to note when something hadn't felt right, even when there was nothing to support the bad feeling. As he talked, his finger trailed over the case documentation, tapping for emphasis on points he thought were of special interest. With his left hand, he held a gleaming brass cartridge that had been standing on its flat end on the desk. From time to time he twisted the cartridge in his fingers, palmed it, tossed it back and forth between his two hands as he talked, clearly liking the feel of its shape and weight.

What it all came down to was that Sig's best guess was that somebody planned to take Andrea Bergstad. He thought that because it was clear whoever she left with hadn't shown up on the video, hadn't wandered around checking things out. It just seemed like they came in, being careful to stay off camera range, got Andrea, and left. Didn't even think about doing a robbery.

"And there was nothing that showed any struggle. She just went with him?"

"I think we have to assume he had a gun. Why else would she have left? One minute she's there"—Sig snapped his fingers—"then she's gone." He sighed. "You know the conceal-and-carry law the legislature passed last session?"

73

"Don't get me started," Mars said.

"This situation that Andrea Bergstad was in. You ask yourself. If Andrea had had a gun that night—would it have made a difference?"

"I can give you my answer," Mars said. "Tell me what you think."

"If she'd had a gun, it would have been in her purse. And her purse was behind the counter. She wasn't anywhere near the counter when whoever it was that took her came into the store. If she'd had a gun in her purse, even if she'd been behind the counter, is she going to have time to get the gun out and point it at the guy?"

"No."

"So, we agree."

"I'll go you one better. If Andrea Bergstad had had a gun in her purse, odds are she'd have lost it or it'd have been stolen before she ever had a chance to use it. Or if she shot it, that she'd miss and hit an innocent bystander. People who say standing on a firing range holding a pistol in two hands, legs spread, taking time to take aim at a fixed target, qualifies someone to shoot a handgun during a crisis situation don't know what they're talking about."

Sig said, "God knows being down here in Redstone, I haven't had many times when I had to decide whether to draw my firearm or not. You—working where you do—even with the training you get handling firearms and making decisions on when to fire or not—is it ever an easy call?"

"Never," Mars said. "And anyone who tells you it is easy shouldn't be carrying a gun. But what really makes me nuts about conceal and carry is the message it sends to kids. Conceal and carry tells our kids that the way you protect yourself, the way you solve problems, is to use a gun."

"I think we're kindred spirits on this point," Sig said. He picked up the cartridge again, turning it in his fingers. "No, even if Andrea Bergstad had had a gun on her hip that night, I can say with certainty we'd still be sitting here today wondering what happened to her."

The cartridge slipped from his fingers and rolled toward Mars over the desk, then dropped to the floor. Mars bent over to retrieve it. He looked at the cartridge before he handed it back to Sig.

"A .308 cartridge. Serious ammo. You a marksman?"

Sig shrugged. "Oh, I used to hunt some. But, no. Not a serious marksman. For sure never shot with anything that fired a .308 hard point."

He reached over to take the cartridge from Mars. "This," he said, holding the cartridge between his thumb and index finger, "is actually the only physical link I've got to Andrea's disappearance."

Mars looked alarmed, as if he'd missed something.

Sig chuckled, then said, "No, not really. What happened was, a couple weeks after she disappeared we had a bunch of volunteers out in a field east of the One-Stop. Didn't really expect to find much of anything, but I picked this up. You can find all kinds of shotgun cartridges in fields around here—but an unfired .308 hard point, that's a find."

Sig gave the cartridge another look, then dropped it into his shirt pocket.

"What *would* have made a difference, Sig? Your best guess?"

Sig sat in silence. Then he said, "Erin Moser. Erin had been Andrea Bergstad's best friend. I've always felt like Erin Moser knew something she wasn't talking about. But Erin Moser never told me what it was she knew."

"Well," Mars said, "that makes five things I need to check."

"Five things?" Sig said.

"The surveillance tape you sent me from the night Andrea went missing. The last you see her on the tape, it looks like she's walking toward the door, as if someone's come in—consistent with what we know about her being on the phone with Erin Moser."

Sig nodded.

"But almost the last thing we see of her is like she's bending over, then she pops up again, then she's gone."

"That's right."

"Seems like an odd thing to do—especially if someone's holding a gun on you. I couldn't find anything in the files you sent that explains why she ducked down like that. Nothing on the scene when you arrived that explains that?"

Sig was nodding his head in agreement, but his response was negative. "I remember that from the tape—but, no. Never got close to anything that would explain what happened there."

"Another thing—when your officer showed up on the scene—what's his name—Hess?"

A grimace passed Sig's face. "Averill Hess."

"Averill Hess. It kind of looks to me like he ducked down in the same place where Andrea ducked. But I didn't see anything in his crime-scene report about why he did that. You ever ask him about that?"

Sig looked troubled. "I'm embarrassed to say I didn't even notice. Nothing Averill did ever made much sense—I guess I must have thought he was picking up a piece of paper or something. A gum wrapper, a cigarette butt. That would be something Averill would do. Can't say it occurred to me when I've looked at the tape that he ducked down right where Andrea did."

"Averill still in Redstone?"

Sig swiveled around and opened a desk drawer, pulling out a small spiral notebook. He turned pages, found what he was looking for, and wrote it down on a slip of paper. He passed the paper over to Mars.

"He was on final notice for inappropriate conduct on a traffic stop when Andrea disappeared. Then he let the couple leave who called in that the One-Stop was deserted without getting any information on them. I was going to fire him, but he quit before I got around to it. Last I heard, he was working security at a big discount store up in Alton, about forty miles south of the Twin Cities. Been years since I've seen him."

Mars nodded. "I'll give it a try. See if he remembers anything."

"Well," Sig said, "if he does, it means his IQ is about eighty points higher than I thought it was."

"You're comfortable he didn't have anything to do with Andrea's disappearance? Some of the case notes I went over looked like you considered that."

"It worried me at first," Sig said. "And he was the last person at the scene to actually see Andrea before she disappeared. You put that together with the fact that he had some pretty consistent problems managing his contacts with young women, and you'd have to worry about it some. But nothing I looked at ever made that connection. We were able to pin his movements down pretty tight that night. Bottom line, Averill cleared early on."

"I stopped by the One-Stop on my way in. Looked like the layout of the store hasn't changed much. That right?"

"Pretty much the same. I can't think of anything significant to the case that's changed. Other than the phone. They took the phone out a few years back." Sig paused. "What else? You said there were five things you needed to check."

"The biggest gap you've got in the case is the couple who called in when they found the store empty. I'd sell my soul to talk to them."

"You can put my soul on the block right along with yours. We even had some reward money out on finding them. Nothing."

"I've talked to some of my colleagues in the Cold Case Unit. They think with our linked-case angle, we might be able to interest a program like *The Get List*. We get them to do a story, who knows what might shake loose. We'd ask them to run the drawings of the couple who called in from the One Stop—the drawings you developed from the video."

"Worth a try," Sig said. "But I have to tell you, those drawings are so general—they could be anybody or nobody."

"How well I know," Mars said. "And the drawings are nineteen years old. We can do a little aging on the images, but . . ."

"Exactly. So. That's number three. National media coverage. It's worth a try. What else?"

"I'd like to talk to Andrea's parents. They available?"

Sig shook his head. "Moved out of town the year after Andrea disappeared. Probably the best thing for them. Their lives were in bad shape before Andrea disappeared. After . . ." Sig shook his head again. "They managed to clear a little cash after they sold what was left of their land and the house. Moved down to the Texas coast, bought a prefab home. Then Bob Bergstad had a heart attack. Didn't die right away. In fact, Ruth died before Bob went." Sig shook his head. "Sad, sad lives. I would have liked to have been able to tell them what happened before they died. That much peace they deserved."

Mars said, "Am I remembering right? That you checked out the parents? No question about their involvement?"

Sig was quick to put Mars's question to rest. "It was in the files. We were able to nail that with the clock. The time Andrea told her friend on the phone somebody was coming in, the time we got the call that the One-Stop was deserted, the time we called Bob Bergstad out at his farm to tell him Andrea was missing. There just was no possibility that Bob could have been involved given that timeline."

"And her mother?"

Sig uttered the kind of laugh that has nothing to do with anything being funny. "How do I explain how impossible it is that Ruth Bergstad could have done anything like that?" He sat, shaking his head for a minute before he said anything. Then he said, "One thing—and this applies to both Bob and Ruth—according to Andrea's friend, the last thing Andrea said on the phone was, 'Somebody's coming in.' Now if it had been her mother or father, I think it's safe to say she would have said as much."

Mars reached over and tapped Erin Moser's statement. "Speaking of Andrea's friend. This is the last thing I need to follow up on. What you said about Erin Moser—your feeling that she knew something worth knowing that she never talked about. Is she still around? I'd like to talk to her."

It had seemed to be a simple question. But Sig looked like Mars had just sucker-punched him.

Sig pushed himself out of the recliner, his back to Mars. He jammed his hands in his pockets and turned. There were tears in his eyes.

"I guess this wasn't in the case files. No reason it would be. You said everybody makes mistakes on cases. But not everybody makes a mistake that means somebody dies."

Mars stared. "Erin Moser is dead? Something happened with the investigation and she died?"

Sig's voice was hoarse. "More like something that didn't happen with the investigation. Something I didn't do. The day she died—little more than three weeks after Andrea disappeared—Erin came to the station in the morning. Said she was just checking in, but that wasn't how it felt to me. I think she was ready to talk. I think she *needed* to talk."

78

Sig punched a closed fist into the palm of his hand. "Fool that I am, I told her I was running late. Told her I'd take a couple minutes, but . . ." He shook his head and dropped back into the recliner. "Why in God's name I thought meeting with a bunch of windbag legislators was more important than talking to Erin, I can't tell you. From the first on this case, I thought Erin was key. And me knowing how reluctant she was to talk, I should have just said, 'C'mon in.' But I gave her an out, and she took it. We said we'd get together the next morning . . ." Sig put his hand up to his forehead, drawing it slowly across his brow. "But by morning she was dead."

Mars's head was spinning. Erin Moser's death complicated everything. Erin Moser's death raised the possibility that his linked-case theory was falling apart, that there was a motive for this case that had nothing to do with a predator who took advantage of lax security at convenience stores.

"What happened?" he said, knowing that the direction his investigation took hung on Sig's answer.

Sig sat silent, his hand lifting gently from the padded arm of the recliner, the heel of his hand coming down in a muted thud, then the same thing again. His lips were drawn into a thin line.

"She was driving on a county road east of town. Had a flat tire. She left the car and walked along the road. It was dark, she had on a dark coat. The road was narrow—hardly any shoulder on the road— and a car hit her. She was dead when I got to the scene."

Something in Mars relaxed slightly. "It was an accident, then."

Sig restarted the slow, rhythmic thud of the heel of his hand against the upholstered arm of the chair.

Mars said, "The person who drove the car that hit Erin—you found the driver?"

"He was at the scene," Sig said. "We had to have a car take him over to the hospital in Knife Lake. He went off the road after he hit Erin, dislocated his shoulder, hit his head against the windshield."

Mars felt more relief. "So there was no question that the driver didn't intend to kill Erin . . ."

Mars's question surprised Sig. "No. Absolutely not. It was an accident all right—I mean, his part of it. He hadn't been speeding, hadn't been drinking. And anybody that saw the guy knew he was taking it hard." Sig turned slightly to get a good look at Mars. "You're asking if there's a chance the driver killed Erin because she was connected to Andrea's disappearance. That's what you're asking?"

"Just a thought. Look, you said it yourself. You had a long career out here with only one domestic homicide. Then, in the space of just over three weeks, Andrea Bergstad goes missing and her best friend is killed in a car accident. What are the odds? But you're right. If the driver was at the scene, that says a lot. What do you know about the driver?"

Sig opened another three-ring binder, but talked mostly from memory.

"There was a detour off the interstate back then. He'd come off the interstate to follow the detour. It was a dark night, he was probably a little tense, disoriented."

"You knew where he was from, where he was headed—and that made sense?"

Sig went back to the three-ring binder, picking up his glasses, holding them up in front of his eyes instead of putting them on. He nodded as he read. "He was from Duluth, on his way to Sioux Falls. His dad had gotten sick."

Sig chewed on the earpiece of his glasses, like he was trying to remember something. "Now that I think about it, I called his parents in Sioux Falls to tell them he wouldn't be getting there until the next day. If I'm remembering right, the hospital kept him overnight in Knife Lake for observation."

"So it made sense—someone who didn't live around here, being out on that road late at night?"

"No question about it."

"Sounds solid," Mars said. "And I trust your judgment about his reaction. So mark it down as a star-crossed night." Mars paused, thinking back to something Sig had said that he hadn't understood. "One thing. When I asked if you were sure it was an accident, did I hear you say *his part of it*—meaning the driver? I didn't follow that."

"When I saw her at the station that morning," Sig said. "I can't tell you how sad she looked."

Mars gave Sig some time. When he spoke again, he softened his voice.

"You think it's possible she committed suicide."

"It's been on my mind."

"Tell me why you think she would have done that."

"Partly what the driver said. That she just came out of the darkness into the road in front of the car. Like she jumped at the car . . ."

"When a driver is startled by something, what they could be describing is their surprise, not what the other person did."

"Oh, I know that. But even so. This was a dark, deserted road. Hard to figure how she wouldn't have seen his headlights. What I think about is, she's just had the worst three weeks of her life, she's been under a lot of stress, probably not sleeping all that much. Then she's out on a back road, alone at night, and she gets a flat tire. The last straw, so to speak."

Sig went quiet again. "I just keep remembering Erin's face that morning, when she showed up in the station parking lot. I didn't think of this right then, I thought about it after she died. What I've wondered is if she was starting to feel she'd made a mistake not telling us what she knew right away. Maybe she was thinking if she'd come forward from the first, Andrea would still be alive."

Sig shook his head. "Just plain sad is how she looked. A sadness I've seen every night I've closed my eyes for the past nineteen years."

CHAPTER

13

"Six weeks is four weeks too long."

Nettie Frisch and Mars Bahr sat opposite each other in the reception area of their office. One of them stretched out on the derelict couch Mars had bought at a garage sale, the other in a chair, feet up on an ottoman that didn't match the couch or the chair.

Their habits of partnering had been established when Mars had hired Nettie from the administrative section at the Minneapolis Police Department. He'd hired Nettie rather than partnering up with another detective. What he'd wanted was someone to handle the documentation end of investigations and to find ways of using the computer to assist in developing cases.

He'd got that and then some. Nettie took to the assignment with a passion and ease that exceeded Mars's expectations and his imagination. In short order she'd become an essential part of his cases and had quickly begun to develop suggestions for databases and applications that were useful throughout the department. As much as anything, their move from the MPD to the State Bureau of Criminal Apprehension's Cold Case Unit had happened because it was an environment that gave Nettie bigger opportunities to drag criminal investigation information management into the twenty-first century.

They'd had one shared dissatisfaction with their new jobs. Neither of them liked working in private offices. After years of working at facing desks in the MPD homicide squad room, they'd missed the casual communication that took place when you were never out of sight of your partner. They missed the ease of asking each other questions without picking up a phone or getting up from their desks.

And while neither of them would have admitted it, they missed each other. So, within a few months of making the move to the new office, they'd rearranged their quarters. They'd moved their desks into the reception area—the largest room in the three-room suite—converted Mars's office into a conference room, and used Nettie's office as a file room, and, even more important, a place to keep the refrigerator for Nettie's Evian water and Mars's Coca-Cola.

The new arrangement felt better right away. With one significant problem: Their close working arrangement made it painfully obvious to both of them that Mars didn't know what to do with himself. If both of them had had trouble settling in, it might have been less of a problem. But Nettie was as well-suited to her new job as Mars was ill-suited to his.

Each of them carried the daily burden of pretending not to notice the contrast between how they were working. Nettie's phone rang five times for each of the times that Mars's phone rang. Nettie had meetings with other state agencies that were involved in the pilot five-state database that was being developed. Nettie was over at the state legislature testifying before budget and data privacy committees. Nettie could work at her computer screen for hours at a time without stopping for anything other than taking a sip from her iced Evian bottle.

Mars had his files. Files piled on his desk and on the floor around his desk. The most he could hope for was that he'd find something in one of the files that would give him a reason to make a phone call. He'd open a file, stare at it for minutes, then reach for another file. Every half hour or so, he'd get up and walk around the office, tossing a paper clip between his hands, working at looking like he was thinking about something he'd read in the files. Three or four times a day he'd go back to the file room to get a Coke. Coke in hand, he'd take time out on the couch, feet up on the couch back, interrupting Nettie with questions that didn't have much to do with what either of them were working on.

She never said, "Mars, shut up." But her patience with him made them both uncomfortable. They both knew that things couldn't go on much longer like this but neither had any idea what to do about it.

When Mars had returned from Redstone Township full of his old energy, Nettie dropped everything she was doing and put in extra hours to get in place what Mars needed to carry forward the investigation into the three convenience-store abductions.

She wasn't sure at first what had made Redstone different from the other cases Mars had started with. After a couple days of working with him, Nettie guessed that it was Mars's connection with the retired Redstone chief of police that had, at last, gotten Mars to warm up to a cold case.

Their first priority had been to get *The Get List* to carry a story on the three abductions. Mars didn't think much would come from media coverage on two of the three cases they'd linked, but identifying the mystery couple from the Redstone abduction could be significant. If they could find the couple who'd called in the report on the deserted One-Stop, it could provide information that would be significant to all three cases.

And now they'd hit a stumbling block that would slow Mars down and let the air out of his reinflated tires.

The earliest *The Get List* could run a segment on the three abductions would be in six weeks. And six weeks wasn't a certainty. It could just as easily be twelve weeks.

"Not acceptable," Mars said, hoisting himself up from the couch and starting to pace. "What are our alternatives? This is the only national media choice we've got?"

Nettie knew she'd get this question, and she was ready with an answer.

"*TGL* has got the best demographics. The biggest audience. We could go for one of the other cable shows, but the viewership is so small I'm not sure it would do us any good."

"So, we do one of the other shows first and run *TGL* on their schedule. We just need to get moving."

Nettie sank back on the chair and shifted her feet on the ottoman. With her eyes closed she said, "It doesn't work that way. Another channel carries our story, *TGL* won't touch it."

"What about that network program on NBC—*Dateline?* They've carried a lot of crime programming."

Nettie didn't open her eyes. When she spoke, she pronounced each word slowly. "What they do is cover investigations that have been resolved. They're not going to be interested in a case—three cases—that haven't been solved. That's why what we're doing is perfect for *TGL.*"

Mars stopped pacing and aimed the paper clip he'd been pulling apart at the wastebasket. It made more noise when it missed than you'd think something like that would.

He blew air through his lips, making a flubbing sound, and dropped back down on the couch, propping his feet up on the back of the couch. "It wouldn't hurt to try. They might be interested in the statistics we've developed on convenience-store crime. Maybe they'd do that story, and we could squeeze in the angle on the mystery couple."

Now Nettie opened her eyes. "Number one. If anything, *Dateline* would take longer to schedule than *TGL.* Number two, the public information office at the BCA would *like* us to hold this story until we *have* solved the three abductions and then get coverage on *Dateline.* Much better publicity for them if we get coverage on three cases we've solved instead of coverage on three cases we can't figure out. So, if I go to the BCA and say, let's try for *Dateline* instead of *TGL,* they'll be only too happy to go for it. And you'll be out of tricks for how you're going to turn up the mystery couple. *Not* a good idea to start pushing that angle."

They sat in silence. Mars knowing Nettie was right, Nettie getting tired of having to tell Mars things he could figure out on his own, if he wanted to.

Nettie sat up. "Look, Mars. I FedExed our package to TGL last week. The producers said they'd get back to me as soon as they'd had a chance to go through it. All they said is, if they accept the story, it'd run in six to twelve weeks, depending on what else is scheduled. So let's not waste a lot of energy worrying about scheduling until I've heard back from *TGL.*"

She stood. "I've got to be in downtown Minneapolis to meet with the FBI people on the database project in a half hour. Depending on when my meeting ends, I may or may not come back here."

Nettie slapped the tops of his shoes as she walked by him. "You're on your own, partner."

Nettie's mind spun with frustration as she came out of her meeting at the FBI's downtown Minneapolis office.

After fighting repeated battles at the legislature on civil liberties issues associated with the development of their Integrated Interstate Data pilot, she'd organized a meeting with the FBI to discuss ways of screening information to assure quality standards. What the local office had just been told by Washington was that the Justice Department was back-pedaling on requirements that the FBI's National Crime Information Center meet data accuracy and timeliness requirements under the 1974 U.S. Privacy Act.

Nettie's response to civil libertarians' concerns about the IID had always been that data that was legal to collect in one jurisdiction should be legally accessible to all jurisdictions. But she agreed completely that expanding access raised the bar on accuracy and timeliness standards for including data.

Now this.

What the DOJ was proposing lowered the bar at exactly the moment the bar needed to be raised. Sure, the IID project could develop more rigorous standards than those followed by the NCIC, but at some point different data standards would work against the very objectives the pilot aimed for: uniform reporting and access. More than that, Nettie knew that the DOJ's proposed easing would strengthen opposition to the IID and heighten suspicion about the public purposes of the IID project.

What she found particularly frustrating were the reasons the DOJ was giving for why accuracy and timeliness standards had to be eased. In essence, they were saying it was too hard to be accurate and complete because NCIC collected its data from so many sources that it was administratively impossible to assure that data being reported was accurate.

"Hell," Nettie muttered as she waited for the elevator, "if they really mean that, they should support projects like the IID, not trash the quality standards."

She hesitated before pushing the button for her floor in the elevator, looking at her watch. It was almost four o'clock. If she went back to the office now, she'd spend most of her time in rush-hour traffic. She was meeting her sister for a walk at six, so what made sense was to grab something to eat on the skyway, then head home. Thinking about going back to the office reminded her that if she did that, what awaited her was certain to be Mars's continuing impatience about scheduling the *TGL* segment.

At last, an easy decision. She punched "2" and headed out on the skyway.

Nettie thought about Mars as she walked, preoccupied with trying to solve the unsolvable. She followed the skyway through several buildings, going into the Orient Express without really thinking about it. She got a tray and a vegetarian entrée, then sat down at a table without mentally registering where she was or what she was doing until someone spoke her name.

"Nettie!"

Karen Pogue stood next to her table holding a foam take-out box. "You're a long way from your office." Karen looked around. "Is Mars with you?"

Here we go, Nettie thought, kicking herself for not being alert enough to avoid Karen.

Nettie gave Karen a polite smile, shaking her head. "No. I had a meeting with the FBI. Thought I'd grab something to eat before heading home."

"Do you mind?" Karen said, holding up her take-out box and gesturing to the chair opposite Nettie.

Damn.

"No." Nettie tipped her head toward the chair Karen was already sitting down in. "It's just that I've got to leave . . ."

"I'm working late. But better to eat here than make a mess at my desk. And you can catch me up on Mars. I'm worried about him. We all knew this job wasn't a good fit, but the last I saw him, he was . . . morose. I mean it. Absolutely despondent. Which is really too bad, now that he and Chris are settled and loving their new place."

This was what Nettie disliked about Karen Pogue. Well, be honest about it. Karen's using Nettie to worm out personal information about Mars was only one of the things Nettie disliked about Karen Pogue. She also disliked that Karen treated her like a fifth wheel. She'd lost track of the number of times she and Mars had been together with Karen when Karen had invited Mars to go out to dinner without inviting Nettie. Not that Nettie would have wanted to go. It was just that the way Karen ignored Nettie was offensive.

"May I have one of your napkins?" Karen said, reaching over to Nettie's tray. "So. What *is* your take on how Mars is doing."

Anyone else, and Nettie would have welcomed an opportunity to talk through what was going on with Mars. In some ways there wasn't anyone better to talk about Mars with. Karen was a forensic psychologist who'd met Mars at professional seminars, eventually working with him on cases. She was smart, she was fearsomely perceptive, and she knew Mars personally almost as well as Nettie. But Nettie didn't trust Karen's motives where Mars was concerned.

"She has designs on you," Nettie had said to Mars after Mars had mentioned he and Karen had had dinner.

Mars had seemed surprised by the idea, which just made the situation that much more maddening.

"She's married," he'd said. This from a man who was a daily witness to human transgressions against morality and decency. It was obvious he did not want to get into a discussion about it.

Nettie had clasped her hand to her heart in feigned shock. "Oh, no. I had no idea. Well, then, of *course,* I must be mistaken." She wadded up a piece of paper and threw it at Mars. "Admit it, Mars, you've said it yourself. You don't understand why Karen stays married to Ted any more than I do."

Mars had given Nettie an impatient look, but when she'd continued to watch him with what he described as a smirk, he'd said, "Okay. If she *was* interested in someone else, marriage would not be an insurmountable obstacle. But that's just the point. Karen doesn't need to be married. They've got no kids, she's got plenty of money, an interesting job . . . if she doesn't want to be married, there's no reason she needs to stay married. I think it's safe to conclude she's married because she wants to be married. Even if you and I don't understand why."

Nettie shook her head. This was another point concerning Karen on which Mars was consistently naïve. "What Karen's income gets her is nice clothes, a nice car, a nice house, a nice vacation twice a year. What being Ted's wife gets her is a spectacular house in Kenwood, the lake place, the apartment in Paris, six-week trips to Turkey and Patagonia and God knows where else, the housekeeper who does the grocery shopping and laundry, their share in the Napa Valley vineyard, the caterers when they entertain more than eight people for dinner, the club memberships, the personal shopper at Neiman Marcus, donations that get her on the board at the Orchestra . . ."

Mars held up both hands. "I had no idea you'd given Karen's lifestyle this much thought. All I'm saying is I don't believe she stays with him for material stuff. And if that is why she stays with him, why is she going to leave him for me? This may come as a shock, Nettie, but my salary is not going to keep Karen in the style to which she is accustomed. Even now that I'm not paying child support."

Mars's response shook Nettie a bit. It was a response that showed that Mars had been thinking about Karen more than Nettie thought he had.

"I'm not saying I think she wants to leave Ted and set up housekeeping with you. I've never said that. I think she wants it both ways. She wants a Ted lifestyle with you on the side."

Mars had laughed and changed the subject, leaving Nettie feeling a little silly about having exposed so much of her feelings about Karen.

And now, with Karen across the table from her, the memory of that conversation came back to Nettie and made her feel, once again, a little silly, and as always around Karen, sort of flat-footed.

As Nettie had not been quick to respond to Karen's question about Mars, Karen jumped in with a second question.

"And what about Evelyn? Has he said anything about Evelyn? I told him when she got back they should come for dinner. He just said he wasn't sure when she'd be back. *Nothing* about *if* she was coming back."

This really was out of line. Even for Karen. She's just admitted that she'd asked Mars about Evelyn and he'd chosen not to say anything, so now she's trying to pry something out of me.

Nettie shrugged, ignoring Karen's last question, then reversed gears and said, "Actually, this case we're working on—the three convenience-store abductions? Mars actually seems interested. He's made a connection with the chief of police on one of the cases that's kind of revved him up. Only problem we've got right now is that we need to get *The Get List* to schedule a segment to give us something to follow up on. That's taking longer than I'd like, but if we can get that going . . ."

Nettie had watched Karen's reaction when Nettie hadn't answered Karen's question about Evelyn. It was a subtle reaction, but it was clear to Nettie that Karen got her point: *I'm not talking about Mars's personal life with you.*

Karen shifted slightly, then tried a more subtle tack. "I told Mars this was the wrong job for him." She took a bite of her lemon chicken, then said, "I suppose he knew how good this move would be for you. He's so generous. Always putting other people's needs ahead of his own . . ."

Nettie felt her cheeks flush. "You're right. Mars did know this would be a good job for me. But he decided to make the move because he couldn't hack MPD politics anymore. He wanted to go, even knowing that it was risky."

It was Karen's turn to ignore what Nettie had said. "What people don't get about Mars is that he's an emotional guy. He gets his energy from other people's emotions. If that's not there, he runs on empty. Classic foster child syndrome."

Nettie looked up at Karen sharply. Karen's assessment had surprised her, so much so that she responded before she had a chance to check her curiosity.

"What do you mean?"

Karen looked smug. "Foster kids that are in care for long periods of time tend to go one of two ways. They become very unstable and have difficulty forming strong emotional attachments or they overcompensate. They have heightened senses of responsibility and are always looking for ways to be heroic. In effect, they want to be the person who was missing during their formative years. Guess which end of the stick Mars grabbed? It's such an obvious part of his psyche. Even his parenting . . ."

This conversation was making Nettie uncomfortable. Why it made her feel disloyal to Mars she couldn't have said. But that was how it made her feel. Disloyal.

"I've got to go," she said, gathering paper onto her tray and shoving back on her chair. "I'm meeting my sister. I've got to get home and change. Good to see you."

She and Karen looked at each other directly before Nettie turned away. There was no question they understood each other. And no question that understanding had not bred trust.

"You're jealous."

Nettie glanced over at Val as they walked, immediately sorry that she'd indulged her need to complain about Karen Pogue to her sister. Nettie's complaints fed right into Val's long-cherished opinion that Nettie's interest in Mars was more than professional.

Nettie walked on without answering Val, trying to decide if she had the energy to go into the whole thing about Mars again. Her past arguments against her sister's ideas on the subject had failed. Did it make sense to try again? Or would trying again only have the effect of affirming that Nettie *did* protest too much?

In the end, Nettie couldn't stop herself, just as earlier she hadn't been able to deny herself the gratification of complaining to Val about Karen.

"If I were jealous," Nettie began, "why would I have gotten along with Evelyn, but not Karen? Evelyn is the only woman I've known who I think Mars was really serious about. But Evelyn and I were close. We would have been closer if she'd stayed around."

"Maybe . . . that's . . . just it," Val said, breathing hard as she struggled to walk and talk at the same time. Val was older than Nettie by almost ten years, and heavier by at least twenty pounds. "You . . . never . . . really saw Evelyn . . . as a . . . threat. You knew . . . from the first . . . she'd be . . . leaving."

Annoyed with Val, Nettie picked up the pace of their walk in revenge. "It doesn't follow. If I was interested in Mars it would have been threatening to me that Mars might follow Evelyn when she left."

"That's crazy," Val huffed. "Mars is going to . . . leave . . . his kid? Like that's . . . going to happen? I . . . don't . . . think so."

Nettie came to an abrupt halt, turning to face Val. "Damn it. You've made up your mind, and nothing I say is going to change what you think. Why even discuss it? Let's just drop the subject. If you want to think I've got a thing about Mars, fine. You're entitled to your opinion. Just don't tell me about it."

Before Val could answer, Nettie's cell phone rang.

"Probably Mars . . . pulling your . . . chain," Val said, catching up with Nettie.

But it wasn't Mars. Nettie recognized the area code and number.

It was *The Get List.*

"Wrong again," Nettie said to Val.

CHAPTER

14

"We're not that impressed with the case detail," the *TGL* producer said.

Nettie's stomach sank.

The *TGL* producer went on. "You've got three cases—or wait, two cases—that are linked by crime site, MO, cause of death, and the time frame in which the abduction took place. Then this third case—where you don't have the abductor on tape and where a body's never been found—all you've got on that is the interstate convenience-store location and—*if* an abduction took place—it took place roughly within the same time frame as the other two abductions. Weak, very weak."

Before Nettie could ask if he was telling her *TGL* wouldn't accept their proposal, he started in again.

"But. We like what you sent us on the convenience-store statistics and we like the angle on these three cases being part of a trial balloon on new investigative techniques. We talked that over with the executive producer, and he agreed. He said go heavy on that and we'd be interested."

Nettie went limp with relief. "That's great. Any idea on scheduling?" She held her breath again.

"That's our other problem," he said. "We've just had three segments tank. Legal complications, some production errors, and a significant change in case facts. So we're in scramble mode. One of the reasons we're calling you is that your production suggestions look doable. If you're willing to blast off on this thing, we need your segment in three weeks. We know that's a push, but frankly, if we don't slot you in that time frame, I can't commit to this season."

He thought he needed the hard sell to get her to agree to the truncated schedule.

Wrong.

"If you can commit to airing our case in three weeks, we'll commit the resources you need on our end to make it happen," Nettie said.

"OUT-standing. Consider us committed. We'll fax you the paperwork in the A.M."

The resources needed on "their end" kept Mars and Nettie fully occupied over the next two weeks. *TGL* segments featured both simulated scenes from featured crimes and interviews with actual victims, family members, and law enforcement personnel involved in the original investigations. Nettie coordinated setting up the "actuals" and both Nettie and Mars reviewed scripts for simulated scenes and the actuals. They supplied victim photos and crime-scene videotapes. They reviewed unedited videos that *TLG* sent via the Internet and provided comments on the videos to *TLG*'s production staff.

When *TLG* crews came to Minneapolis to film the actuals, Nettie traveled with them, so she was out of the office for three days running. With Nettie gone, Mars focused on the procedures *TGL* had in place to handle tip calls. This was the part of their strategy that gave him the most concern. He'd started by saying he wanted all incoming calls to *TLG*'s tip lines recorded and he would personally review all the calls.

TLG staff had been confounded by this request.

"Do you have any idea how many calls we're going to get on this?"

"A lot," Mars said.

"Let me tell you about 'a lot,' " the production assistant had said. "We will get more calls than you will live long enough to listen to. And probably seventy-five percent of the calls are not going to be worth listening to. Another twenty percent will wash out in the next review cycle. That will leave us with five percent of the calls that will be worth your time—and five percent is still a big number."

Mars winced. "It's just that the smallest detail can make a difference. Something you'd miss unless you were involved with the case . . ."

"Where your time means something is in working on the form our tip takers will use. Everybody on our tip lines has been trained on interviewing callers and they're instructed to pass on anything to our investigators that they have any doubts about. Believe me, after you've been doing this a while, you develop a sixth sense of what's real and what's not. Trust us on this and give us your best shot on the interview form. That's where your involvement will make a difference."

Mars knew what they were saying was right, but it still made him nervous. He couldn't think of a single case he'd handled where some small detail hadn't been important to clearing the case.

In the end, he recognized he didn't really have a choice. He'd just have to hope these guys were as good at screening calls as they said they were.

Mars went back to Redstone with the *TGL* production team to interview Sig Sampson.

"He was sensational," one of the producers said after they'd completed the interview and were heading back to the Twin Cities. "Nineteen years later, and he still has the details at the tip of his tongue. Those black binder case files—how many on the shelves—a dozen? You ask him a question and he knows just which file to go to, which page"—he turned toward the back of the gigantic Lincoln Navigator the *TGL* team had rented and said to the cameraman—"it shot great, right?"

"Fabulous," the photographer said. "Passion always shoots great. This guy cares as much about this case today as he did on day one. It'll blow everybody else off the screen."

The cameraman turned to the last row of seats behind him where Nettie was sitting with a young woman who was the *TGL* production assistant.

"Except for you, gorgeous," he said, leering at Nettie. "Smart shoots great, too. Smart and beautiful. Nothing beats that."

Nettie put her hand on his face and pushed him in the other direction. He thought she was kidding around with him.

"I mean it," he said. "You managed to make all that crap about your data whatsits interesting. And the statistics—the workplace mortality numbers—that's going to work. I was worried about that, but with Miss Frisch doing the numbers, it'll sell." He looked over his shoulder and gave Nettie a big grin. "All we need to work on is your wardrobe. I see you in a black lycra blouse, top four buttons open, black lace bra . . ."

Mars looked at Nettie through the rearview mirror.

What he saw on Nettie's face made him rethink his discussion with Sig Sampson about conceal and carry.

The cameraman owed his life to the fact that Nettie wasn't permitted to C&C.

The producer sitting next to Mars said, "I was disappointed the victim's parents weren't living in Redstone anymore. But Sampson was great. Couldn't have done better. All these grieving parents look alike, anyway."

"Only the ones that are dead look like the Bergstads," Mars said, pissed at how crass the producer's attitude was. It was Mars's turn to think about the possibility that C&C had some virtues. But his next thought was that what the producer had just said was not that different from how Mars himself had felt on the first cold cases he'd worked.

The *TGL* team dropped Nettie and Mars at their office, where they'd both left their cars. It took extra effort on Nettie's part to separate herself from the cameraman, who was intent on taking her out for a drink.

Mars started making excuses for Nettie, saying they had things to finish up, but Nettie interrupted him.

Facing the cameraman head-on, she said, "I don't have anything to do tonight. But if I didn't have anything to do every night for the rest of my life, you'd get the same answer: *No,* I do not want to go out for a drink with you. Get it?"

"I think you just guaranteed yourself some unflattering camera angles when they edit this tape," Mars said as they walked over to their cars.

"Like I care," Nettie said. The troubled look he'd seen on her face when she'd been talking with the *TGL* production assistant came back. "Mars—when the producer was talking to you about the fact the Bergstads didn't live in Redstone anymore?"

"Yeah?"

"The production assistant was asking about that. She wanted to know if they were dead or what. I told her what Sig Sampson told you, that the Bergstads had moved to Texas the year after Andrea disappeared and had died after that. The PA said she thought that was odd. That most of the families they meet who have missing relatives never leave the place they lived when their relatives disappeared. Especially when it's a kid. They want to be there in case the kid comes back. The PA said she couldn't ever remember a family who had a missing kid who moved away that soon after a disappearance."

A sour feeling started to ooze in Mars's gut, taking the edge off how well the day's shooting with the *TGL* crew had gone. It was the same feeling he'd had when Sig Sampson had told him Erin Moser was dead, and Mars had thought his theory about a predator trolling convenience stores had just tanked. As soon as Nettie had raised the question about the Bergstads moving away from Redstone, he knew the point needed to be thought through.

But not now. For now they had to stay focused on *TGL*.

"There's always somebody who's different," is what Mars said.

Mars's phone rang as *The Get List*'s closing credits rolled.

Glancing at the caller ID, Mars said, "So, Sig, how does it feel to be a television star?"

"I can tell you it's positively painful. Lord, I knew I was getting old—but that fella on the program tonight looked like he had one foot in the grave. And talk about a muddle mouth. I don't think I said one coherent sentence . . ."

"As usual, you're being way too hard on yourself. The cameraman said after the shoot that you were terrific and you were. I had some concerns about how they'd edit what they had, but all in all, they hit the points we wanted to come across. The theory about a single predator, convenience-store risk, what we're doing with the database—and I think they did an especially good job on putting out a call for our

97

mystery couple. That's what I'm really hoping will pan out of what ran tonight."

Sig said, "You and Nettie came across real strong. I'm keeping my fingers crossed on finding those two. I suppose our senator renewing his reward offer helps, but I have to tell you, he annoys the daylights out of me. Always looking for an opportunity to score political points. The other thing—with that offer out there, TGL is going to get twice as many false leads as they otherwise would. At least that was our experience back in 1984 when he first offered a reward."

"I think I agree with you," Mars said. "But my colleagues in the Cold Case Unit tell me reward money can make a difference. My idea is that it only helps if you've got someone who has something to lose by coming forward. Give them a big enough incentive, and what they've got to lose seems less important. But I guess we're about to find out how the reward is going to work, one way or another."

"How'd he get involved in this thing, anyway?" Sig said, talking about the senator's reward offer.

"His office here must have clued him in," Mars said. "Probably picked up on the local coverage that's run about the TGL program. TGL called me a few days ago. They seemed pretty pleased about the reward. They're the experts on what works in generating new information. And they're the ones that have to sift through all the chaff that comes in. Let's hope they're right."

"What's next for us?" Sig said.

"We wait. TGL will forward electronically what they consider to be the solid tips in the next forty-eight hours. What we do then depends on what the tips are."

"How do they decide what to send on?"

"Three categories. TGL says category one is easy, the nutcases, the calls that don't even connect to our cases. They expect those calls will be about seventy-five percent of what they get. The second category is calls from people who say something specific about our cases—the caller knew a victim or has some kind of connection to the scene—but what they say kind of stops there. Nothing they say gives us anything to follow up. The third category is what TGL will forward to us.

Callers who say something specific about our cases and what they say gives us something to follow up."

"Any idea what the volume's going to be?"

"*TGL* says they'll get anywhere from several hundred to several thousand tips. Like I said, the tips that cover the information we asked for—the category two callers that get forwarded to a second level of reviewers, mostly retired or volunteer law enforcement folks from what I'm told, will be about twenty-five percent of the total. So, it could be a couple hundred or a couple thousand. *TGL* says if thirty to fifty percent of category two turns out to be solid, we'll be doing well."

Mars heard Sig sigh. Then Sig said, "You'll always kind of wonder about the ones you don't see, won't you?"

"I've talked *TGL* into giving me a random sample of tip sheets from the first and second screenings. Just so I can get a feel for what we're missing."

Sig sighed again. "So, now we wait."

"That's it," Mars said, feeling his own tension starting to build at the prospect of waiting. Then he heard the silence on Sig's end of the line.

"Sig?"

"Yeah?"

"Another forty-eight hours isn't anything like nineteen years."

CHAPTER

15

"Seventy-six solid tips," Nettie said as she scrolled through the file that *TGL* had sent as an e-mail attachment. "There was a total of eleven hundred and thirty-three tips, two hundred and forty-one of those made it past the first screen, and seventy-six are solid."

"What about the random sample of the rejected tips?" Mars said. "We agreed to a random sample of one of every fifty rejected tips."

"Give me a minute," Nettie said as she continued to scroll through the file. "So, one of every fifty rejects and there were . . ." she mumbled as she did the math in her head.

Tapping a calculator on his desk, Mars said, "If there were eleven hundred and thirty-three tips and we got seventy-six solid tips, there's a reject pool of one thousand and fifty-seven, which . . ."

Mars punched the equal sign and looked over at Nettie. "Twenty-one point one four. What did they send?"

Nettie looked back at him with a smug smile. "Twenty-two. Satisfied?"

Mars leaned back on his chair, stretching his legs. He clasped his hands on top of his head and started making popping sounds with his lips. Never a good sign.

He straightened up. "Twenty-two out of one thousand and fifty-seven. That makes me nervous."

"Not as nervous as all eleven hundred and thirty-three would make me," Nettie said. "Twenty-two plus seventy-six is ninety-eight. Still a lot of work."

"If we're lucky," Mars said, "it will be a lot of work. But how much work it ends up being depends on what's there. If it's not a lot of work, we're in trouble."

They worked the tip sheets as they agreed they'd do. Nettie printed out all ninety-eight of the tip sheets, because that's how Mars wanted to work. He wanted to be able to touch and feel each tip sheet. It would be the first fresh evidence he'd handled since starting the investigation, and he wanted that evidence to be tactile, to stir all his senses. He'd never get that from a computer screen.

With the tip sheets printed, they each took thirty-eight of the solid tips and eleven of the randomly selected tips. The plan was they'd each go through their tip sheets, ordering them by which tips would receive priority investigation. Then they'd switch tip sheets and if either disagreed about priorities, they'd pull those sheets and argue priorities between them.

The tip sheet information was basic: name, address, and age of person providing information and contact information. There were boxes that were checked to indicate which of the three cases the tipster had information about and whether their information concerned suspects or victims. After that was a series of questions about the caller's relationship to either the suspect or the victim. Callers were then asked to give a brief narrative of their information that the *TGL* screeners would enter on the computer tip sheet, reading it back to the caller before saving the file.

TGL had cautioned Mars and Nettie that while some tips warranted immediate follow-up and referral to the local law enforcement agency—like, "my brother used to live in Redstone Township and he told me five years ago that he's the one who took Andrea Bergstad in 1984"—most did not.

Mars had suggested they mix the randomly selected tip sheets with the solid tips so they'd give the same level of attention to all the reports. They weren't more than a half-dozen tip sheets into their respective stacks when they'd each hit a randomly selected tip. It stuck out like a neon light. They took to reading them out loud to each other for comic relief.

101

"Mr. Ernest Kleinmetz (age 62) of Knife Lake, Minnesota, reports that he delivered bread to the One-Stop in Redstone Township between 1989 and 1993 and personally knew all the staff working at the One-Stop. While he doesn't remember any staff names, he would be able to identify them if shown pictures."

"Mrs. Maude Getz (age 73) of Richmond, Indiana, reports that the convenience store she frequents was robbed two weeks ago. She has photocopies of the two perpetrators posted by local police and will forward the photocopies upon being assured that she is eligible to receive the $25,000 reward."

"DeeDee Kipp (age 19), Vermillion, South Dakota, says that the photo on TGL of the Redstone Township abduction victim resembled her babysitter. She has pictures of herself with the babysitter and will send them upon request."

"Abel Johnson (declined to specify age or place of residence) had a vision in which the name 'Damien Will' was repeated. Mr. Johnson said he heard the name repeated every time Chief Sampson of Redstone Township spoke during the TGL segment."

Of the randomly selected tips, they were twenty-two for twenty-two on the useless scale. Lots of psychic visions, lots of somebody who looked like somebody without any meaningful tie to any of the three investigations, and lots of stretching thin connections to tie the tipster to the reward.

"So," Nettie said, "feeling better about not being able to see all eleven hundred and thirty-three tip sheets?"

"Better, but not a hundred percent. You know how it is, Nettie. The smallest detail." He shook his head. "But what I really feel bad about is the solid tips. I don't see anything here that gets us near our mystery couple. Slim pickings all around."

"There could be more. *TGL* said sometimes the most solid tips come two or three days after the show airs. Or through their Web site. People who have something serious to say take time to think it over before they call in."

Mars got up and walked around the office, flexing his fingers, stretching, then coming back to his desk and scooping up the tip sheets.

"Okay. Your best shot. Where do we start with what we've got?"

"We got—what?—three tips about guys Andrea went to high school with . . ."

"All of whom Sig Sampson checked out backward and forward in 1984."

"So why does someone call in nineteen years later unless there's something to it?"

"Because some people never get past high school. For some people, something that happened to them in high school is still the most important thing in their lives. Then there's a national television program that talks about what happened in their hometown, where they went to high school when they were teenagers, and their old grudge is reborn."

Mars shrugged. "It won't hurt to nudge around on those three guys. See where they are, what they've been doing. But . . ." He held up both hands and let them fall.

"What about you? Anything you think we should start on right away?"

Mars picked up the tip sheets again, fingering through them. "I don't know. Maybe the fellow who said he was at the One-Stop earlier that night and there was a guy hanging around the store. At first I thought it was the same fellow who told Sig Sampson there was a car in the lot but he didn't see anybody in the store other than Andrea when he went in. But I checked and the names don't match. Guess I'll talk to him. Try to get more details."

He dropped the tip sheets on the floor next to his chair. "Amazing. Nineteen years later and we're still getting calls from people about Averill Hess."

Mars sat up straighter, rubbing his eyes. "Which reminds me. I need to talk to Averill about a question I had on the videotape." He yawned and looked at his watch. "Geesus, Nettie, it's almost three o'clock. C'mon, let's get out of here. Tomorrow's another day. Maybe something will pop out of this crap tomorrow that we're too tired to see now."

"And if it doesn't?"

"Doesn't what?" Mars said, too brain numb after hours with the tip sheets to follow the conversation.

"If nothing pops out of the crap, what then?"

Mars stared at nothing in particular. As they started for the door, he said, "It's what you said. If nothing pops with what we've got now, we better hope it pops in the next day or two.

"If not, we're right back where this thing started in 1984. Not a good place to be."

CHAPTER

16

The first pop came in a phone call at 10:39 the next morning.

"Detective Bahr? I'm Marvin Brustein. I represent a client who believes he has information that is responsive to questions raised on *The Get List*. My client prefers to have me contact you directly rather than calling the program's hotline."

"And your client's name is . . ."

"My client prefers not to be identified. He has authorized me to provide you with his information, but his preference is not to be directly connected to the information or your investigation."

Without knowing if what he said next was true, Mars said, "Is your client aware that by failing to identify himself he won't be eligible for the reward offered in the case?"

Brustein's tone was dismissive. "My client is not motivated by a twenty-five-thousand-dollar reward."

Good for him and better for you, Mars thought, tapping his right index finger on the desk as he thought about what to say next.

"You're an attorney, Mr. Brustein?"

"Yes."

"Criminal law?"

Brustein didn't answer right away. Then he said, "Yes." Nothing else, just "yes."

"Good," Mars said, his tone conciliatory, collegial—he hoped flattering without being an obvious suck-up. "Then I'm sure you can understand that the value of any information you provide is reduced if

I don't know who is providing the information, if I don't have the ability to question that person regarding specific aspects of the information . . ."

"I expect we could arrange a written interrogatory if you felt it was necessary after reviewing the information I provide. I doubt it would be necessary . . ."

"I appreciate that—but I have to tell you, it would be a poor substitute for a face-to-face interview. You're from the Twin Cities, Mr. Brustein?"

"Yes."

"And your client? He's from this area as well?"

Another silence. Then, "I don't believe that information is relevant to your interests."

Mars processed Brustein's response quickly. He thought it likely that Brustein's client was another attorney in the same firm. It didn't take him more than five seconds to reach that conclusion and his sixth sense told him Brustein was following Mars's thought processes on the other end of the line. It made Mars feel like he'd gained some ground.

Mars tried to laugh in a way that sounded friendly. "I'm sure you can appreciate that I'd prefer to be the judge of what's relevant to my interests."

Brustein didn't say anything.

Mars shifted on his chair and in his tactical approach.

"Look—Marv? You said your name was Marvin?"

"Marv is fine."

"What I'm having trouble with here is understanding your client's motives. It would help me if you could explain why he doesn't want to have a face-to-face. Are you prepared to say your client has no direct involvement in the commission of a crime?"

Brustein came back at Mars fast.

"Absolutely. As to my client's motives . . ." Brustein drew a deep breath. "My client is concerned that the circumstances surrounding the information in question could subject him to charges for which he would not . . ." Brustein had gotten twisted in his own words, and he stopped.

Mars said, "Just say it, Marv. Then we'll decide where to go next. Give me what your client gave you."

In a weary voice, Brustein said, "My client believes he is the individual you are looking for—the individual who called the Redstone police in October of 1984 to report that the One-Stop convenience store was not staffed."

A warm, melting sensation spread under Mars's skin, followed by a cold prickling.

His voice had dropped an octave and sounded fuzzy around the edges when he said, "Why in God's name, Marv, does your client think telling me that himself is a problem? He must be an attorney, right?"

"Again, I don't believe that information is relevant . . ."

"Okay. Forget whether he is or isn't an attorney. I just can't think of another reason why anyone would dance around on coming forward with information as nonculpatory as what you've just said."

The line was silent for a long time before Brustein said, "My client is concerned that someone might hold him culpable for leaving the One-Stop before law enforcement officials arrived. He has assured me that he was not asked to stay— was not even asked to give his name or contact information—but he feels if it was falsely asserted that he had been asked to stay and didn't . . ."

"Marv," Mars said, "it is a matter of record that the individual who made the call was not asked to stay at the scene. The officer who failed to request that the caller stay at the scene was subject to disciplinary action for that omission. Nobody—*nobody*—is going to accuse your client of leaving a crime scene against police instructions. Is that it? Because if that's all that's worrying your client, he's got nothing to worry *about*."

Mars could hear Brustein breathing on the other end of the phone.

"I'm relieved to hear that. You'd be willing to fax me a statement to that effect? Confirming that my client was not asked to remain at the scene?"

"If I had your client's name I would. I am not prepared to fax you anything that says an unspecified person was not asked to remain at the scene."

A deep sigh.

"We are still left with the simple fact that what I've just told you is all my client has to say. He does not believe he has anything substantive to contribute to the investigation."

"You said you're a criminal attorney. I take that to mean you understand implicitly why I want to talk to your client about that October night in 1984 at the One-Stop. Give me his name and your fax number and I'll have the exculpating statement to you in the next five minutes. Then we can go from there."

This time Brustein didn't hesitate.

"Larry Shawn. 612-340-1199."

The story Larry Shawn told in his downtown Minneapolis office was straightforward.

He and a woman he'd been dating—a woman he was in the process of dumping, he added, with an offensive degree of self-pride in the statement—were heading back to Madison, Wisconsin, after attending a fraternity brother's wedding in Nebraska.

Shawn interrupted himself to reach across his desk, rising slightly off his chair to pull a humidor toward him. He took the top off and made a job of selecting a cigar.

"Cuban," he said to Mars, briefly lifting the obscenely long and thick object toward Mars, then cutting it with an elaborate scrimshaw and silver instrument. "El Rey Del Mundo Choix Supreme. A robusto. Very complex, a woody finish . . ."

He stopped himself, some vestigial sense of good manners distracting him. He held the robusto toward Mars. "Have one. Nothing like it."

Mars shook his head.

Shawn took a small box of matches from a vest pocket, made a single strike, and began the ritual of lighting the cigar, drawing quick, short breaths, his lips flexing on the end of the cigar until the ash glowed. This was a practiced routine on his part, full of self-conscious symbolism. As the first haze of smoke rose, he lifted his eyes toward Mars and said, "Never light a cigar with a chemically fueled lighter.

The taste will saturate the leaf. Ruins a great cigar as soon as you draw."

He shook the match out with one hand, and as smoke filled the room, leaned back, raising one foot to his desk. "Where was I?"

"Heading back to Madison with a woman you no longer loved."

Shawn grinned, pleased with Mars's answer. "No longer lusted after, truth be told. Love never was part of it." He gave Mars a conspiratorial look, assuming that between men this was a circumstance that required no explanation.

"I was shot," Shawn said, "and we still had a long drive ahead of us. Maria, the gal I had on the skids"—he repeated his knowing grin—"had to pee like every fifty miles. So I'm pissed about having to stop. I stay in the car, she goes in, comes right back out. She was spooked because there was no one in the One-Stop. Wanted me to go in with her while she peed. Just to get her out of there faster, I went in. While she peed, I called nine-one-one. Like I said before, like my lawyer said, no one asked me to stay. No one even asked for my name. End of story."

"I'm curious. Why didn't you call in when you saw the news coverage about Andrea Bergstad's disappearance?"

"How about because I didn't see or hear anything. Even if there was something in the Madison papers—and I don't think there was—I was a senior in law school. I had finals coming up. It wasn't like I was sitting around reading newspapers much."

"And Maria? She didn't hear anything about the disappearance?"

Shawn laughed. "Maria? Read newspapers? I mean, the *news* part of newspapers? Give me a break." Shawn's cigar had gone cold, and he went through the motions of relighting before he spoke again. "Tell you the truth, I wouldn't know if she heard about it or not. I saw her once—briefly—after that trip. A school the size of UW-Madison, it doesn't take much effort not to see someone you don't want to see. I will say this. *If* she'd heard about it, I'm pretty sure she would have gotten in touch. She was a do-gooder type."

"Any idea where she is now?"

"Not the slightest. Not even sure if she graduated from Madison.

When I was seeing her she was talking about going abroad instead of spending more time in school."

He tapped the cigar ash into a long crystal ashtray that looked like it would have made a fine blunt object murder weapon.

"Good luck trying to track down someone named Maria Carlson. If that's still her name."

"And you called my office rather than the *TGL* hotline number because?"

"You were local. And I wanted to talk to my lawyer first. He suggested we just call you directly."

"Fair enough. I want to go through your memory of that night. Step by step. Start with when you drove up to the One-Stop. Nothing seemed wrong about the place to you—or to Maria?"

Shawn made a deep shrug with both shoulders, his cigar raised in one hand. "No—I was just anxious to get back on the road."

"And your friend, Maria. She didn't notice anything, say anything . . ."

"Not before she went in. I mean, she kept trying to get me to respond to her, she'd been doing that all weekend. But she didn't say anything about the . . ."

Shawn stopped abruptly. He sat forward and for the first time seriously thought about that October night nineteen years ago. He brought the cigar to his lips and drew deeply, squinting as the smoke seeped out of his lips.

"When we drove up. She said something when we first drove up to the One-Stop. She kept trying to get me in a good mood. And she said . . ."

He hesitated. "Something about—who was that guy? The fifteen minutes of fame guy, white fright wig?"

"I'm not following," Mars said.

"I didn't either." Shawn snapped his fingers. "Warhol. She said the One-Stop looked like an Andy Warhol painting."

"An Andy Warhol painting?"

Shawn opened both arms in a gesture of futility, the movement causing the ash on his El Rey Del Mundo to collapse and drift toward the carpet. "Go figure. Classic Maria quote. Don't expect it to make sense. She was a fucking fine arts major. I thought it was sexy when I met her, but it wore out fast. She was always saying something like that."

Mars scribbled a note and said, "I have a DVD dupe of the scene at the One-Stop when you and Maria were in the store. I'd like you to watch it, see if it jars any memories . . ."

Shawn popped forward, looking at his watch. "I gotta get over to the courthouse for a deposition. Long as I can get out of here in the next forty-five minutes, give it a shot."

Mars set up the DVD player on Shawn's desk. "The visual quality is poor. But I think you'll recognize yourself and Maria."

He punched the play button and the gray, grainy image of the One-Stop, circa 1984, emerged, the counter clock in the lower right-hand corner being the only motion on the screen. After a few moments, Maria walked in, hesitated, then turned, leaving the camera range. Her presence was all the more eerie for the slightly slowed motion of the tape, the way any movement she made created a faint trace of light before it dissolved back into the image.

Shawn was bent forward, elbows on knees, hands clasped, swiveling the El Rey between his lips. "God," he said when Maria appeared, "she did have a pair on her. I'll give her that." Then he whooped as he and Maria reappeared. "This is surreal. Seeing this now, after all this time. Sur-*real*."

Like any egomaniac, Shawn was only interested in what was going on when he was part of the action. His concentration was complete as he watched himself walk behind Maria toward the rest rooms.

"Stop it here, can you?"

Mars hit the pause button, then turned to watch Shawn.

Shawn was staring at the screen. He looked at his cigar, drew on it, then looked back at the screen. "Right here," he said, pointing the cigar at the screen. "What I said earlier—about Andy Warhol?"

"About the One-Stop looking like an Andy Warhol painting."

"Yeah. I think I got that wrong." He sat silent and motionless, his eyes fixed on the screen. Then he pulled the crystal ashtray toward him, tapped the ash, and looked at the screen again. His elbow was on the desk, the cigar between his index and middle finger. He brought

111

the cigar closer to his face, his thumb moving back and forth across his lower lip.

"Edward Hopper," he said.

Mars raised his eyebrows to signal he didn't get Shawn's point, but said nothing that would break Shawn's concentration.

"I actually liked Hopper's paintings. What Maria said when we drove up to the One-Stop wasn't about Andy Warhol. When we drove up to the One-Stop she said it looked like an Edward Hopper painting. And it did. Real isolated in the dark, all the light coming out of the windows. The light just making the place look isolated." He drew on the cigar and exhaled. "What she said about Warhol? She said that about this spot right here. Where we are right here on the tape."

Right where, Mars thought, but did not say, *Andrea Bergstad ducked down just before she disappeared and right where Averill Hess ducked down when he walked into the One-Stop just after Andrea disappeared.*

"Why?" was all Mars said.

Shawn continued to stare at the screen. "I'm not remembering this exactly. What I'm remembering is something on the floor. Like the clerk had been stocking shelves, maybe. I don't know . . ."

"And that's where Maria said something about Andy Warhol?"

"Not something. She said the same thing she said about Hopper. She said, 'It looks like an Andy Warhol painting.' Just like when we drove up to the One-Stop she'd said, 'It looks like an Edward Hopper painting.' "

They watched the rest of the tape until they came to the point where Larry Shawn and Maria Carlson left the One-Stop.

Shawn looked at his watch, then tapped the ash off the end of the cigar, leaving it dead. "I have to get going. Sorry I can't tell you any more than that. Bottom line is, I can't believe anything that happened while we were at the One-Stop is going to help you out."

Mars stood up, snapping the DVD player shut. "Sometimes it takes a long time to figure out what is or isn't helpful."

"What you don't know after nineteen years seems to me like something not worth knowing," Shawn said, pulling on his suit coat and shooting his cuff-linked shirtsleeves.

Mars considered giving Larry Shawn his take on all the things Shawn hadn't learned in the past nineteen years.

It took only a moment's consideration for Mars to decide he had better things to do.

CHAPTER

17

Better Thing to Do Number One was to ask Nettie to track down someone named Maria Carlson who was a fine arts major at the University of Wisconsin-Madison in 1984.

Having made a mental note on that point, Mars let his mind play as he drove back to the office with what Shawn had told him. Whether Shawn knew it or not, what he'd told Mars explained what had been inexplicable: Why had Andrea Bergstad and Averill Hess ducked down at precisely the same spot in the One-Stop?

Problem was, what Shawn had told Mars didn't really answer that question. It raised more questions. What Shawn remembered was that it looked like someone had been stocking shelves at the spot where Andrea and Averill had ducked. That didn't explain why Andrea would have ducked down at that point. Someone comes into the One-Stop with a gun, her first thought isn't going to be, *I've got to finish stocking shelves before I leave.*

For that matter, it didn't explain why Averill would have ducked down.

Mars pulled the car over and picked up the case file, looking for the report on the crime scene. His finger traced down over the scene description. Nothing about unshelved products on the floor.

Maybe Averill put things back on the shelves when he bent down. Sig had said it would be just like Averill to notice something like a gum wrapper or a cigarette butt on the floor and pick it up. Except

Averill's head had dipped out of sight for what?—at most a three count. Hardly enough time to stock a shelf.

Better Thing to Do Number Two was to contact Averill.

Nettie'd left him a note on his desk.

She was meeting with the IID project team near the State Capitol and wouldn't be back in the office until midafternoon. The note also said a man had called twice for Mars, but had not left his name or a message. *Feels like another pop to me,* the note said.

Nettie had told Mars more than once that he had problems with delayed gratification. That she was right hadn't been any help at all in curbing his impatience. He wanted Nettie to find Maria Carlson ASAP, and he wanted to talk to Averill Hess now.

Nettie not being available, Mars tried calling Averill at the number Sig Sampson had given him. Predictably, Hess was no longer at that number and the easy things you do to find a new number didn't work. This was a job Nettie could get done blindfolded and exactly the kind of job Mars didn't want to do under any circumstances.

He looked at his watch. Probably another hour before Nettie got back. He thought about what Shawn had said about the place on the video where both Andrea and Averill had ducked down.

It looks like an Andy Warhol painting.

Shawn's description of Warhol as the fifteen minutes of fame guy with a white fright wig had brought an image to Mars's mind, but that image did not include any idea of what Warhol's paintings looked like.

Mars sat down in front of his computer and Googled "Andy Warhol's Paintings."

The hits numbered in the thousands. He picked the first site that included pictures of Warhol's paintings.

The first painting he saw, a highly stylized pastel portrait of Marilyn Monroe, connected Mars to Warhol's work right off. Pop art. "And pops are what I need, right?" Mars said to himself as he scrolled through Warhol's popular culture images from the fifties and sixties. Mao Tse-tung, Richard Nixon, Jackie Kennedy . . .

And Campbell's soup cans.

The warm, melting feeling, followed by a prickling sensation, Mars had felt when he knew they'd connected to the mystery couple hit him again.

He forced himself to stay calm, to think through everything he knew about the case that could possibly connect to an image of Campbell's soup cans. There was something vague, abstract, about why it felt to Mars like this image was important. He was tense with fear that if he missed the connection now, it would be lost forever.

He slipped the DVD dupe of the One-Stop surveillance tape into the drive on his computer, fast-forwarding to the point where Andrea had ducked down for a moment.

What if, he asked himself, *at this moment, Andrea bent over, took a Campbell's soup can off the shelf and put it on the floor?*

Her doing that fit perfectly with what he saw on the video image. More than that, it fit perfectly with the image of Averill Hess bending over, picking up a single soup can, and putting it back on the shelf.

The question was, *Why* would she do that?

No. The question of why Andrea would do that was premature. The first question Mars had to answer was an absurdly mundane one—the answer to which might well be impossible to find.

He got Tom Fiske's phone number in Redstone from directory assistance. That was the easy part. The tough part was dealing with Tom Fiske's attitude when he took Mars's call.

"Thanks a lot for trashing convenience-store managers on national TV," Fiske said as soon as Mars identified himself.

"I don't remember anybody trashing convenience-store owners," Mars said. "The point we wanted to make was made with the numbers we gave about convenience-store employee deaths and injuries. And what could be done to make those numbers smaller."

Mars didn't add, but he thought, *If the shoe fits, wear it.*

"That's not what people who saw the program think," Fiske said. "I've been taking shit ever since the program ran. People saying I didn't care about the people working for me, that I'm responsible for Andrea's death. I haven't worked at the One-Stop for seven years, but after the *TGL* program, that's how people around here are going to think about me. How do I shake that?"

It gave Mars the perfect lead-in to his question.

"You can help me answer an important question about the One-Stop the night Andrea disappeared. And I know this is a long shot, but trust me, it's important."

"What?" Fiske said, still sounding belligerent.

Mars played his angle hard to flip Fiske from belligerent to cooperative.

"Like I said. I know this is asking a lot. But Sig Sampson said you were a hands-on kind of manager, so I'm hoping you'll remember. If you can't—no hard feelings. It's a lot to expect, but I've got to give it a shot."

"So give it a shot," Fiske said, the edge already off his voice, sounding a little cocky, like he welcomed a chance to show off what he knew.

"Don't think this is crazy—and even I don't know at this point why this is important, I just know it is—but did the One-Stop sell canned soup in 1984?"

Fiske guffawed. "This is a hard question? *Yes,* the One-Stop sold canned soup in 1984."

"Good," Mars said. "But that wasn't the hard part. The hard part is, where in the store was canned soup stocked?"

Fiske was silent for seconds. Then he said, "I can tell you that, too. Corporate had product floor plans for all their One-Stops. The way they shelved product was based on customer demand—the last-minute impulse purchase, chips, snack food, candy bars, stuff like that—on the first shelf in front of the cashier. Which was fine, except canned goods were walking out of the store in pockets and purses. So we moved the big bags of chips to another rack near the front of the store. Nobody's gonna get a big bag of potato chips into a purse or a pocket without pulverizing the product, making a lot of noise, so it worked fine. Then we moved the canned goods to the bottom shelf directly opposite the cashier. That way, anybody wants a can of soup, they've got to bend over to get it, right in front of the cashier. We cut our losses on canned goods to almost zero immediately. You go into the One-Stop today, it'll be the same setup. And that was my innovation. My idea. I think Corporate used that plan in all their stores after they saw the way it worked for us."

What was on Mars's mind was that Fiske and One-Stop Corporate had put more thought into protecting cans of soup than they had put into protecting staff.

"That's what you needed to know?" Fiske asked when Mars didn't respond immediately.

"It gets me started on what I need to know," Mars said. "I appreciate your cooperation. It will be noted in my report."

Mars kept his hand on the phone after he'd talked to Fiske. Was it possible that the most important contribution One-Stop management would make to the investigation of Andrea Bergstad's disappearance would be a decision on where they'd shelved canned soup?

He couldn't answer that question until he answered the most important question, the question he'd started with.

Why had Andrea Bergstad put a can of Campbell's soup on the floor before she left the One-Stop?

When Nettie came back into the office she saw Mars standing at the office window, obviously in deep thought mode. This was not unusual. What was unusual was the image on Mars's computer monitor. A pop art image of Campbell's Tomato Soup.

"Soup's on?" Nettie said as the door closed behind her.

Still deep in thought, Mars turned toward her. It took him a minute to connect to what she'd said.

"Soup is definitely on," he said, moving back from the window. "It just isn't hot yet."

He told her what he'd found out from Shawn and Fiske.

"Am I crazy," he said, "or does this make sense to you, too?"

"It makes sense to me, too," Nettie said. "But I also agree it's not hot yet."

"I've been standing here doing free association on words. Can. Soup. Campbell's. Tomato. Warhol did paintings of vegetable soup cans, too. Vegetable. Red and white. Trying to see if anything clicks with what we know about Andrea Bergstad. Nothing."

Nettie said, "Campbell, Mars. Alan Campbell offered the first reward in the abduction case. When he was a congressman in the Redstone district. The same Alan Campbell who is now the junior senator from Minnesota, the same Alan Campbell who just offered a reward when *TGL* ran our case. The same Alan Campbell who is trying to position himself as a vice presidential candidate in the next election."

"The same Alan Campbell who's counting on the incumbent vice president falling over dead," Mars said.

"That's the one," Nettie said. "Personally, I can't stand the guy. But you've got to give him credit for parlaying poster-boy looks and no brains or morals into a pretty successful political career."

"Tell me this," Mars said. "How does Alan Campbell connect to a convenience-store predator?"

Nettie dropped down on the couch. "The only thing that comes to mind is that there isn't a connection between Alan Campbell and a predator. That Alan Campbell *is* the convenience-store predator. Just not the convenience-store predator we thought we were looking for. I mean, somebody who was trolling around at night picking off store clerks working alone."

She swung her feet up on the couch, grabbing her thick black hair into a topknot with one hand. "I have the sinking feeling my database connection just tanked."

Mars started making popping sounds with his lips. A bad sign. Then he said, "Shit."

"Eloquent," Nettie said. "Tell me, Mars. How do we go about investigating a connection between a sitting senator and a 1984 abduction of a seventeen-year-old convenience-store clerk?"

In unison they said, "Carefully. Very carefully."

CHAPTER

18

It was dark by the time Mars and Nettie left the office.

They'd spent almost two hours on the Internet trying to find something that would tell them where Alan Campbell had been the night Andrea Bergstad was taken from the Redstone One-Stop.

After repeated futile searches, Nettie said, "Nineteen eighty-four is too long ago to find what we need to know on the Internet." She picked up her phone. "I'm going to call Linda Van Cleve and see if she can get me into the History Center tonight. They'll have local newspaper files going back forever."

"This could wait until tomorrow," Mars said, not really meaning it.

Nettie waved a hand at him in dismissal as she started to explain to Linda Van Cleve, director of the State Historical Society, that if at all possible, it was important that she have access to the History Center to check something prior to a legislative committee meeting that was scheduled for the next morning. She told Van Cleve what she needed, nodding as she listened to Van Cleve's response.

"That's great," Nettie said, giving Mars a thumbs-up. "I'll be over in a half hour. That gives you time to reach security at the Center?"

Masterful, Mars thought, listening to her.

Nettie put the receiver down hard. "I'm set. I'll call you when I have something."

Certain that he and Nettie had been the last occupants to leave their office building, it half surprised Mars when another car followed him out of the parking lot, making a right turn after Mars as he headed back to downtown Minneapolis. Mars kept his eyes on Nettie's car ahead of him until she took a left. Then he checked his rearview mirror to be sure the car didn't take a left after Nettie.

It didn't. It stayed behind Mars. Sometimes directly behind him, sometimes in a lane behind him to his right or his left. A light blue, late-model Buick LeSabre. Mars couldn't make the plates, but as much as he could tell, it looked like an Iowa tag. For no good reason, other than that Iowa and evil weren't two words you put together in the same sentence very often, he took comfort in the fact that the car was from Iowa.

Mars took the Delaware exit off I-94, turning left off Delaware onto Washington Avenue. This took him through the University of Minneapolis East Bank Campus, across the Washington Avenue Bridge over the Mississippi, past the West Bank Campus, then into downtown Minneapolis.

It wasn't the most direct route back to the condo, but he didn't want direct just now. He wanted indirect. And he wanted to see if the blue Buick from Iowa stayed on his tail as Mars wound his way home.

No way the blue Buick from Iowa was still going to be on his tail on that route unless its plan was to follow Mars.

Which was exactly what it did. Mars signaled his turn just before he took a right off Washington between Marquette and Second and dived down the ramp to the garage. He had just enough time to see that the blue Buick from Iowa had slowed to miss the light at Second and was idling near the garage entrance. Just before Mars drove through the key card-operated garage doors, he saw the Buick's tail-lights flash and the Buick move east on Washington.

"What was that about?" Mars said as he got out of the car. Since moving out of a uniform into street clothes, there hadn't been many times on the job when Mars felt scared. He didn't feel scared now, but he was more than curious about what the Buick had been up to.

The phone was ringing as he opened the front door. Without taking his key out of the door, Mars moved quickly to the kitchen wall phone.

"Dad!"

"How are you?" Mars said, more grateful than he could say to hear his son's voice. Their new living arrangements in the downtown condo suited them both, but for Mars, when Chris was gone, the perfection was blighted.

"I'm good. We've confirmed my return flight, so Mom said I should let you know."

Mars shook his head without saying anything. Only Denise did things like confirming flights.

"I'm anxious for you to be back," Mars said. Then he talked about the reasons why, none of which got close to his feelings. "The place is starting to look pretty grungy. And I haven't had a decent meal since you left."

"Ten days," Chris said.

"Ten days," Mars repeated.

He'd barely reset the receiver before the phone rang again.

"Mars?" Nettie said. "When we drove out of the parking lot—did you notice that blue Buick behind us? I don't think there was anyone else in the building when we left, but the car stayed behind you after I turned . . ."

"Iowa plates," Mars said. "It stayed on my tail until I turned into the garage."

"Iowa plates," Nettie repeated. "That doesn't sound so bad. What do you think was going on?"

"Damned if I know," Mars said, turning toward the refrigerator for a Coke. He had just started to open the refrigerator when he saw the man standing in the front hall, his hand raised to knock on the partially open door.

"I'm sorry," the man said, seeing Mars seeing him. "I called your office today—but I think maybe this is a conversation we should have in person. I wanted to catch you as you came out of your office, but . . ."

Mars held his hand up to signal the man that he should wait. Then he said to Nettie, "I have to go. I'll call you later tonight."

Mars switched the hall light on to get a good look at the guy. He looked like somebody who would drive a blue Buick LeSabre with Iowa plates. Maybe five feet ten or eleven, putting on a little weight, but basically fit, hair starting to go gray in a good way—good clothes, clean, pressed, coordinated. Probably fifteen, twenty years older than Mars. He looked like the kind of guy you'd find at a golf club on weekends or a Rotary Club lunch weekdays. Looking at him, Mars knew what the guy's glove box and car trunk looked like. Nothing in either place that didn't belong there.

What the guy didn't look like was somebody who'd lurk in parking lots and tail strangers.

"How'd you get past security at the front door?" Mars said.

Again the guy apologized. "I called a couple times downstairs. Got a busy signal on both calls. I was standing there when one of your neighbors came in with her dog. She asked me who I was trying to reach, and when I said your name, she said your son walked her dog. She brought me up . . ."

He looked around for a moment. "I hope I'm not waking your son."

Mars didn't answer. Instead he said, "You'd better come in." Maybe not the smartest decision Mars had ever made, but he was way too curious about what was going on not to sit the guy down and find out. "Your batting average on the phone is lousy."

"That's pretty much how it seemed to me." The guy held out his hand. "I'm Jim Baker. Decorah, Iowa. I caught part of *The Get List* program the other night. Didn't see all of it, but what I saw made me want to talk to you."

"Let's go into the living room," Mars said. "I was just getting a Coke. Want one?"

Baker hesitated the way someone does who wants something to drink, but not what's offered.

"Sorry," Mars said, "but Coke is what we've got. Maybe a bottle of Evian water . . ." He opened the fridge and peered in. There was nothing in the fridge other than Coke. "Nope. Coke is it. Tap water, if you don't mind drinking river water. Dry as it's been the past few weeks, the Mississippi brew is a little ripe, to my mind."

"A Coke would be fine," Baker said. He rubbed his face with both hands. "What I need is caffeine and liquid. I left Decorah early this morning and have been sitting in the parking lot at your building for the last three or four hours."

Mars caught him looking in at the empty refrigerator. "My son's out of town," Mars said. "I don't eat in much." Mars handed Baker a can of Coke and a glass and led the way into the living room, switching on lights as he walked.

Mars and Chris weren't set up for guests. Since they'd moved, the only people who came by the condo were Chris's friends and Nettie. Now, as lights came on, it occurred to Mars that the living room looked like the inside of the refrigerator.

Chris's futon that he'd used when he'd visited Mars's old efficiency apartment was draped over a bare pine frame. The steel frame shelves Mars had used for general purpose storage at the apartment were against the wall next to the sliding-glass doors that opened onto the small terrace. Their major purchase since moving to the condo was a giant flat screen TV and DVD. It had been set up more or less in the middle of the room and had never been moved. Piles of DVDs surrounded the TV. Two collapsible fabric chairs from Target were positioned in front of the TV.

"You just got divorced, right?" Baker said, taking the room in.

"Half right. Divorced. Almost nine years ago. But we just moved."

Baker nodded. "Looks like a real guy place."

Mars took his first objective look around the room. "That's probably right." He pulled over one of the fabric chairs and sat. Baker followed his lead.

Mars took a deep swallow of Coke and said, "I let you in because I really want to know why a guy who drives a blue Buick LeSabre with Iowa plates would follow me home from the office."

Baker's face tightened with tension. "You noticed me." It was a statement, not a question.

"Probably an occupational habit. Paying attention to what's going on around you. Being more suspicious than the average guy."

Baker turned the glass in his hand. "I don't know where to start. I'm afraid I'm not going to be able to tell this story any way that'll make sense to you. That's really why I drove up here instead of calling."

"Just start," Mars said. "We'll sort it out along the way. Patience is on my job description."

"This is going to sound crazy," Baker said, looking at Mars like he wanted absolution before a confession.

"Crazy is also part of the job."

Something hollowed out on Baker's face as he thought about how he wanted to start. The carefully maintained veneer of his exterior self lost its cohesion and exposed—what? Grief, fear, guilt? It was impossible to say. All that Mars could say for sure was that whatever Baker had on his mind had the power to alter the man as soon as he started to let it come to the surface.

"I need to tell a story," he said. "A story that starts a long time ago."

"The story I'm working on is nineteen years old," Mars said. "You work cold cases and you get used to old stories."

Baker bent forward on his chair, head down, then raised his eyes toward Mars, keeping them on Mars's face.

"If I'm right about the story I'm going to tell, your story is older than that. If I'm right, your story starts at the same time my story starts.

"Thirty-two years ago," Baker said.

CHAPTER
19

"I was in Vietnam in 1971," Baker said.

He let that stand, not saying anything else right away, assuming it was a statement that had its own meaning.

"It was the worst possible place for me to be. Me and a lot of other guys, but guys like me especially, because I've always liked things to be clear-cut. I like to know why I'm doing something, and I need to know that I'm doing something for the right reasons. I went into Vietnam as a Marine because I thought that would make things clear-cut. I thought being a Marine would guarantee doing things for the right reasons."

He shook his head, making the sound of a muffled, unformed laugh.

"Vietnam in 1971. Probably Vietnam anytime. Nothing clear-cut, and for sure no right reasons. I just tried to keep my head down, do my job, stay alive."

Baker told his story slowly. The story of a straightforward man who went to Vietnam believing simple truths. A man who found a reality more complicated than anything his character or experience had prepared him for.

If it had ever been an original story, Mars thought as he listened to Baker's soft voice, it no longer was. The story Baker told had become, since the end of the Vietnam War, a kind of Everyman's story of Vietnam. Men went bravely and returned disillusioned. They went believing in something and returned believing nothing.

That was Jim Baker's Vietnam story.

Nor was it a story that brought Mars nearer to understanding why, on this July night thirty-two years later, a stranger from Iowa was sitting in his living room telling Mars his story of disillusionment.

Not until Baker told Mars what had happened at Khe Ranh.

"There were two sounds I'd never heard until Nam.

"Two sounds I never want to hear again. The Vietcong's SKSs. Chinese- or Russian-made semiautomatic rifles. You can hear them from miles off, if the air is right, if they're at one end of a valley and you're at another.

"You'd think a rifle would sound like a rifle. Not the SKSs—all my internal organs just sank when I heard them. Especially when it was a surprise that there were VC around.

"But the SKSs—how they sounded—was nothing compared to the little beep you'd get from the sensor you wore if you were part of an advance team doing recon at night . . ."

"A sensor?" Mars said.

Baker looked directly at Mars. "If you were on patrol at night, moving a position, doing recon—you'd wear a sensor around your neck. That way, if an enemy sniper was using an infrared sighting scope, you'd hear this little beep when his sight picked you up . . ."

Baker made the muffled laugh sound again, the look in his eyes hollow. "Lot of good it did you. Somebody told me Quantico's timed it. When you hear the beep, you've got one-fifth of a second to hit the ground. I never saw anyone that made it down in time. All the beep really does for the guy that gets sighted is advance warning he's gonna die. Doesn't even give him time to cross himself."

They both sat in silence for seconds before Baker spoke again.

"But the beep saved me. On a trail out of the Khe Ranh Valley. My squad was heading back to base camp. It was dark, intelligence told us there were no VC in the area. We thought we were home free.

"Then I heard it. Heard the beep. I dropped without even stopping to think that I wasn't wearing a sensor. I was three men back from the head of our line. Our squad leader must have been wearing a sensor. What I heard was his sensor. He went down almost in synch with me—it was like he exploded. He had to have got hit with a hollow point. Then the guys all around me started going down. I got dinged—friendly fire I'm pretty sure—but nothing serious. Not that I could really tell. I was covered in blood. Mostly other guys' blood, not my own.

"I crawled on my belly off the trail into the underbrush. And I stayed there I don't know how long. Until someone grabbed my ankle. I'll tell you the truth. I shit myself . . ." Again, the empty laugh. "Only reason I didn't piss in my pants is I'd sweated myself dry while I was lying there. It was nighttime, but the temperature still must have been in the high nineties—and the humidity, the humidity was off the scale. I was seriously dehydrated.

"The guy who grabbed my ankle was Myron Godfrey. Maybe the sweetest guy I've ever met. A young black guy from Washington, D.C. Enlisted right out of high school. You know the expression 'A.J. Squared Away'?"

Mars shook his head.

"A real buttoned-up Marine. Somebody who buys the whole deal. Perfect marksman scores. Stays sharp lying in the mud in the jungle. That was Myron Godfrey. The only man I met in Nam who never lost faith."

Baker stared, thinking back over the years. "So, I'm lying there in my own shit, worrying about how somebody was going to find me and take me home, and Myron has been crawling up and down our line checking bodies.

"He says to me, real quiet, 'Baker—it's you, me, and Al Dente. We're not going to get the bodies out now. We need to stay under cover, off the trail, and get back to base camp for help. Then we need to be back here before dawn to get our guys. So we gotta move fast.'

"Al Dente," Myron said. "What I thought was, there is no justice in the world. Of all the guys to make it through, this would be the one guy who least deserved it. Any situation, Al Dente would be the guy you'd say not only didn't deserve to make it, he was a guy the world would be better off without. A real Skivvy Honcho, a skirt chaser. That said, I can also tell you that of all the people you'd expect to make it through in any cluster fuck situation, Al Dente would be it. Charmed life. Undeserved, but charmed."

Baker sighed, shifted in his chair, then got up, walking around. He stopped by the sliding doors that led out onto a small terrace. He turned to Mars.

"Would you mind if we moved our chairs out here?" he said, nodding toward the terrace. "It's a nice night, and I need all the air I can get to tell this story."

Mars stood, picking up both their Target folding chairs, while Baker slid the doors back. Mars switched off the overhead light in the living room before he pulled the doors shut behind him to minimize bugs on the terrace.

"I don't usually use the good furniture out here," Mars said, "but I'll make an exception tonight." Baker looked confused. He was still too much into his story to get a clumsy joke.

Being out on the terrace was a good move. Even surrounded by high-rises and the muted noise of traffic on the street below, it felt right. Mars guessed Baker had another motive for wanting to be on the terrace. He wanted to tell his story in the dark.

Darkness suited Baker's story. And Baker's voice, disembodied in the darkness, took on a tone of gravitas as he, Myron Godfrey, and Al Dente made their way off the trail in the Khe Ranh Valley back to their base camp.

"Godfrey was a lance corporal, I was a second lieutenant, and Al Dente was a captain. But the way things worked on this trek, Godfrey was the honcho. Godfrey was in the lead, Godfrey was taking the compass readings, Godfrey was making decisions on when to halt, when to move. It was an unholy adventure, I can tell you that. We could hear SKSs firing—Godfrey said about three miles off and not in the direction we needed to move. He said he thought we were about six miles from base camp, but it was impossible to tell how much ground we were covering. There was no path, it was severe dark, and we were forever getting tangled up in the undergrowth or tripping on roots underfoot . . ."

Mars said, "Severe dark?"

"Utter darkness," Baker said. "My term, I guess. I have a friend who's a pilot. He used the term 'severe clear' to describe a perfect flying day. A day when visibility is limitless." Baker paused. Mars could feel Baker turn toward him. "September 11, 2001, New York City. Pilots described that day, that place, as severe clear."

The information stayed in the soft night air between them, until Baker spoke again. "I asked my friend what the opposite of severe clear was, and he said zero visibility. That didn't quite do it for me. I said, maybe 'severe dark,' and my friend liked that. We've used it between us ever since. Mostly to describe a situation where you're bum fuck nowhere—mentally, physically, emotionally. And severe dark, in all its meanings, was where we were on that trek."

Baker lifted his feet, resting them on the terrace rail. "Al Dente, who was doing nothing to get us where we were going, starts complaining about being dehydrated, saying that we needed to find water. Hell, if you'd rung out the three of us you wouldn't have come up with a teaspoon of liquid. Godfrey, who's still calling me and Al Dente 'sir,' says there's a village on our route, that we can try and get water there, but what he thinks would be best would be to tough it out. To get back to base camp as quick as possible.

"Al Dente says he needs water now, we'll check out the village. He looks at the map. The village isn't far from the base camp, and there's a good road between the village and camp. He says he's sick of slogging through shit. We'll go to the village for water, then take the road back to camp."

Baker stopped. "What I'm going to say next—it's a hard thing to explain to anyone who's never been in Vietnam. But nothing was what it seemed. A village—three or four huts with old people and women and children—could be dangerous. When we came into that village, that's what we found. A clearing surrounded by jungle. A few huts, women and kids, a couple of old ladies and one old guy . . ."

Baker drew a deep breath, and when he spoke again, his voice was trembling. "What worried me—what worried Godfrey—was that one of the villagers was a young girl. I don't know, maybe eleven, twelve years old. Fragile-looking. Not five feet tall, probably eighty-five, ninety pounds. Long black hair, hanging down her back."

Baker shook himself hard before going on. "Southeast Asia was a flesh pot. If there was a guy in your squad, in your platoon, who had deviant tastes, he had plenty of options for satisfying himself. And if he did, it got talked about. Guys on leave tended to partner up based on their tastes, and it was no secret that Al Dente liked young girls. He bragged about it. Hell, he got his nickname because of his reputation for liking young girls.

"So when Godfrey and me saw Al Dente watching the girl, we got nervous. The people in the village gave us water, offered us food, but Godfrey waved them off. Asked Al Dente very formally for permission to continue to lead to base camp.

"I knew right off what Al Dente was going to do just by looking at him. He had this sick look on his face. He wasn't looking at anything but the girl. Godfrey says, 'Sir! We need to leave now in order to make it back to the trail tonight to complete our mission'—meaning, to get the bodies. To a Marine, nothing's more sacred than that. We don't make it back to the trail where we took fire before dawn, the VC are going to take the bodies.

"Al Dente waved us on. Said he wanted to complete inspection of the village. That he'd come right after us. Godfrey stood his ground . . ."

Baker bent forward, elbows on his knees, dropping his face into his cupped hands. When he raised his head, Mars saw the shine of tears reflected on his cheeks from the streetlights below. Baker's voice was hoarse when he said, "I can still hear Godfrey's voice. 'Sir! Permission to assist in inspection!' 'Sir! Permission to remain under your command until further orders!'

"Me?" Baker said, "I stood there with my ass hanging out. Not saying anything. To this day, it just feels to me like if I'd said something to support Godfrey . . ."

He shook his head again and drew a deep breath. "Finally, Al Dente gets really pissed. He shouts at Godfrey, 'Alpha Mike Foxtrot, Lance Corporal. Is that an order you can read?' "

Before Mars could ask Baker what the order meant, Baker said, " 'Alpha Mike Foxtrot' is Marine talk for 'Adios, Mother Fucker.' To say something like that to an A.J. Squared Away Marine like Godfrey . . . well, it just goes to show how FUBAB Al Dente was." He waited only a second before he added, "Fucked Up Beyond All Belief."

"It strikes me," Mars said, "that Marines had a whole dictionary to describe screwing up."

"You're right about that," Baker said, sounding tired. "And we needed the whole book in Vietnam."

Mars let Baker take time before he spoke again, but the silence gave Mars time to consider that he still had no idea how this increasingly ominous and compelling story was going to connect to Andrea Bergstad.

"After Al Dente's Alpha Mike Foxtrot farewell, we didn't have much choice. We left the village and headed back onto a jungle path that would take us to the base camp road. At that point, even I could have gotten back on my own.

"We hadn't gone more than a hundred yards when we could hear screaming behind us, from the village. An older woman's voice, yelling in Vietnamese"—Baker's voice cracked—"and the girl's voice."

In a strangled whisper, Baker said, "What I especially remember was the two words the girl kept repeating—'No, please. No, please.' Except the words came out, 'No-ah, plea. No-ah, plea . . . ' "

He sobbed as he said, "I remember being so touched that she was trying to speak English. This little girl, trying to speak English to save herself. And her mother's voice making this high electronic sound . . ."

Baker straightened himself. "Godfrey said, 'I'm going back.'

"All I said was, you can't. I didn't say, we'll both go. I just said, you can't. But of course, he did. Because that's who Godfrey was. Godfrey was the kind of guy who went back.

"Me, I was the kind of guy who just stood there on the path, dried shit on my pants, tears running down my face. Then I heard Godfrey going through his 'Sir!' routine again. I couldn't hear what Al Dente was saying, but I could tell he was yelling at Godfrey, getting madder.

"Finally I got myself off the dime. I headed back. I figured with both of us there, seeing whatever was going on with the girl, Al Dente wouldn't have a choice. But by the time I got to the edge of the clearing, standing in the undergrowth, Al Dente had drawn his sidearm. He had it pointing directly at Godfrey. Godfrey, bless him, was standing there looking right back at Al Dente, not blinking.

"What was really bad was the girl. Al Dente had her by the hair. She was down on her knees in front of him. His pants . . . his pants . . . were unzipped, hanging loose on his hips. I can't . . . I can't tell you . . . how obscene . . . The girl was crying, but trying not to make any noise. The mother, too, kneeling behind Al Dente, her hands up in front of her face. I think when Al Dente drew his sidearm it must have shut them both down.

"So what do I do? I start thinking about consequences, justifying why it doesn't make any sense for me to intervene. I tell myself, Al Dente won't have the guts to actually shoot Godfrey. But if I suddenly come out of nowhere, it might rattle Al Dente. He might fire in reaction to seeing me.

"How it seems to me now is that right when I had that thought— that if I came out into the clearing, Al Dente might fire—there's a shot. *Crack!* Next thing I see is Godfrey, Godfrey lifting up, then Godfrey goes down. I'm not taking any of this in. I'm thinking Al Dente shot Godfrey, but I know I didn't see his sidearm fire.

"While I'm trying to understand what I've just seen, too scared to move, this figure moves into the clearing. Tall, lean, and . . . green. I know that sounds crazy, but he was green. Green body paint. Carrying a sniper rifle. Then I get it. This is who shot Godfrey. And just when I'm realizing that's what happened, this guy—the Green Man—lifts his rifle with one hand, not even putting it to his shoulder, and fires a single shot into the girl's forehead. Her mother screams, and he shoots her. Casual. Like he doesn't care one way or the other."

Baker stands up. "I think I must have run then. I don't remember. What I remember is hearing more shots while I ran. Sometimes a double report—which had to mean Al Dente was firing, too. I'd made it all the way back to the road when I fell, tripped over my own feet. I broke my ankle, but I still got back to base camp on that broken ankle.

"And that ankle got me a medical discharge."

Baker was silent for a long time. Silent for so long that Mars guessed his story must be over. Mars was, at once, shaken by the story, moved by the horror of the scene, and touched by Baker's honesty. He was also confused. He still didn't know why James Baker had come all this way to tell his thirty-two-year-old story—no, not just a story, a *confession*—to him.

Mars couldn't ask the question at that moment, couldn't say, "Too bad. What's this got to do with me?"

Instead he said, "And nothing's ever happened to Al Dente for what he did that day? He made it out of Vietnam, too? And the Green Man? You know any more about who he was?"

Baker was trembling. The summer night was still warm, but Baker was trembling. Mars stood up next to him, putting his hand on his shoulder.

"Let's go back in. We can talk inside."

Mars turned the wall light on as he walked into the living room. When he looked at Baker in the light, he was shocked. Baker's smooth, well-maintained middle-aged self looked ten years older than how he'd looked when Mars had first seen him at the door. He looked ravaged. And the trembling had increased to an almost spastic shaking.

"I . . . I've never . . . told anyone . . . not anyone . . . what I just told you. When I got home from Vietnam, my wife knew something was wrong, but I never told her. Not even my wife. How could I . . ."

A tremor shook Baker so hard he staggered. Mars forced him down on the futon couch, went into the bedroom for a comforter, then wrapped Baker in the comforter. Then he went into the kitchen and ran the hot water tap. When the water was as hot as it would get, Mars filled a glass and took it out to Baker.

"Drink this," he said. "I think you're going into shock. You don't stop shaking in the next couple of minutes, I'm taking you over to the Hennepin County Medical Center ER . . ."

"No," Baker said, sitting up, clutching the comforter around his shoulders, one hand extended to hold the glass of hot water. The water splashed wildly as he lifted the glass to his lips with his shaking hand.

Baker gulped the water, and Mars moved behind him, grabbing

134

both of Baker's shoulders, massaging them deeply. "Stamp your feet," he said, and Baker, like an automaton, stamped his feet.

Mars wasn't sure what the medical rational was behind what he'd just put Baker through, but the improvement was immediate. The shaking stopped and Baker's color returned to normal. He breathed deeply, consciously, leaning back onto the futon frame, looking for all the world like what he wanted to do was sleep.

With his eyes closed, Baker said, "They made it back, all right."

He opened his eyes and looked at Mars.

"If Al Dente hadn't made it back, I wouldn't be here."

Mars shook his head. "Your story is extraordinary. But I have to tell you. I'm not getting the connection to the Andrea Bergstad case—what am I missing?"

Baker closed his eyes again, then opened them.

"I forgot the most important part. I told you Al Dente got his nickname because it was a well-known fact he liked young girls. But I never told you his real name . . ."

"Al Dente is a nickname?"

Baker nodded. "We started by calling him Chicken Noodle. Suited him. But—you being a cop, you must know how men can be about nicknames. You start with one, then you spin another name off that one. The farther out you go from the original, the happier everyone is. So Chicken Noodle became Al Dente. Al Dente for *firm,* with reference to the fact that he more or less had a permanent hard-on for young girls."

The warm, melting sensation, followed by prickling, was, once again, flooding Mars's senses.

"And Chicken Noodle," Mars said. "You called him Chicken Noodle because of his real name."

Baker nodded. "Yeah. From Alan Campbell to Chicken Noodle wasn't more than a hop, skip, and jump."

CHAPTER

20

"I was in Minneapolis a week ago on business," Baker said. "I heard a news story about *The Get List* doing a segment on the convenience-store abductions.

"The news piece mentioned that Minnesota Senator Alan Campbell had renewed a twenty-five-thousand-dollar reward offer for information leading to the victim's return or identification of her body. The piece I heard didn't say much more about the victim or about Campbell's connection to her, but I got a kind of sick feeling in my stomach. I made it a point to watch *The Get List* program. When I saw the picture of the girl, heard how young she was—well, all I could think was if I'd done something about Alan Campbell thirty-two years ago, that girl would probably still be alive."

Mars shook his head. "I can't imagine being in the situation you were in back in Vietnam. Or that you'd know then that Campbell could possibly get involved in something like this when he got back to the States. For that matter, we're a long way off from establishing Campbell's connection to Andrea Bergstad . . ."

Baker said, "But you weren't surprised when you found out Al Dente was Alan Campbell. You knew who I was talking about before I said his name. You must think . . ."

The phone rang. Mars looked at his watch, and was startled to find it was after midnight. Then he remembered that Nettie had gone over to the History Center.

"I've got to get this," he said to Baker.

"Well, partner," Nettie said, "our pop art forensics just went fizz."

"Meaning . . ."

"Meaning I've got an article from the *Duluth News-Tribune* that says on the October 1984 night in question, Alan Campbell was the keynote speaker at the annual St. Louis County Republican Bean Feed."

"Damn," Mars said, his warm, prickly feeling drying up fast, "I didn't even know Republicans ate beans."

"It was too much to hope for," Nettie said. "Not that Republicans eat beans—I mean that our pop art soup can was a message from Andrea. It seemed providential at the time, but . . ."

"Nettie, I can't talk just now. Something has come up—but given what you've just said, I'm not sure anymore what it means. Can you be at the office at seven?"

"Like *what* has just come up?"

"Not what. Who. A guy from Iowa who drives a blue Buick has come up. To my condo, as a matter of fact. Talk to you in the morning."

"You're right," Mars said, returning to the living room and to the point Baker had been making before Mars took Nettie's call.

"We have been looking at a possible connection between Campbell and Andrea Bergstad's abduction. But what we had to establish that connection was thin. Very thin. And now"—Mars nodded in the direction of the kitchen—"the call I just got pretty much blows even that connection, thin as it was, out of the water."

Baker said, "I know what I've told you doesn't help much, but every instinct I have is telling me there is a connection. I'm just sorry I can't give you anything else . . ."

"Tell me," Mars said, "what happened after you got back to base camp."

Baker drew a deep breath. "What could I say when I got back to base camp? If it had been just Campbell shooting Godfrey, the girl, maybe I could have held my ground. But it would be Campbell and the Green Man against my word. I don't know about the Green Man, but I can tell you, Campbell was a hell of a good liar. Even I could think of a dozen ways Campbell would tell the story that would get him off the hook. And if I could think of a dozen ways, Campbell could have come up with a hundred ways. That was the thing about Vietnam. There were always a dozen ways things did or didn't happen, always a dozen ways why you were right and somebody else was wrong. Somebody else?

"I was in base camp for only about twenty-four hours after I got back. My ankle break was bad, especially after I'd walked on it for as long as I had, so I got helicoptered out the next day."

"And when Campbell got back to camp?"

"He got back a few hours after I made it back. He had the Green Man with him. They were carrying Godfrey's body. Said Godfrey'd taken fire in the village and they'd had to take action to clean up the village."

"And Campbell never said anything to you?"

Baker gave Mars a hard look. "Oh, Campbell talked to me all right. He came into the hospital tent. Came up to me real quiet, and said, 'I want you to know that I've decided not to charge you with deserting the scene of action. I know what went on back there was pretty dicey, pretty confusing, so I'm going to look the other way on this one. We lost enough guys on this mission,' is what he said."

Baker shook his head. "I read his message loud and clear. 'You say anything about me ordering you and Godfrey out of the village, anything about Godfrey coming back to the village, and I'll come after you.' "

"You don't know if he knew you'd seen what happened with Godfrey, with the girl?"

"I'm sure," Baker said, "he didn't know it at the time. If he'd known I'd been there, in the undergrowth, just on the perimeter of the village, I wouldn't be alive now. They would have got me then. But I'm willing to bet he thought about it plenty afterward. And his message covered that possibility. What I'm really sorry about is that Al Dente read me just right. Chicken shit that I am, I left it where he wanted it left."

"And the Green Man," Mars said. "What did you find out about him?"

"The Green Man," Baker said. "He made quite a stir when he came into camp. Kind of the 'Bigfoot' of Vietnam was how it sounded to me. Half myth, half legend, larger than life. And *green*. Always covered in green body paint."

Baker looked preoccupied for a moment, then said, "Vietnam was the perfect environment for a guy like the Green Man. A perfect scenario for a guy who wanted to do things his own way and didn't want to be bothered by bureaucracy. Word had it that the Green Man had been useful to some of the brass. They'd pretty much given him carte blanche to operate on special assignments and, when he wasn't on assignment, on a freelance basis. He went wherever, did whatever. Most snipers work in pairs—a spotter to assist in sighting the target, and the guy with his finger on the trigger.

"The Green Man worked alone. There was something about him . . ." Baker rubbed his right hand slowly across his chin as he considered what he was going to say.

"Snipers. A breed apart. Extraordinary discipline, extraordinary skill. Most people think being an ace sniper means you're a good shot. End of story. But there's so much more involved. You've got to know how wind conditions, humidity, and temperature are going to affect your shot. You've got to be able to plan a tracking strategy, camouflaging strategies, you've got to maintain a precision weapon under impossible conditions—and you've got to be able to integrate all of that information in the instant that you pull the trigger.

"Hard to know exactly what motivates a guy to be a sniper. Most of them just have a real taste for the challenge, the precision of the job. I mean, every guy with a gun in Vietnam was a potential killer, but most of us really didn't want to think about killing an individual. We did what we had to do to stay alive, to accomplish our mission. But we didn't take any pleasure from the idea that we were killing some mother's son, some baby's father.

"What snipers do is much more specific, more focused. Most of the time it's hard for them to ignore the fact they're killing an individual. Part of their mental—their emotional—discipline is to handle that. To keep a guy in your scope long enough to see him think, to see him scared, to see him tired, to see him do brave things—and then, in an instant—to pull the trigger on him.

"Not easy," Baker said. "For most guys, not easy. And you wouldn't want it to be easy. Every once in a while, you run across a guy who likes the idea of killing. The thing about the Green Man—what I saw of him that day in the Khe Ranh Valley and what I heard about him after—is that he was as close to being a blank slate emotionally as you're going to get. He didn't kill for pleasure, but killing didn't much bother him, either. You manage that balance, you're going to be a sniper to remember."

"And the Green Man," Mars said, "he never talked to you after you were back at camp? You never found out his name?"

Baker shook his head. "Doubt that was something he'd do under any circumstances. And I never heard the Green Man's name. I asked a couple guys—nobody I knew had any idea. As it happened, a few hours after I got to camp, another guy from our squad—a guy we'd left for dead—made it back to camp. That was a considerable distraction.

"I tried to talk to my squad mate," Baker said, tears welling in his eyes, "but he didn't want to talk to me. Can you blame him? He heard us leave him . . ."

"And you never talked to Campbell again?"

Baker said, "My last memory of Campbell is seeing him lying in his tent when I got carried out on a stretcher to the copter. Lying on his cot, head propped up, smoking a cigarette. He had his cassette player on, full blast, playing this over-the-top, mid-sixties make-out song. He played that song all the time, especially after he'd come back from leave. But to play it then—after what he'd done the day before? That memory alone . . ."

Mars figured Baker had suffered enough remembered guilt for one night. He thought the best thing he could do—for the investigation and for Baker's sake—was to give Baker hope.

"What happened in the past," Mars said, "is done. Over. What I need to know is if I can count on you to help in the future. If our investigation into Andrea Bergstad's abduction takes us back to Alan Campbell, are you prepared to come forward then?"

140

"Why do you think I'm here now?" Baker said, genuinely incredulous. "Anytime, anyplace—"

He stopped to draw a deep breath, his emotion obvious.

"I'm there."

CHAPTER

21

Mars sat in the living room with the lights out for a long time after Jim Baker left.

More than he had been prepared to admit to Baker, he agreed that what had happened to Baker in Vietnam was relevant to what had happened to Andrea Bergstad. At the perimeters of Mars's consciousness was a vague awareness of talk about Campbell being a ladies' man. What he couldn't remember hearing was anything specific about young girls.

If they had been able to prove that it was possible for Campbell to be in Redstone on that October night in 1984, Mars would have felt like they'd scored a direct hit in making the connection. Instead, what they had was what sounded like conclusive evidence that Campbell was not in Redstone on that night.

Mars decided to put conclusive evidence on hold and think about motives. In October of 1984, Alan Campbell was one political season away from becoming the junior senator from Minnesota. Why the hell would he get himself involved in abducting a teenage girl?

The answer to that question seemed simple. The teenage girl had become a problem for Campbell.

She was talking about her relationship with Campbell.

Mars thought about that. It didn't really work. If Andrea Bergstad had talked about her relationship with Campbell, that would have surfaced before now. And, if Andrea Bergstad had talked about her relationship with Campbell, abducting her would be the last thing you'd

142

want to do. It would just complicate Campbell's involvement when the abduction was investigated.

Maybe Andrea Bergstad had started to put pressure on Campbell. Maybe the romance was wearing off, and Campbell wanted to take preemptive action to end the relationship in a way that would prevent her being a problem in the future.

That made more sense. But it didn't answer the question of how Campbell could have been in Redstone at the same time he was eating beans with Republicans in Duluth.

Mars got up and walked back out to the terrace, taking comfort from the warm, humid air. He stared out at the city, appreciating the sight of the City Hall clock tower. He'd loved working in that building, even if the people and politics he'd shared that space with had made it impossible for him to stay at the Minneapolis Police Department.

He thought back to Jim Baker's thirty-two-year-old story. A story that had seemed remote, unconnected, to Mars's nineteen-year-old story. Now he was certain the two stories were connected. If he just could find a way to do it.

Severe dark, Mars thought, recalling Baker's words. A situation of utter darkness. A situation that left you adrift, mentally, physically, emotionally.

"I can relate to that," Mars said out loud. The extraordinary thing about this case was that understanding what had happened thirty-two years ago, nineteen years ago, kept slipping further out of reach the more they knew.

"I'm missing something," Mars said out loud.

That was obvious. But what Mars meant was that he could *feel* that he was missing something. That meant the thing he was missing was within reach. It was there. It was something he already knew, that he hadn't yet connected. He just needed to concentrate.

Concentrating didn't happen. He was tired, his brain was still permeated by Baker's story. So he gave up trying to force the missing connection. Instead he thought about the first thing he needed to do tomorrow.

That, at least, was easy.

He needed to drive down to Redstone and talk to Sig Sampson. They needed, the two of them, to sit in Sig's cool, dark den and bang heads over what Sig knew about Alan Campbell and Andrea Bergstad. They needed to . . .

The connection came. Just like that. It came from the image of Sig Sampson, sitting in his den, fingering the .308 cartridge.

The image burned the fatigue off Mars's brain like a flash fire.

He went into Chris's room and turned on the computer. Then he did a Google search on "Marine Sniper" and "Ammunition."

It took scrolling through the first two entries to find what he wanted to know. "This," Mars said, "is getting to be the case that Google got."

There was no way he was going to bed now.

He looked at his watch. Nearly 2:00 A.M. Three hours to drive to Redstone. That would get him there too early, but it was better than staying here, pacing the floor.

Remembering that he'd told Nettie he'd be at the office by seven, he called her office phone and left a message. Then he took the elevator down to the garage.

He was on the road to Redstone before 2:30 A.M.

CHAPTER
22

Mars was wakened almost simultaneously by a lightening sky and Sig Sampson tapping on his windshield.

He shook himself to reclaim consciousness and pushed open the car door, his legs stiff as he swung them out. It was already hot and morbidly humid. Mars felt soggy and dull. He had no doubt he looked even worse.

"Good Lord," Sig said. "I thought when I came out the front door, *What's this town coming to? People sleeping on the street in their cars.* Then I saw it was someone I knew, and I really got worried."

"I've come to tell you a story," Mars said. "Make me a cup of coffee?"

"I'll do better than that," Sig said. "I'll buy you breakfast down at the Harvest." Sig took another look at Mars. "I'll be risking what reputation I've got left in this town to sit at a table with a stranger—particularly a stranger who *looks* like he's slept in his car—but hell, at my age, why not live dangerously?"

"I'm going to save your reputation, Sig," Mars said, taking Sig's arm and moving him back toward the house. "This is a story that needs to be told in private, in a dark room. And I know just the place."

With efficiency, if not inspiration, Sig made Mars scrambled eggs and toast while the coffee perked. Neither of them said anything about why Mars had come to Redstone during the dead of night, but as soon as Mars had finished his eggs, Sig cleared their plates from the table and said, "Let's go back to the den."

The air conditioner had been off, so the room was close and airless. The shades had been open, but Sig pulled them shut before he turned on the air conditioner. In moments, the air conditioner began to feed its condensation in soft plinks into the coffee can on the floor. The sound reminded Mars of how far they'd come since his first conversation with Sig Sampson in this room.

"I'm going to tell you a story without telling you where the story comes from," Mars said. "I want you to focus on the story, then we'll talk about why I think this story is true."

Without thinking about it, Sig reached for the brass cartridge. Seeing him do that, Mars was reminded that until he'd moved to the CCU, he'd always played with a pack of cigarettes. A new habit born of an old habit. A bad old habit. It had begun to feel infantile to him, playing with a pack of cigarettes, and when he'd left the MPD, he'd told himself it was a habit he could do without.

Watching Sig now, the cartridge moving in his hand, Mars realized it was a habit he'd broken because there hadn't been anything in his new job that he'd thought deeply about. Until now. And for the first time, he missed the cigarette pack.

"I'm going to tell you what I think happened the night Andrea Bergstad was abducted," Mars said. "A lot has come together in the last couple days—some of it pretty thin—but thin or not, it feels right to me. After I've told you what I think happened, I want you to tell me if it makes sense to you."

The cartridge had stopped moving in Sig's hand. His eyes were riveted on Mars's face. But he didn't say anything. Sig had enough sense to know that saying something now would just slow down hearing what Mars had to say. And Sig had been waiting nineteen years to hear this story.

"I think," Mars said, "that Andrea Bergstad was having a relationship with an older man . . ." Mars saw a frown begin to cloud Sig's face. "Not her college boyfriend. A married man. A married man with a public reputation.

"On the night she disappeared, I think an associate of that man came to the One-Stop. I'm still not sure what his purpose was, but what

I think he told Andrea was that his associate—the man Andrea was having a relationship with—wanted to see her. My guess is he said the man was waiting for her in the car. I think that's why Andrea left the store the way she did. I think she thought she was just going out to the car to talk to this man, that she'd be coming back to the One-Stop.

"But something was worrying her. Because before she left the store—the point on the tape where she ducks down?—she took a can from the shelf and put it on the floor. That can was a signal. To whom, I can't say. My guess is it was just a desperate gesture. The point is, I think she was already suspicious, scared, before she left the One-Stop.

"When Andrea got to the car, she realized the man she was involved with wasn't there, and she tried to get away. I don't think she went back to the One-Stop, because that probably felt to her like a dead-end trap. I think she ran away from the One-Stop. To that field east of the One-Stop. Where you had witnesses who reported seeing someone running . . ."

Sig closed his eyes. Then, not being able to contain himself, he said, "But nothing they said checked out . . ."

"The people who give you the eyewitness accounts that fit best are often the least reliable," Mars said. "Not intentionally. But they've read news accounts, they've internalized what it is you want to hear. By the same token, the people who come up with half-baked eyewitness accounts that don't seem to make any sense at all—sometimes those are the people who are telling you what they really saw. They aren't embellishing, they aren't cutting and pasting to make their information fit—they don't even understand it themselves . . ."

"Tell me what you think happened after Andrea ran."

"I think the man who came to get her had been a Marine sniper. I think he had a sniper rifle with him, but I don't think he'd planned to use the rifle right then, at the One-Stop. I think he made a mistake in not being ready for what happened next. I think by the time he got the rifle out of the car, got a scope on the rifle—I don't even know if he'd anticipated needing an infrared scope—I think Andrea was gone. That he had to go after her.

"I think he went after her in that field, and I think he fired. A lot of sniper rifles have a five-round magazine. I think he fired all five rounds, and still wasn't sure he'd gotten her. So he stopped and reloaded . . ."

Sig had gone very pale. "And he dropped a cartridge when he reloaded."

"Exactly," Mars said. "A .308 cartridge is a common type of ammunition for sniper rifles."

Sig stared down at the cartridge in his hand. Then he got up and put the cartridge down on his desk. His back was to Mars, but Mars heard the sound of the cartridge as Sig set it down.

Sig needs a new finger toy, is what Mars thought.

"Your story," Sig said. "Does it have a happy ending? Did Andrea get away?"

"I don't know," Mars said. "But I have to guess not. Where's she been for nineteen years if she got away?"

"So he found her in the field," Sig said, still with his back toward Mars. "One of his shots hit home, he found her in the field, and he carried her out of there, back to his car."

"That would be my guess," Mars said, "except I'd guess he moved his car away from the One-Stop first."

Sig turned toward him.

"The man," he said, "not the sniper. The man Andrea was involved with. You know who that is?"

"I'm going to tell you who I think it was," Mars said. "Let me warn you. This is the thin part. I'm relying on you to tell me if you think it's possible."

Sig watched Mars as if he were afraid to hear what Mars was going to say next.

"What I said about Andrea putting a can on the floor before she left the One-Stop?"

Sig nodded.

"I'm pretty sure what she put on the floor was a can of Campbell's soup."

Mars waited. He didn't want to give Sig any more than that. He wanted to see if Sig would make the connection on his own.

Sig's emotions were visible on his face. A moment of uncertainty, dawning realization, followed by shock, disbelief—then, a sour resignation and disgust.

He made eye contact with Mars.

"Alan Campbell," he said.

Mars nodded, and Sig began to pace. He didn't speak for a while, then he said, "It fits with how I was reading Erin Moser."

Mars turned his head toward Sig, not certain what he meant.

"Erin must have suspected that Andrea was involved with Campbell. I don't think she knew for sure. If she'd known for sure, I think she would have said. She must have been wrestling with what she should say, what she shouldn't. I think she hoped right up to the day before she died that Andrea would come back, and if Andrea did come back, she didn't want to be the one who'd spread the word that Andrea and Campbell were involved. She would have thought about how that'd be for Andrea to have people know that.

"The morning of the day she died, the morning she came by the station, she must have decided Andrea wasn't coming back. I think she was going to tell me then what she thought about Andrea and Campbell."

Sig sighed. "It all fits. But what I don't understand is how you found out about the soup can," Sig said. "There wasn't anything on the tape . . ."

Mars said, "This gets me to the part of the story about how I know what I know. We found the guy who called in that the One-Stop was deserted. He's a criminal lawyer in the Twin Cities. He and his girlfriend were passing through on the interstate on their way back to Madison, Wisconsin. They never heard anything about Andrea after they'd left. But the guy saw *The Get List* segment and contacted us.

"He gave us the link to the Campbell's soup can on the floor in the aisle," Mars said. "And I confirmed with Tom Fiske that soup was stocked on those shelves shortly after the One-Stop opened."

Sig's forehead was rutted in deep concentration. "But I swear, Mars, when I came by the store—it was hardly anytime later—I don't remember seeing anything like that . . ."

"Remember what you said before, Sig. About Averill Hess on the tape. He ducks down at the same place Andrea did. You said it would be just like Averill to pick something up off the floor. A cigarette butt, a gum wrapper. How about a can? I tried to contact Averill, but he wasn't at the number you gave me . . ."

Sig snorted. "Don't waste your time. If Averill did do it, he probably wouldn't remember doing it. And if he remembers, he'll figure out he shouldn't have done it. So he'll lie."

Mars smiled. "Good old Averill."

Sig wasn't in a mood to be humored. "Some mistakes you live with a lot longer than others."

"Sig—what I really need you to think about is Alan Campbell. Did he know Andrea? Was there anything you heard back then that connects him to Andrea?"

"Nothing that I heard about," Sig said, but then he thought about it. "This is a bit of a stretch, but . . ."

"Stretch is good, Sig."

"Well, before he went bankrupt, Bob Bergstad was real active in the Republican Party. County chairman, on the state steering committee Sponsored a lot of fund-raisers—some at their farm, before it went to hell. Campbell was this district's congressman back then. I remember one event, Campbell had some fellow Republicans from other states at a big barbecue out at the Bergstads'. Our department provided security for the event." Sig shook his head. "But Andrea would have been just a kid then. Not more than ten, eleven years old . . ."

Sig looked over at Mars, saw the look on Mars's face, then turned away. Both of them were quiet for a long while.

Sig said, "Something else. I asked Bob Bergstad if he knew any elected officials that could get us support on the investigation. He said he'd call everybody that he knew—then he said that Andrea had helped out on some campaigns. Doing door knocks, literature drops, things like that. My impression was he was talking about recently—I mean recently in 1984. He said both Andrea and Erin had done that . . ."

Sig stopped, rubbing his chin. "So, yes. I guess there's a good chance Campbell would have known Andrea. Probably even likely he knew her. But you know what I can't figure?"

150

Mars gave Sig a look that said, *What?*

"If Alan Campbell *is* responsible for what happened to Andrea Bergstad, why would he put up a reward? First in 1984, then renew that offer for *The Get List* program? You wouldn't think he'd do anything to encourage people to come forward—or to associate himself with the case. Except for that, I could say, maybe. *Maybe.* But that piece of it just doesn't make any sense to me."

Mars had thought about the same question. It bothered him less than it bothered Sig, but it deserved thought.

"I'm not sure what Campbell was thinking. In 1984, he was running for the Senate. It was good publicity. Now—well, it's common knowledge he's positioning himself to be a vice presidential contender-in-the-wings. Stepping forward on national television can't hurt—can't hurt, that is, if he's confident there's no way anyone's going to tie him to what happened in 1984. Let's face it. He has good reason for feeling confident about that. Even what we *think* we know now—a can of soup—isn't much. And I don't see any clear path to turning what we know into solid, admissible evidence. We're a long, long way from having what we need."

Sig said, "What about the fellow you think shot Andrea that night, the sniper?"

"That's the other story I need to tell you," Mars said. "It doesn't give us anything much more solid, other than a possible tie between the sniper and Campbell, but I'm sure it's key."

"You know his name?" Sig said.

"The Green Man," Mars said. "I need to tell you a story about the Green Man."

CHAPTER
23

Driving back to the Twin Cities, Mars considered his options for investigating Senator Alan Campbell's connection to the Green Man.

Sig hadn't been able to tell him anything other than that there was a man who drove Campbell's car at the Bergstad barbecue who might have fit the Green Man's description. Sig was going to try to pin down dates when Campbell had been in Redstone in 1984. He was sure Campbell had been there—at least in the summer, as Redstone was in Campbell's congressional home district, and it was an important base for his senatorial campaign.

Investigating a suspect on a cold case was tricky for all the reasons that investigating a suspect in a current crime could be tricky. There were times when you didn't want the suspect to be aware that he was under investigation. Times when you particularly didn't want the suspect to know the specifics of what you were interested in. Most times, you didn't want to implicate the suspect by investigating him—not unless you were real, real sure about what you had.

The only thing Mars was sure about in this investigation was that he wasn't sure about what he had. But not being sure about what he had was an altogether different thing from being sure he was on the right track. On that point, he was dead certain.

How to prove his instincts when all the difficulties of conducting the investigation were compounded by the fact that the principal suspect was a powerful political figure? Mars didn't give a shit that Campbell might use his political power to hurt him professionally. He did want to avoid having Campbell use his political power to stymie the investigation.

What he needed was an insider. Preferably someone outside Minnesota. Someone he could trust implicitly to keep Mars's suspicions confidential.

Mars drove for miles across the flat Minnesota landscape without a single name coming to mind. And then, without consciously thinking of the investigation where he'd first encountered Boyle Keegan, Boyle Keegan's name came to him.

Boyle Keegan. An FBI specialist in domestic terrorism who'd assisted Mars and Nettie on a case a couple years back. At the very least, Keegan would be a place to start. If Keegan didn't know anything, he might know somebody who did.

Mars leaned forward, stretching to reach the glove compartment. He squeezed the release, then fumbled in the open box to see if by chance he'd left his personal directory there. No luck.

Just as well. Mars was too tired to articulate the questions he wanted to ask Boyle.

Mars tuned the car radio to a golden oldies station. He needed golden oldie energy to get him back to the Twin Cities after having only a couple hours' sleep the night before.

It wasn't really working. He continued to feel groggy. At the next rest stop, he pulled over, parked, and cranked the seat back, leaving the car running to keep the air-conditioning going.

It was a golden oldie that woke him almost two hours later. He was awake without being conscious of waking up. Somebody, he didn't know who, was singing "You've Lost That Lovin' Feeling."

Mars got out of the car, used the john at the rest stop, then got a Coke from a vending machine. He drank half the can before getting in the car and backing out.

An unformed thought stopped him. He pulled back into the parking spot and sat, waiting for the idea to crystallize. What came first was Jim Baker telling him that Campbell had been in his tent, listening to a "make-out" song the day after the massacre at Khe Ranh.

Where was that coming from? Why did that memory come to mind?

Probably just something that bubbled into his consciousness from listening to golden oldies, Mars thought, pulling out again. He drove another nine miles before he noticed he needed gas. It was when he pulled up at the convenience-store gas pump that the memory came back. Something from Sig Sampson's case files. Something about the radio being on full blast at the One-Stop. And, if he was remembering right, something in Erin Moser's statement about a song that had been on the radio when she'd been talking to Andrea.

Mars remembered something else, then. From the surveillance tape. He remembered Andrea walking away from the phone toward the counter, and reaching up. They never had figured out why she'd done that.

Mars forgot about the gas and called Sig Sampson, asking him if Mars was remembering right—that Erin Moser had mentioned the name of a song that had been on the radio when she'd talked to Andrea Bergstad the night she'd been abducted.

"That's right," Sig said. "Let me just check here, and I should be able to tell you the name of the song. We used it to confirm the time Averill was at the One-Stop . . ."

Mars could hear Sig fumbling with the three-ring binders. Then Sig came back on the line. "Here it is. 'Hold Me, Thrill Me, Kiss Me.' Mel Carter. That's what you need to know?"

"That's it, Sig. Thanks. I'll talk to you later. Just checking an idea."

"You must be back home by now, right?"

"Not quite," Mars said. "I took a rest break. Talk to you soon."

Mars punched 411 on his cell phone and got three numbers for James Bakers in Decorah, Iowa. He got his James Baker on the first call.

"One detail I wanted to check," Mars said. "Probably nothing, but who knows. You said Campbell listened to a tape on his cassette player. That you heard him listening to it the day after the massacre at Khe Ranh . . ."

"That's right," Baker said.

"You remember the title by any chance?"

It was a moment before Baker said, "No. I don't. I'd know it if I heard it, but the title doesn't come to mind."

"Do me a favor," Mars said. "See if you can get hold of a song called 'Hold Me, Thrill Me, Kiss Me,' by Mel Carter, then let me know if—"

"That's it," Baker said. "Those words are repeated over and over in the song. That's it for sure. I didn't know that was the title, but I remember those words in the song."

Mars drove away from the gas station without getting gas, invigorated by yet another connection between Andrea Bergstad and Alan Campbell. A moment's reflection tempered his excitement. He put his two major pieces of evidence at this point—a soup can and a golden oldie—in the context of filing a criminal charge against Campbell in connection with Andrea Bergstad's 1984 abduction.

As his car sputtered, lost power, then coasted to a stop on the shoulder, Mars could imagine hearing the prosecuting attorney's laughter.

Mars had run out of gas forty miles south of the Twin Cities.

CHAPTER

24

By the time Nettie arrived with a five-gallon can of gas, it was getting dark.

They'd driven back to the cities in their two cars—stopping to pick up something to eat, then on to the condo to eat their dinner on the terrace while Mars briefed Nettie on what had happened over the past twenty-four hours.

Nettie was a good listener. She didn't interrupt unless she found something being said to be unclear or unbelievable. And because Mars knew he was being listened to by a discerning critic, it made him a more objective judge about his own information.

Nettie didn't interrupt while Mars told her about Baker in Khe Ranh, Sig's take on the connection between Andrea and Campbell, and the connection between Andrea, Campbell, and a golden oldie.

All she said was, "Why is it always the circumstantial evidence that feels right in your gut? The stuff that's way out on the edge. I mean, you could tell me that five people in Redstone believed Andrea and Campbell were romantically involved, and I'd have more doubts than I do based on what we've found out about the soup can, the Khe Ranh massacre, and the golden oldie."

Neither of them said anything for a while, then Nettie said, "What do we do next?"

"I was thinking on the way back," Mars said. "I'm going to ask Boyle Keegan if he can find out anything about Campbell and the

Green Man. Or if he can't, if he knows somebody who can. Somebody we can trust."

Nettie nodded, seeming preoccupied. "Good idea."

Mars watched her closely, which wasn't easy to do in the dark. Boyle Keegan had had a thing about Nettie when they'd last worked together. Nettie hadn't seemed interested and Boyle wasn't the kind of guy who pushed, so it hadn't gone anywhere. Still, Mars was curious. In a paternal way.

"You've already called him?" Nettie said.

"I called him while I was waiting for you to show up with the gas. Got his answering machine. So I just said we had a sensitive case involving Campbell and a Marine sniper, and we needed some inside-the-beltway advice on sources."

"You left Campbell's name on the message?" Nettie said, her voice sounding disapproving.

"Nettie. This is Boyle Keegan's answering machine we're talking about. Boyle encrypts everything. I'd asked him about security when we worked with him before. He said as long as I used the number he gave me there was no problem."

"Still," Nettie said. "This case feels a little scary to me."

Mars thought she was talking about funding for their office. State budget cuts had decimated government agencies. Mars and Nettie, as the newest team in the BCA's Cold Case Unit—with no notches of accomplishment as yet on their professional belts—were vulnerable.

They both knew that. Mars didn't care. Nettie did.

"Nettie, we haven't been on this job for a year, and you've already established a state-wide reputation. Hell, you've got a region-wide reputation. There'll always be a job for you. And you know how I feel. If it's over, it's over."

Nettie looked over at him, wondering how he could be so cavalier. Of everybody she knew, she could think of no one with fewer career choices than Mars. Not because he didn't have the ability to do other things, but because there were so few things he wanted to do. And so many things for which he had no patience.

"I know that I'm making a contribution, Mars. And I know other people know that. But until we prove that what we're doing really accomplishes something, it won't count. We need to prove ourselves on a big case."

"This could be that," Mars said.

"Besides," Nettie said, "I wasn't talking about this case being scary because it could affect our funding. I meant scary-scary. What you said about Campbell in Vietnam, and about this Green Man character abducting Andrea Bergstad. These are scary people."

"Scary people keep us in business, kiddo."

Nettie didn't answer him. They sat in the dark, swatting bugs and looking out at the city. A low front had settled over the city in the past few days, bottling up the heat, deadening the air. During the day, the air looked slightly yellow. At night it had texture.

Mars said, "I forgot to turn out the living-room lights. We're getting bugs."

"It's okay," Nettie said, "I need to go anyway. This air is getting unbreathable."

Mars said, "You've got fifteen seconds. 'I don't trust air I can't see.' "

Nettie felt a sudden, uncontrollable urge to cry. It was the first time since they'd worked on a cold case that Mars had played the movie-line game.

He's back, she thought, grateful that the unbreathable darkness was a cover for her emotion.

"The clock is ticking," Mars said.

"I know it was Gene Hackman. But I'm drawing a complete blank on the movie."

"Crimson Tide," Mars said, standing. "Chris and I watched *The Conversation* and *Get Shorty* before he went to Cleveland. If there is any doubt that Hackman is one of the great actors of our time, you just need to watch those two movies. The difference in the way he plays the two characters is nothing short of brilliant."

"The new Jeff Bridges," Nettie said. For as long as she'd worked with Mars, he could, with very little provocation, go crazy with indignation at what he considered to be the greatest cinematic injustice of the last century: that Bridges hadn't gotten an Academy Award for his performance in *The Fabulous Baker Boys.*

She recognized her mistake in mentioning Jeff Bridges immediately. Mars was winding up to go crazy. She took preemptive action and interrupted him.

"Mars? Something kind of weird. I've been going through the tip sheets we got from *TGL,* pulling out the random sample tips—the ones that we thought were worthless—to scan them for our files. I looked again at the one we got from the nineteen-year-old girl in Vermillion, South Dakota. DeeDee Kipp. And it just hit me. When we first started the convenience-store project? When we were deciding on criteria to use to select cases?"

"Yeah," Mars said, starting to feel tired again.

"We started with convenience-store victims who'd been shot in the five-state region."

"Which, in our wisdom," Mars said, "we quickly decided was a far too inclusive criterion." He pulled back the door to the living room. "C'mon in. Before we get West Nile Virus."

They stood blinking in the living-room light.

"This time, when I saw the name of the town DeeDee Kipp was from—Vermillion, South Dakota—I realized that one of our 1987 shooting victims was from Vermillion, South Dakota."

Mars blinked hard. "So?"

"So, I thought it was unusual. Someone who calls in to *TGL* is from the same small town in South Dakota as one of the shooting victims that we picked using our original selection criteria."

Mars walked away from Nettie, over to one of the metal shelves. He fingered through a pile of stuff on one of the shelves, pulling out a road atlas. Flipping to the back of the atlas, he drew his finger down the page. When it stopped, he turned to Nettie, reading out loud.

"Vermillion, South Dakota. Population nine thousand seven hundred and sixty-five. It's not a stop on the road, Nettie."

"If it were ninety thousand plus, I might be impressed. I still think it's unusual—two people connected to the investigation from the same small town."

"Admit it, Nettie. You wanted an excuse to interrupt me. You didn't want to listen to me on the subject of Jeff Bridges not getting an Oscar. True?"

"It was on my mind," Nettie said.

CHAPTER

25

The Green Man had misjudged a seventeen-year-old girl. The mistake had been that simple, even if the consequences of the mistake had not been simple.

He understood how he had made the mistake. He had violated his basic operational principle: anticipate all possible outcomes and be prepared to respond to any possible outcome.

He also understood why he had violated his basic operational principle. After years of planning operations that had brought down sovereign governments, that had eliminated clients' personal and political enemies, that had resulted in the deaths of international terrorists, that had foiled complex trade restrictions—a request to eliminate a seventeen-year-old schoolgirl had seemed like an afterthought.

Andrea Bergstad hadn't even been a target he considered worthy of his skills. He had agreed to take on the assignment for two reasons. First, Campbell was an established client. It was always a good idea to maintain a relationship with past clients. Second, Campbell was likely to become a U.S. senator. Political connections were as important as established relationships.

So he'd agreed to take on the job, allowing himself four days to complete the necessary surveillance, do the job, dispose of the body, and disappear.

In plain terms, he had underestimated his target.

At the time, four days had seemed like more than enough. More than enough right up to the moment when Andrea Bergstad stopped cold as he led her to his car, parked outside the One-Stop.

"He's not in the car," she said.

He reached for her quickly, but not quickly enough. She ran from him, inches away from his hands, then out of sight.

She made a mistake as well. She didn't go back into the store where there was a phone. No doubt she viewed going back into the store as a dead end. What she hadn't considered was that to follow her, he would have come within range of the security camera. He wouldn't have done that. But she hadn't known he wouldn't have done that.

So she ran.

In the instant when Andrea disappeared into the night, he weighed his choices. Follow her without the rifle or take time to get the rifle out of the trunk. The idea of physically capturing her, having to kill her with his bare hands, wasn't how he wanted things to work. Having that much physical contact with a target was too risky. And it wasn't something he did. He killed with his rifle, not his hands.

So he traded time for having the gun. A mistake he'd spent the past nineteen years regretting.

He had monitored the Bergstads' phone records after that night in 1984. Three years after Andrea disappeared, a number that had never appeared on their records turned up repeatedly over a two-month period. He traced the number to a pay phone at a convenience store in Vermillion, South Dakota. He knew as soon as he saw the place that she'd be there. And she was. He'd sat in a car across from the store for several nights before just the right opportunity presented itself.

It had satisfied him that he'd shot Andrea Bergstad at a convenience store. Mission accomplished. He'd regained control. The most important thing.

And now this.

Campbell had called him as soon as he heard that Andrea Bergstad's disappearance was being reopened by Minnesota's Cold Case Unit. What the Green Man knew of the angle being investigated hadn't worried him. He had watched *The Get List* program and felt more confident. Let them spin their wheels looking for a convenience-store predator. It would keep them from spending their time on more troubling possibilities.

He'd told Campbell to offer the reward as a way of keeping a hook into what *The Get List* turned up. Not because he expected *The Get List* to turn anything up, but because, this time, the Green Man wanted to be sure. Underestimating this assignment had gotten him in trouble nineteen years ago. It wasn't going to happen again.

And now this.

Another goddamn teenager. And potentially a much more dangerous link between Campbell, Andrea Bergstad, and himself.

The Get List had supplied Campbell's office with a copy of the tip sheets forwarded to the Cold Case Unit. One of the ninety-eight tips had come from a nineteen-year-old girl named DeeDee Kipp. The tip had been innocuous: her childhood babysitter resembled the photo of Andrea Bergstad.

What hadn't been innocuous was that the girl lived in Vermillion, South Dakota. *Maybe* a coincidence. Maybe not.

Coincidence or not, he didn't like it. It wasn't immediately obvious how that tip could tie back to Campbell or to him. But if the Cold Case Unit followed up on the tip, who knew what they might turn up?

Another thing he didn't like was the girl's age. Nineteen. Meaning she would have been born in 1984. Andrea Bergstad hadn't looked pregnant in October of 1984. But if she'd been four months' pregnant then, a premature delivery in late December wasn't out of the question. What he knew of Campbell's relationship with Bergstad was that it was possible that Bergstad could have been four months' pregnant in October of 1984.

He needed to do a record's search on DeeDee Kipp's birth. But that wouldn't satisfy him. He had personal knowledge of how easy it was to falsify birth records. He needed something more than a document. He needed to see DeeDee Kipp with his own eyes. To assure himself that the girl in the flesh could not have been Alan Campbell and Andrea Bergstad's daughter.

He was preparing to leave for Vermillion, South Dakota, to track down DeeDee Kipp when he noticed that her phone number area code was 507, not South Dakota's 605.

Using an untraceable cell phone, he dialed the 507 number and got a three-voice message that changed with each name.

"Hi. You've reached Amanda . . . and DeeDee . . . and Cheryl." Then the three separate voices said in a chorus: *"You know what to do when you hear the tone."* Another voice piped in, *"If you don't, you're too dumb to talk to us."* Laughter in the background.

He hung up before the beep. Then he checked a map. Mankato State University was in the 507 area code. He went to his laptop and found Mankato State's Web site. There was a listing for Deandra Kipp in the student directory that matched the number on the tip sheet. What she must have done was given the name of her hometown where she'd known the babysitter she'd mentioned in her tip. Then she'd given her current phone number in the contact information.

The Green Man stared at the name on the directory. *Deandra.* Except for the second "d," the same letters as *Andrea*. He continued to stare. It was too close for comfort. He needed to go to Minnesota. He needed to see her.

Forty-eight hours later he returned from Minnesota. He didn't need to bother with birth records. He had known on sight that DeeDee Kipp was Andrea Bergstad's daughter.

He'd hardly had time to take a position across from the tall, narrow Victorian frame house that had been converted to a duplex when a young woman who could have been Andrea Bergstad wheeled away from the house on a bicycle. Dark hair, soft, pretty features, a lithe body, sparkling brown eyes.

The resemblance was so strong that his first impulse had been to cover his face for fear that she would recognize him. She had looked right at him as she turned her bike from the driveway onto the street. If she had been her mother, she would have recognized him, he was sure of that.

After that single encounter he had left Mankato. There was no question about who her parents were. The only question that remained was, what was he going to do about DeeDee Kipp?

* * *

164

It was getting dark when he returned to his home base. He purposely did not turn lights on. The dim room suited his purpose. He sat back in a chair and considered his choices.

He had known before he'd left for Mankato that eliminating DeeDee would only complicate his problems as long as there was a possibility that she was a subject of the investigation. He looked again at Kipp's tip sheet. Her tip was so ambiguous it was possible—maybe likely—that nothing would come of it. To act now, to take preemptive action now would only cause more problems.

What he couldn't get out of his mind was DeeDee Kipp's resemblance to her mother. The real risk was that the investigators would see DeeDee Kipp. They had photos of Andrea Bergstad. If they saw DeeDee the connection would be made immediately. At that point, the investigation would spin out of control.

What he needed to do was track the investigation more closely. He needed to know if the Cold Case Unit investigators went to Mankato.

At that point, his only option would be to eliminate the investigators and DeeDee Kipp.

CHAPTER

26

It surprised Mars that it had taken Boyle three days to return his message. Boyle was a guy who stayed in touch with his answering machine, no matter where he was, no matter what he was doing.

More surprising was the message itself.

"It's Boyle. Got your message. Sorry about the delay on the fishing trip. I won't be able to get up there for another day or two. Problems on this end. What you said about my phone sounding like it was tapped? I had it checked. All clear. Hope all is well with you. Be in touch."

On first listen, Mars thought Boyle had mistakenly dialed Mars's number in response to another message.

On second listen, Mars had second thoughts.

On third listen, Mars translated the meaning of Boyle's message. He heard *"sorry about the delay on the fishing trip"* and *"problems on this end"* as *it's taken me longer than I expected to follow up on your problem.* He heard *"I won't be able to get up there for another day or two"* as *I'm coming to Minneapolis.* He heard *"what you said about my phone sounding like it was tapped"* and *"hope all is well with you"* as *have your phone checked.*

Mars sat still after he'd figured out Boyle's message.

What the *hell?*

Mars couldn't believe that he'd told Boyle enough about Campbell and a Marine sniper for Boyle to uncover anything that merited this level of secrecy.

More than that, it was unlike Boyle to be this cautious. He was a savvy, cynical, careful guy, but not somebody who was easily unnerved. Mars had the distinct impression that Boyle was unnerved and that Boyle not only knew something about Campbell, but that Boyle knew more about Campbell than Mars did.

And what Boyle knew about Campbell wasn't good.

Mars picked up the phone to call a friend in the local FBI office to ask if Mars could get someone to sweep the apartment for bugs. Then he thought again. Thought again about using his phone to ask if someone could check to see if his phone was bugged and thought again about asking his Feebie friend.

He was starting to feel like this was a case where knowing where you were going before you actually went was a good idea.

And he was starting to feel the full impact of the case's political complexities. He'd thought he'd dealt with political complexities when he'd worked out of City Hall, but this case was making those issues look like small potatoes.

So instead of calling the Feebie friend to ask for a sweep, Mars called Danny Borg for lunch.

They had Jucy Lucys at Matt's on Thirty-fifth and Chicago.

Mars numbered Danny Borg as one of the four people on the face of the earth that he trusted implicitly, right there with Nettie, Chris, and John Turner. John Turner had been chief of the MPD before moving on to San Diego a couple years earlier. His departure had been the tipping point for Mars's decision to leave the MPD. Mars had gone through the political wrangling and infighting that inevitably followed a change in chief twice before, and he'd decided three times was not the charm. That, and Mars knew that no matter how good a new chief would be, he wouldn't begin to fill Turner's shoes.

Danny Borg had been in uniform out of the Downtown Command when Mars had first met him. Danny was an intuitively good investigator who never took things at face value. And Danny had two essential qualities you couldn't train for. He had a naive, unshakable belief in truth and justice. And he had a good heart.

His devotion to Mars was also unshakable and frequently embarrassing. Mars, with Turner's support, had been instrumental in getting

Danny promoted out of his uniform and into a suit as a detective in the MPD. Danny would go to his grave being grateful for that support.

Once promoted, Danny had invested in a new wardrobe of double-breasted, slightly iridescent suits, and ties that were long on primary colors and bold designs. Sitting opposite Mars in a booth at Matt's, he positively glowed.

"So, how's it going?" Danny said. And then, without waiting for Mars to answer, "You know what? You look better. This is the first time I've seen you since you moved to the CCU where you looked happy. Things are going good then, right?"

Mars nodded as he ate around the edges of his Jucy Lucy. A Jucy Lucy was two slabs of beef molded around a dollop of cheese, then grilled crisp, slid into a bun wrapped in paper, and dropped on a table for a diner to eat at his own risk. Bite directly into a Jucy Lucy before it had cooled from infernal to hot, and you would forever alter the interior of your mouth.

"Going better," Mars said. "An interesting case. Part of why I called you for lunch. I need my apartment, my phone, swept for bugs." Mars took a bigger bite of his Jucy Lucy, thinking while he chewed. "Actually, probably my apartment, the office, and Nettie's place. Just to be on the safe side. But I don't want to ask somebody to do it myself. Can I ask you to make the arrangements and keep it under your hat?"

Danny nodded slowly as he chewed. "Sure. Your apartment or your condo?"

Danny had this way of being real literal. It was a virtue in an investigator, but in conversation it could make you nuts.

"Condo. I still say apartment. I gave up the apartment when we moved to the condo."

"Smart move," Danny said. "That apartment of yours was a felony waiting to happen."

"But cheap," Mars said. "And when I was paying child support, cheap mattered."

"You're lucky you got out of there alive," Danny said.

It was an attitude Mars had noticed among a lot of street cops. Profound distrust for anything or anyone that fell below the lower middle class rung on the socioeconomic ladder. Danny's distrust was as deep as anyone's and, in Mars's judgment, was Danny's only character flaw.

"You want to be there when they do the sweep?" Danny said.

Mars shook his head. "I'd like to give you the key and have you take them in. And I'll get you Nettie's key. The office can be done anytime during the day between eight and five. That okay?"

"Absolutely," Danny said. He wiped his mouth with a napkin and sat back in the booth. "Tell me about the case."

Without knowing why right off, Mars hesitated. It only took a second to recognize that you didn't do anyone any favors by telling them about the possibilities in this case. At least not now, not before Mars knew more about what they were up against.

"Not ready for prime time," Mars said.

Danny's face immediately reflected disappointment. And something more. Hurt. Danny was taking Mars's reluctance as a personal slight.

"Danny," he said. "I was thinking when I called to ask you to take care of this security thing at the apartment. You're one of four people in the world I trust implicitly . . ."

"So trust me," Danny said.

"This time I've gotta ask you to trust me," Mars said. "Trust that if I thought it was in your interest to know what I know, I'd tell you. Not telling you doesn't have anything to do with not trusting you. It's just that right now I'm feeling like anyone who doesn't need to know about this case is better off not knowing."

"That sounds to me like something you should tell me about. Maybe I could help."

"You're helping by taking care of this security check. For now, I'm sticking to my instincts on this, Danny. For now, you're better off not knowing anything about this case."

They stood out in front of Matt's for a while before going to their cars.

"Okay if I get the sweep done later this afternoon?" Danny said. "I know someone who can take care of it off the books."

"This afternoon is great. If there's a charge, Danny . . ."

Danny waved Mars off. "It's my brother, Mars. And if you want him to do some follow-ups—just give me a call."

169

Mars grinned. "Perfect."

As they parted, Danny called back, "Mars? When you feel you can talk about it, give me a call?"

Mars lifted his hand to signal he would.

Danny walked backward. "How long before you think you'll be able to say something?"

"The sooner the better," Mars said.

"And if I don't hear from you . . ."

"Not good if you don't hear from me, Danny."

CHAPTER
27

Mars's phone rang right after he'd gotten back to the apartment from the office.

He picked up the receiver while he read the note that had been left on the kitchen counter

Clean, it read. *Your place and Nettie's. We'll do the office tomorrow.* Below the message was a scribble that Mars recognized as Danny Borg's signature.

"Hello," Mars said into the phone, thinking about the fact that Danny's note had given him a flash of relief that was surprising. His mind was wandering to what he'd be feeling if Danny's note had read *dirty* when Boyle Keegan's voice came through the receiver.

"I'm downstairs. Beam me up, Scotty."

Mars pushed the buzzer to release the lobby door, then opened his own front door and waited for Boyle.

Mars heard him before he saw him. Boyle was huffing as he came down the hall. He was a big guy, six-three, six-four. Tall enough to be an NBA point guard, if he'd had a mind to shoot hoops. And meaty. Thinning, wild reddish hair. A flushed face that revealed many truths about Boyle, including that all by himself he drank more than would have been good for four adult males.

Mars stepped out into the hall to greet Boyle, and was too surprised by how Boyle looked to even say "hello."

Boyle carried a duffel bag in one hand, a couple of fishing rods in the other. He wore a squashed-down fabric hat that was covered with fishing flies, and one of those vests with four hundred zippered pockets.

"You really *are* going fishing?" Mars said.

Boyle lifted a finger to his lips. Then, as he dropped his gear on the hall floor and moved to the kitchen, where he started taking apart Mars's phone, he said in a booming voice, "You've got your shit ready? I'd like to get started first thing in the morning."

Mars took the pieces of his phone from Boyle and held up Danny Borg's note. "The apartment was swept this afternoon, Boyle," Mars said.

Boyle was immediately relieved. "So. You got my message. I mean, you *got* the message. It was a little subtle, I have to admit, but I thought I could count on you." He started moving through the condo, appraising what he found.

"Shit. I wish I'd known you'd got a clean sweep before I spent a thousand bucks on all this fishing crap."

"A thousand bucks?" Mars said, incredulous.

"You don't fully appreciate how stupid people are until you see how much they pay for stuff like fishing gear, ski gear, all that junk. Don't worry about it. I can take it back. Just that it's a nuisance dragging it back and forth on the plane."

He turned around in the living room.

"This is great. You know why? You haven't ruined it with a bunch of useless furniture. I knew my first wife and I were headed for court when she bought this thing called an—oh, hell, I can't even remember what you called it. Some fool French word. A shelf tower thing is what it was. Then, after she buys this shelf tower, she's gotta go out and buy a bunch of crap to put on the shelves. Crap you're never going to use for anything. It just sits on the shelves. Then she's gotta hire someone to clean the house because there's so much crap to dust and whatever. That was when I told her. This isn't going to work. She got all the crap in the divorce settlement, which was fine with me. With my second wife, I told her up front: no French shelf towers that you've got to hire someone to dust."

"I didn't know you were still married," Mars said, thinking about Boyle's evident interest in Nettie.

172

"I'm not," Boyle said. "What I found out second time around is that a French shelf tower is just one of a lot of things that can go wrong in a marriage."

Boyle stopped his tour of the apartment and slapped his forehead. "Shit again," he said. "I forgot. You don't drink. You keep anything for guests?"

"Well," Mars said, "we had some dead-cat-infused ice cubes, but I think we're out of those. Other than that . . ."

"Point me toward a liquor store that sells single malt whiskey," Boyle said, "and order pizza. Thin crust, sausage and pepperoni for me."

As he left, he said, "Nettie joining us?"

"Now that I know you're here, and what's on the menu for dinner, I'll give her a call."

"Surdyks' is a great liquor store," Boyle said as he came back in with a narrow brown bag under one arm and a twenty-four-can pack of Classic Coca-Cola dangling from his other hand. "My single malt was three bucks cheaper than anywhere I could get it in D.C."

He spotted Nettie in the kitchen, dropped the beverages on the counter, and gave her a bear hug. "I'm a happy man," he said, "good liquor and the company of a beautiful woman. It's all I've ever asked from life."

They sat in the living room, Boyle and Nettie on the futon couch, Mars on one of the collapsible Target fabric chairs, pizza boxes and a roll of paper towels on the floor between them.

Boyle didn't want to talk about why he was there until they'd finished the pizza. Then, tearing off a sheet of paper toweling and wiping his hands, he said, "I've got a lot to tell you about your Senator Campbell and his Marine sniper. But I'm going to start at the end, because I don't want the two of you to miss how serious this thing is you've gotten yourselves into."

They looked at each other, then back at Boyle.

Boyle considered what he was going to say before he said it. Then he gave them each a direct look.

"When I first heard what I'm going to tell you, I didn't believe it. I thought it was part and parcel of all the noise that passes for fact inside the D.C. beltway.

"Then, last summer, something someone in the administration said about a war with Iraq got published. No doubt you heard it. This administration guy was asked about the possibility of the U.S. going to war with Iraq in August. And his response was, 'You don't roll out a new product in August.' "

Doyle picked up his whiskey bottle, poured himself a generous splash, took a deep, wincing gulp, then set the bottle back down.

He belched, loudly and without apology, then said, "After I heard that, I started believing what I was hearing."

Nettie said, "And what you were hearing was . . ."

"Let me tell this my way," Boyle said. "It's a complicated story, and I don't want to miss the important parts.

"Number one. I can't prove anything I'm about to say is factual. I'm basing what I'm going to tell you on what I've been told by people I respect, people who've had their feet on the ground in a lot of different places for a long time. Then I've done a gut check on what I've been told, processing it against my own experience. So I'm not going to tell you anything that I think is completely off the wall. What I tell you is, in my judgment, plausible to one degree or another. But do I know for certain what I'm going to tell you is true? No."

Boyle looked at each of them. "Understood?"

Mars and Nettie nodded, without having a clue what they were agreeing to.

"What really complicates this picture is that you've got the CIA splintered into guys who've left and aren't happy about how they left, you've got guys still in the CIA who feel like they're getting dumped on for everybody else's mistakes, and you've got the FBI which has been the principal government whipping boy—deservedly so—over the past fifteen years . . ."

There was something on Mars's and Nettie's faces that told Boyle they were having a hard time figuring out where he was going.

"Bear with me. I need you to understand the context. If you don't get the context, you're not going to understand your own risks."

174

They both shifted their positions as if hunkering down for what was to come. Boyle took that as his signal to continue.

"The bottom line in this context is that we have chaos at the highest levels of the government's security community. And do you know what chaos breeds?"

Mars and Nettie took Boyle's question to be rhetorical, which it was. They waited for him to go on without saying anything.

"Chaos is the red flag of opportunity for clandestine activity. And clandestine activity is what we've got in spades on the most sensitive political mission this country has undertaken.

"Capturing Osama Bin Laden."

Boyle drew a deep breath.

"That said, let's get to the nut of the issue—why the context I've just described matters.

"Boys and girls, there is not one hunt for Osama, there are three.

"One is the official hunt. This is the hunt that gets coverage on CNN. The official hunt involves special forces troops crawling through caves in Afghanistan. All this with official cooperation from the CIA, the FBI, and so-called assistance from the Pakistani and Saudi Arabian governments.

"The second hunt is made up of mercenaries associated with foreign governments and a few former disaffected CIA operatives. This group has people in Karachi, Damascus—in other words, their search is not where the official search is concentrated. Their motive is to find Osama to either embarrass the U.S. government or to trade Osama for concessions the sponsoring governments want from the U.S.

"The third hunt is much like the second, but different in motive and different in terms of sponsorship. The third hunt is headed up by Campbell's pal. The Green Man. He has his own intelligence sources and his people are principally in Pakistan and Syria. At the highest levels, there is probably Saudi involvement. I could speculate on the connections between the Green Man's hunt and specific individuals inside and outside the administration, but it doesn't serve any purpose to do that . . ."

Mars held up both hands. "Whooooa. I know you want to tell this story your way, Boyle, but back up a little. Why shouldn't there be three hunts? A hundred hunts for that matter . . ."

Boyle stood, jamming his hands in his pockets, walking around the room without looking at Mars and Nettie.

"You're right. I guess I didn't make that clear. It doesn't matter how many ways we try to get Osama. What's wrong," he said, turning to face Mars and Nettie, "is that the 'official hunt' is bogus. It's chewing up resources—read lives and taxpayer dollars—and it's being fed intentionally misleading intelligence. We are spending millions of dollars every day to make sure we don't find Osama. Worse than that, we're playing with the hopes of people whose lives have been devastated . . ."

Nettie got up and started to pace. "Now you've lost me. You're saying someone in the administration doesn't want to find Osama? How is it possible that this administration—any administration— wouldn't want to get him? That they'd waste resources the way you're suggesting?"

"Oh, they want to get him, all right," Boyle said, "but they want him gotten on their timetable. Remember: 'You don't roll out a new product in August.' "

It took Mars and Nettie a minute to think through what Boyle was saying.

Boyle said, pronouncing each word slowly, "Timing is everything. The Green Man's hunt group wants to 'roll out' the capture in a way that will be most beneficial politically. My sources say that would be announcing Osama's capture in 2004. The closer to the election, the better.

He let his words sink in. Mars was on his feet now, almost bumping into Nettie as he paced.

"I just don't see how it would work," Mars said. "You're saying they've got Osama but they're holding him until a year from now— more than a year from now?—how are they going to keep something like that quiet? For that matter, what's to keep Osama from speaking up when their captures are announced?"

Now Boyle sat down, stretching his legs in front of him. "You need a footrest or something," he said, not looking satisfied with his

176

position. "One of those whatever you call it. A hassock. You need a hassock."

He shifted forward, drawing his legs back.

"Look. I said it before. What I know for sure is a lot less than what I don't know. I don't know if they've got Osama yet. And I don't know what their strategy is for announcing the capture when and if they do get him. But I'm a betting man, and I'd bet that when Osama gets rolled out, there'll be wheels on his coffin. At that point, there could be a hundred explanations for why the body isn't warm. That's the easy part, really. And there's another reason why the administration wouldn't want Osama captured alive. There's talk that there will be a court challenge at some point to the United States's authority to extradite war criminals for prosecution in the U.S., particularly if the war criminals are captured by paid operatives. Anyway, my point is, I don't think there's a chance in hell that Osama is going to have a pulse when his capture is announced."

Mars said, "What about Saddam? Is he part of the political strategy?"

Boyle held up both hands in a gesture of uncertainty. "That I can't say. When I first heard the story about the Green Man's hunt, it only involved Osama. But that was before we went into Iraq. Before Saddam was part of the equation. And now? Before the insurgency started, I would have said timing the capture of Saddam would be part of the political strategy. Things going the way they are now in Iraq, I think they're going to have to get Saddam when they can. The political costs of not getting him, with our troops on the ground there getting hits every day, are just getting to be too high."

Boyle took another deep draw on his drink. Then he gave Mars and Nettie a hard, cynical smile.

"Like I said. Timing is everything.

"And now is the time to tell you about the Green Man."

Boyle refilled his tumbler with whiskey. He stared at the glass, swirling it gently, before he spoke again.

"The Green Man showed up on intelligence radar for the first time during the Vietnam War. He made himself useful. To people who counted. He started with the Marines, went into Special Forces at one point—but eventually, even Special Forces were too structured for him. He freelanced mostly, then and now. Still making himself useful to people who count . . ."

"What's his name?" Mars said. "His background?"

Boyle looked tired, disinterested in Mars's question. He sipped his whiskey, then said, "The thing about the Green Man is that it's very hard to sort out legend and reality. He went to Vietnam as an enlisted man. Even before he went to Vietnam he used aliases. I could tell you the name he enlisted under, but that doesn't tell you any more—probably tells you less—than just calling him the Green Man. His history follows that name. It does seem clear that he picked up the 'Green Man' in Vietnam because . . ."

"Because he was a sniper and always wore green body paint," Mars said. Then he told Boyle what Jim Baker had told him and about what Mars and Nettie suspected about Campbell's and the Green Man's involvement in Andrea Bergstad's disappearance.

Boyle nodded when Mars had finished talking. "Fits," was all he said, still looking vaguely bored. He was quiet for a time, then he said, looking more alert, "This Baker. Who's he told about what happened in the Khe Ranh Valley?"

"Nobody," Mars said. "He was clear about that. The conversation he had with me was a confessional."

"Make sure he keeps it that way," Boyle said. "And make sure you keep it that way. Don't tell anybody what you know about the Green Man. Not your other colleagues, for sure not anybody on *The Get List*. The Green Man gets a whiff that somebody's onto him and you've got big, big trouble."

Boyle clutched his right hand into a fist, and extending his index finger toward Nettie and Mars, said, "The Green Man is the reason you don't have to worry about anyone telling about when the capture takes place. The Green Man will make sure there's nobody left to embarrass his clients. That's how he's defining completing his contract."

Mars shook his head. "Global issues aside, Boyle, this is a problem for us back here in fly-over land handling our picayune cold case. We don't have anything on Campbell. To get Campbell, we have to use his connection to the Green Man. That's our only chance to resolve our cold case."

Boyle sat forward. "Damn it, Mars. A girl who's been dead nineteen years isn't worth putting your life—Nettie's life—at risk. Back off. If you can find a way to work your cold case without getting close to the Green Man man, do it . . ."

Nettie said, "He won't try to protect Campbell? I mean, Campbell must have been his client . . ."

Boyle shook his head. "The Green Man doesn't care shit about Campbell. He is scrupulous about meeting the terms of his contracts. Once he's delivered on a contract, the relationship—his responsibility—ends. As a matter of fact, nobody cares shit about Campbell. As bad as the Green Man is—and I'll tell you more about just how bad he is—there's something kind of noble about the guy. Campbell is a sleazebag. Everybody knows that and there isn't anybody who isn't ready to throw Campbell overboard if he becomes a problem. Matter of fact, you'd be doing your state and your country a public service putting Campbell away. So you can get as close to Campbell as you want. Just don't do anything—anything—that puts Campbell and the Green Man together."

"And you're sure the Green Man is working for the side that wants to conceal the capture of Osama," Mars said.

Boyle said, "What motivates the Green Man is a challenge, the ability to work independently. The clandestine operation is his style. It's harder to pull off. And he probably knows the official search is bogus. His intelligence sources are always better than anybody else's."

"No political motives?" Mars said. "Moral quests?"

Boyle guffawed. "God, no. Remember back in the eighties when some of the big banks were in up to their eyeballs with bad loans to South America? What I heard was the Green Man went down there and talked to key people. Told them to pay on the banks' terms or he'd stop insulin shipments to the country. For a while he ran an operation that involved 'harvesting' organs for transplants. Donors—including slum kids in third world countries—didn't survive, but . . ."

Mars was beginning to understand why Boyle had been blasé about the Green Man's actions in the Khe Ranh Valley. "I'm having a hard time putting 'noble' and the Green Man together in the same sentence," Mars said.

Boyle made a motion of indifference. "If the Green Man said he was going to do something, it was done and it was done right. In his world, that's a kind of nobility. When he came back from Vietnam he had an 'asset conversion' business. Converted illegal drugs and diamonds into cash for all kinds of clients for all kinds of purposes . . ."

"And his clients were?" Mars said.

"Anybody who could afford his fees and who could offer him a challenge. Never more than six clients, sometimes only one or two. He has to be his own boss. 'Plays well with other children' never showed up on his report cards."

Boyle shifted. "This is the part that connects to your case. What do you know about Alan Campbell's first political campaign?"

Mars and Nettie looked at each other, shrugging.

"Nothing," Mars said. "First I heard of him was when he was running for the Senate, around the time Andrea Bergstad went missing."

"Campbell's first campaign was for Congress. Ran against a very popular incumbent. All that Campbell had going for him was a rich daddy, his war record, and a good haircut. Then his opponent was killed in a car accident . . ."

"Campbell got lucky," Nettie said.

Boyle shook his head.

"No," Boyle said. "Campbell got the Green Man."

Boyle nodded toward Mars. "I don't know what the Green Man's original connection was to Campbell—probably Vietnam. After you called and said you needed to talk to me about Campbell and a Marine sniper, I knew from what I'd been hearing for years that the sniper had to be the Green Man.

"So, before I came out here I checked with a couple people. They told me, based on deep background intelligence reports, that the Green Man continued to have a connection to Campbell after the war. At least up until the time that Campbell ran for Congress in the mid-seventies.

"I didn't ask about the Bergstad situation because I didn't know

180

about it. But it doesn't take a lot of imagination to believe that Campbell was having a problem with the girl and called in the Green Man to take care of it."

Nettie said, "Like he did with Campbell's first political opponent."

"Exactly," Boyle said. "What my source told me is that Campbell's opponent had a flat tire on a rural road one night. The accident report said he was struck by a passing car. Nobody in the intelligence community believes that. They believe the Green Man shot the tire out, shot Campbell's opponent, then staged the accident with the other car . . ."

Mars let out a wail. "Erin Moser," he said as Boyle and Nettie stared at him.

"Erin Moser didn't get unlucky," Mars said, "she got the Green Man."

Boyle stood up after Mars told him about what had happened to Erin Moser.

"How much more do you need to know to convince you that you've gotta stay away from this guy?" Boyle said.

Mars shook his head. "It's just hard to think that Andrea—Andrea *and* Erin—will never get justice *because* we know what happened, how it happened . . ."

"Your choice," Boyle said, "but unless you and Nettie can find a way to nail Campbell without involving the Green Man, you better prepare yourselves to become a couple of cold cases yourselves."

Mars invited Boyle to stay the night, but Boyle was restless.

"Nah," he said. "I'm getting out of here on the first plane that's going anywhere. And I'm leaving as soon as the two of you promise you'll back off on this. You're smart enough to figure a way to get Campbell without coming near the Green Man."

At the door he said, "The good news is your apartment wasn't bugged. If it had been, I'd say you were already in over your head. That it wasn't bugged says the Green Man doesn't have you on his radar yet, even with *The Get List* program. Or if you are on his radar, he doesn't think you're getting close to him. All that noise about a sexual predator trolling convenience stores probably convinced him you don't know what the hell you're doing. And that's what's saved your butts. Keep it that way."

"Let's go for a walk," Mars said to Nettie after Boyle had gone. "I need oxygen."

They walked through the soft summer night from the apartment, down Nicollet to Orchestra Hall, not talking much, each of them preoccupied with what Boyle had told them and what it meant for their investigation.

Reaching the plaza next to Orchestra Hall, they sat down on a bench and talked randomly about their choices, neither of them willing to give the case up—or willing to go forward until they better understood their risk.

"What I don't understand," Nettie said, "is how the Green Man decided to go after Erin Moser. I guess what I'm saying is that I'd like to understand how he targets people. It might make me feel a little less jumpy."

The same question had been half formed in Mars's mind. Erin had died almost three weeks after Andrea had disappeared. Why then? It only took a moment's thought after Nettie's question before Mars realized he knew the answer.

And it was only another moment before he realized that Sig Sampson *had* made a fatal error in the investigation of Andrea Bergstad's death.

"Let's go back to the apartment," Mars said. "I've got some of Sig Sampson's case files locked in the trunk of the car. There's something I want to check."

Mars went to the file that included news coverage on Andrea Bergstad's disappearance. He found the article he'd remembered. The article that said Sig had refused to comment on whether or not Erin Moser knew the identity of the last person entering the One-Stop before Andrea disappeared.

With hindsight, it was obvious Sig had given an answer that put Erin at risk. Mars knew how Sig would feel knowing that now.

182

What Mars also knew was that it was an answer any officer in that investigation, at that time, would have given.

For that matter, when Mars had first found out that Erin had died after Andrea had gone missing, he hadn't questioned the conclusion that her death was an accident. He had to acknowledge that he hadn't wanted to consider the possibility that it wasn't an accident. If it wasn't an accident, it meant that his theory that there was a sexual predator taking advantage of lax security at convenience stores didn't work.

Mars put his head in his hands as he thought about how he'd let his passion to prove a point about convenience-store security blind him to other possibilities.

Fool.

Mars checked the date of the article.

Two days after that date, Erin Moser was dead.

"What do we do now?" Nettie said, as chastened by what Mars had found as he'd been. "I just don't see that we've got anything on Campbell without the Green Man. We're still stuck with a can of soup, a golden oldie, and an unfired rifle cartridge."

Mars left the file with the news clip open on the table, walked over to the sliding doors, and stared out the black glass at the unseeable night. He remembered Jim Baker's phrase *"severe dark."*

Severe dark. That pretty well summed up where they were.

"It's what I've been thinking about this case since I got Boyle's message," Mars said. "I think we'd better be sure about where we're going before we actually leave." He blew air, taking a little kick at an invisible target on the carpet.

"I think we need to take some time before we move ahead."

CHAPTER
28

Mars waited near the secure doors on the baggage level of the Minneapolis-St. Paul Airport. Behind the Plexiglas doors, escalators flowed in a hypnotic rhythm.

It was a slack time for incoming flight arrivals, and the escalators were empty. Mars walked over to the Northwest Airlines flight arrival board. Flight 1571 had arrived seven minutes ago.

Mars glanced at his watch, then made a bet with himself as to when he'd see passengers coming down the escalator. It was 8:09 A.M. He bet on 8:15. The second bet he made with himself was that Chris would be the first passenger he'd see descending the escalators.

Mars lost the first bet by four minutes, but he won the second bet easily. Chris, accompanied by an airline employee, was at the top of the escalator just after 8:19. He was almost at the bottom of the escalator before another passenger appeared.

Watching Chris from a distance gave Mars a chance to really look at his son in a way a father rarely has a chance to do without exposing more emotion than a father wanted to reveal or that a son wanted to see. What Mars saw from this protected vantage point was that Chris had changed in the four weeks and two days since Mars had last seen him. Still a few months short of twelve, Chris was getting an early jump on an adolescent growth spurt. Or was it that adolescence was getting an early jump on Chris?

Probably both. Whatever the cause, it was the effect that startled Mars. Chris was taller, leaner than he'd been just four weeks ago. And more than the obvious physical changes were the subtle differences in the way Chris carried himself, in a kind of self-consciousness Mars hadn't seen before.

That self-awareness had never been more evident than at this moment as Chris walked next to his accompanying attendant. Chris had his mother's natural sense of good manners, which prevented a public display of his embarrassment at being escorted. But for someone who knew Chris as well as Mars did, Chris's discomfort was evident in the distance he maintained between himself and the airline employee and in the slight twist of Chris's mouth as he glanced at his attendant or responded to her when she spoke.

"How long do I have to be an UM?" Chris had asked after his first airplane ride as what Northwest Airlines classified as an unaccompanied minor.

"Until you're fourteen," Mars had said. "With any luck, your hormones will kick in before that and you'll get a good-looking stewardess to be your escort. Then being an UM will be a plus."

"No way," Chris said. "And they don't call them stewardesses anymore. They're flight attendants."

"I stand corrected," Mars said, taking Chris's invention of the UM acronym and his correction on the proper nomenclature for flight attendants as the first signs that Chris would become a flying aficionado in the same way that he became expert about anything in his life he cared about.

Chris had already evolved the UM concept into a fairly elaborate set of observations. He catalogued what to him were the absurdities of the process by which NWA kept track of him when he flew from Minneapolis to Cleveland to see his mother. He maintained a computer file titled UMdom and kept track of UMdomisms, a rapidly growing list of dumb things people said to Chris when he traveled as an UM.

"I don't see why we can't sign something that would say I didn't have to be an UM. Tell them you're a cop. If you say it's okay, they shouldn't care."

"It would embarrass me to ask," Mars said. "So resign yourself to a couple more years of UMdom."

As a matter of objective fact, Mars had complete confidence that

Chris could negotiate any airport in the United States on his own, including making connecting flights. Even in the event of a crisis, Mars was confident Chris would be able to think his way clear of harm's way. But as a father, he was unwilling to give up any degree of security for Chris, even if Northwest Airlines had been willing to accept a waiver, which Mars thought was highly unlikely.

Watching Chris approach with an attendant who must have been three inches shorter than her charge and notably less quick on her feet did make Chris's UM status pretty absurd.

"Are you Christopher's father?" Chris's escort said as the automatic doors slid open before them. "Not that I really need to check," she said as she compared Mars's ID to the UM's paperwork. "It's so obvious you're father and son." Then she reached up, giving Chris a pat on the cheek. "You've been a great little traveler, young man."

"UMdomism number seventeen," Chris muttered as they headed toward their baggage carousel.

Mars put his hand loosely on Chris's shoulder as they walked. "What held you up deplaning? Seemed like you were slow getting down here."

"You ever been to Gate A14?" Chris asked. "I went up to the ticket counter when we got back to the terminal and asked if they had a flight leaving today for Gate A14. The lady at the counter just kind of looked at me like, duh? But the guy standing next to her laughed. He knew what I was talking about. It's a mile away, Dad, I'm not kidding. It's way down by where you drive into the airport, out by Highway Five. When Mom and me went down to Florida for spring break— after Cleveland? We connected through the Atlanta airport. Atlanta has trains for gates that are far apart. What if I was some ninety-year-old lady? How would they expect some ninety-year-old lady to get from Gate A14 down here? There's no way you could even go on an electric cart. There are two different levels, and these narrow corridors . . ."

And so it begins, Mars thought. *Give Chris a year and another couple of flights and he'll be a leading authority on domestic airports.*

They dodged through the heavy flux of travelers entering the terminal to catch departing flights, Mars turning sideways more than once to avoid being sideswiped by a laptop computer case swinging from the shoulder of a business traveler oblivious to anything other than his need to get where he was going faster than anyone else. Mars didn't know what it was that changed people from human beings into robots when someone else was paying for their ticket, but based on his airport observations, that's what happened.

"How's your mom?" Mars asked while they waited for Chris's duffel bag to drop through the carousel chute.

"Good," Chris said, nodding his head, sounding like he meant it.

"I won't ask about Carl."

Chris shrugged. "I hardly saw him. He's getting his new business going with his brother. He wasn't around all that much. Fine with me." He looked over at Mars with a knowing grin.

As Mars turned off the airport approach road onto Highway 5, he said, "You want to go into the office with me tomorrow morning—I can take you to soccer camp from there."

Chris shook his head. "Can't. I told Lisa Schoof I'd be back today and could start walking Basil tomorrow afternoon."

Mars glanced sideways at Chris. "How is the dog walking going to work with soccer?"

Chris kept his eyes straight ahead, staying quiet.

Mars looked back at the road before glancing over at Chris again.

"I've sort of decided not to do soccer anymore," Chris said.

Mars stayed silent until they'd taken the Highway 55 West exit. Then he said, "*Sort of* decided not to do soccer anymore. Is that the same as you *have* decided not to do soccer anymore?"

"I guess."

More silence as they drove, the Minneapolis skyline coming into view to the west of Highway 55.

Mars spoke first. "It's always been your call—play soccer or don't play soccer. But I'd like to know how you made the decision. You've put a lot of time into soccer, and you're good. You're sure about this?"

Chris nodded hard. "Yeah. It just takes too much time. There are other things I want to do. I've got six people signed up for dog walking. That's eighteen dollars a day. Five days a week is ninety dollars a week . . ."

"You don't have to give up an activity because of money, Chris. Not before you started living with me and not now. We're good. I've got more money than I've had since your Mom and I got divorced, and your college fund is in good shape. It doesn't make any sense for you to give up something you've worked hard at because of money."

"It's not just the money. I *like* doing the dog walking. Plus I don't like the new soccer coach. And three of the guys on the team are pains in the ass . . ."

Mars sighed. Chris's inability to tolerate people he didn't respect had been an emerging character trait over the past two or three years. He'd lost patience with Scouts two years earlier, and he was showing less and less interest in any kind of team or group activity.

Mars sighed because he recognized that Chris was getting more and more like Mars. Not an easy path to follow.

"The other thing," Chris said, his voice sounding very tentative, "is that I may be able to work at Restaurant Alma part-time . . ."

"Chris. You're not even twelve. There's no way they can hire you to work at the restaurant."

"Yeah, they can. As long as you sign something saying it's okay with you. And I can only work certain hours. It wouldn't be like a real job. I'd help with cleaning and getting stuff set up before their dinner service starts, like maybe two or three weekdays. Depending on how busy they are, they'd let me help with prep in the kitchen. I'd be finished before six. And on slow nights, like when the weather isn't good or on Mondays and Tuesdays when they don't have a special group in, Alex would show me how to do stuff in the kitchen. Weekends Jim would let me watch him bake bread . . ."

Mars was shaking his head.

"The best part, Dad, is that we could go for dinner on Sunday nights. For free, except for the wine—and you don't want wine, anyway. Wouldn't that be great? I'd rather have that than money. I mean, I can make plenty of money walking the dogs. I've got a waiting list of people who want me to walk their dogs, and if I add a second shift, I know I could get another six dogs which would mean I'd get thirty-six dollars a day . . ."

"Do you mind telling me how you're going to do two shifts of dog walking and work at Restaurant Alma until six and get homework done—not to mention maybe having some free time?"

"I can get my homework done at school. Or after I get home from the restaurant."

"Let's leave it like this. Your call on soccer. One shift of dog walking on school days and one after-school-day-a-week at the restaurant. Weekends we'll play by ear. Depending on how that schedule works, *maybe* one more weekday at the restaurant. And all of that depends on you keeping your grades up."

Chris nodded, but Mars, glancing over at him, recognized the expression on Chris's face. He was already planning a strategy for upping the ante on more dog shifts and more time at the restaurant.

As they turned off Washington Avenue into the condo's underground garage, Mars said, "Does this feel like coming home?"

"I love this place," Chris said. "It's perfect for us." He looked at Mars with a grin. "How's the refrigerator?"

"Canned Coke is all I've used it for. Works fine."

"Dad?"

"Chris?"

"Could we go to Restaurant Alma for dinner tonight? I'll pay. Then you could talk to Jim and Alex about me working there."

"I was going to suggest going to Alma for dinner. To celebrate your coming home. And I'll pay."

Apart from the prospect of great food in a comfortable place, one of the pleasures for Mars of having dinner at Restaurant Alma was the walk from their condo to the restaurant. It wasn't more than three or four blocks from their front door to West River Parkway, a couple blocks along the parkway to the Stone Arch Bridge, then over the bridge and up the hill on Sixth Avenue Southeast to the restaurant.

More than 150 years after its founding, Minneapolis had awakened to the fact that it was sited on one of the world's great rivers and, as much as anything, it was the reopening of the Stone Arch Bridge as a pedestrian walkway that had brought that awakening about.

Mars would have paid admission to walk over the bridge, a beautiful structure in its own right, and from which there was a view up the Mississippi to St. Anthony Falls. Downriver from the bridge was a wooded gorge, with the east and west banks of the University of Minnesota rising above the river. At either end of the bridge were the flour mills that had been the city's founding industries. Flour was on its way out in the new century, rapidly being overtaken by residential and civic development.

The bridge had significance in Mars's personal history, as well. It was impossible for him to walk on the bridge without thinking about Evelyn Rau, a woman who'd entered his life as a dramatic figure in a dramatic investigation that had involved the bridge and the Father Hennepin Bluffs at the bridge's east end. Evelyn. She who had left his life—temporarily? permanently?—to complete academic research in England.

Mars and Chris always made it a point to stop on the bridge midpoint and look upriver at the falls. The falls was not in top form. After drenching rains in May and the first half of June, skies had been severe clear for the past several weeks. The concrete apron that had been built to prevent the falls' erosion was partially visible under the river's reduced flow, looking rather like ribs under thin skin.

"Evelyn said she doesn't know when she's coming back," Chris said, interrupting Mars's train of thought and revealing that his and Mars's thoughts were following the same track. Contrary to a central principle in Mars's personal parenting guide, Chris and Evelyn had, through happenstance, become friends. A friendship, Mars often felt, that might well outlast his own connection to Evelyn.

"Yeah," he said. "That's what she told me, too."

Chris looked at Mars. "She called while I was gone?"

Mars shook his head. "No. I got a letter."

Chris looked back at the falls, his feelings transparent on his face.

"I thought you guys didn't write letters. She sends me letters, she sends you postcards. No words, just the postcards."

Mars wondered if there was another eleven-year-old kid who

would know without being told that Mars having gotten a letter from Evelyn didn't bode well for their shared future. There wasn't any question that Chris understood. As much as Mars had understood when he'd held Evelyn's letter in his hand, before he opened the letter, that it wasn't good. Just like he'd understood that getting blank post-cards from Evelyn *was* good, even though he'd never been able to explain why that was true.

"I think she decided there were things she needed to say. Evelyn's a writer, more than a talker. I guess that's why she decided to send a letter."

Chris pushed away from the bridge rail and started walking again. Mars followed him, considering what to say before he decided there wasn't anything he could say that would add meaning to the simple fact that Mars had gotten a letter from Evelyn.

They had just started up the hill on Sixth Avenue Southeast when they saw the dog.

"It's a Chesapeake," Chris said. "A Chesapeake Bay retriever. What's he doing out here by himself?"

Chris had wanted a dog for as long as Mars could remember. They'd agreed they'd get a dog after he'd gotten back, and Chris had bought a dog encyclopedia, making a study of his choices. His single constraint was that their condominium association limited dog own-ership to breeds that weighed thirty-five pounds or less.

"He's a beautiful dog," Mars said. "And he's got a collar. He must have gotten out of a yard somewhere. That dog won't be on his own long."

The dog was as interested in Chris as Chris was interested in the dog.

"Here, boy," Chris called, holding out a hand.

The dog stared at Chris, looked over his shoulder, then back at Chris, before moving slowly closer.

"C'mon," Chris said, dropping down on one knee, still holding out his hand.

Mars tensed. A strange dog. A dog that was clearly spooked.

"Chris—I think we need to leave him alone. We don't know any-thing about him. Except he doesn't seem all that friendly . . ."

"He's a Chesapeake, Dad. Retriever breeds are all friendly, except Chesapeakes don't trust people right off. But they're not aggressive. He's looking me in the eye, his hackles aren't up, his ears are down, he's okay . . ."

Up close the dog had a shrewd, canny look. A short, rough, liver-colored coat, golden eyes, pink around the edges, a pink nose and lips. Handsome and weird.

Chris took the dog's head between his hands, putting his own cheek down on the dog's forehead.

"Good boy," Chris said, stroking the dog with one hand while he felt for the dog's collar with the other hand.

"Gunner," he said, reading a brass tag on the collar. "But there's no last name, no address. And he doesn't have a license tag."

Everything about the dog tightened at the sound of his name. He fixed his gimlet eyes on Chris as if, having heard his name, he expected something.

Chris looked up at Mars. "We can't just leave him out here, Dad."

"And we can't take him home. You know the rules. This dog is not thirty-five pounds or less."

"I don't mean keep him. He must have an owner. I just want to take him home until I can find the owner. I'll look in lost and found in the paper. And if there's nothing there, I'll put an ad in . . ."

"And how do we handle the condo board?"

"Mrs. Dorphy is the board president, Dad. She's got a beagle. She's one of the people on my waiting list to have her dog walked. I'll talk to her . . ."

Chris stood up, and Gunner immediately moved closer to him. Mars felt like if he'd ever had any control in this situation, it was long gone.

"Chris. I know how you are about animals. What happens if we can't find the owner? You're prepared to give Gunner up if we don't find an owner?"

Chris didn't look at Mars when he said, "I'll find the owner." He looked toward Mars without meeting his eyes. "I will."

They turned back toward the bridge, dinner at Restaurant Alma forgotten.

Gunner walked at Chris's side, Chris's hand stroking him as they walked. At one point, Gunner looked past Chris at Mars.

The look in the dog's eyes said it all.

As far as Gunner was concerned, his owner had been found.

Before Mars went to bed he cracked open the door to Chris's room. Gunner, who'd been lying lengthwise next to Chris on the bed, immediately raised his head, his body tense and alert. On seeing Mars, his body loosened. He blinked in a amiable way and continued to look at Mars.

The dog's expression carried meaning.

It's okay. I've got him. Go to bed.

The dog's look brought a conscious realization to Mars that had been in his subconscious since Denise had moved to Cleveland.

He hadn't realized until Denise was gone how comforting it had been to have someone else around on a daily basis who had Chris's well-being as their primary purpose in life.

Not that Chris took a lot of looking after. If anything, Chris's capacity for independence was what caused Mars anxiety. If he'd been a clueless kid, an irresponsible kid, setting limits would have been easy and clear. Setting limits with Chris, who gave no evidence of needing them, got harder every day Chris got older. As a father—maybe more to the point, as a father whose job gave him daily evidence of human mortality—it was Mars who needed Chris to have limits for his own peace of mind, not Chris's well-being.

Now, meeting Gunner's gaze, Mars felt the peace of mind that had been missing since Denise had left, for the simple reason that there was now another being in Chris's life who loved Chris as much as Mars did.

As Mars started to step away from the door, Gunner edged closer to Chris, dropped his head on Chris's hip, and gave a deep sigh of canine purpose and contentment.

Maybe another being in Chris's life who loved Chris more than Mars did, Mars thought as he went back to his own room.

If that was possible.

CHAPTER

29

It was typical of Nettie that she was able to carry on with the routine details of an investigation in the face of false starts and obstacles.

Just as it was typical of Mars to become restless and unfocused in response to facing an insurmountable roadblock on the Bergstad investigation. On a hot case, there was no shortage of angles to follow if one approach went flat. But with the Bergstad case, everything Mars could think of doing led directly toward the Green Man.

Nettie, who had begun the thankless, tedious task of following up on the tip sheets that had come in through *The Get List,* watched Mars pace, watched him sit down, get up, sit down again, watched him flip listlessly through the case files.

"You need your cigarette pack," she said, thinking the pack might have the effect on Mars a pacifier has on a restless infant.

He stood at the window, looking out, hands in his pockets, his back to Nettie.

Turning around, he said, "That thought occurred to me when I was talking to Sig Sampson. He was playing with the cartridge he found the way I used to play with a cigarette pack. Did make me miss it—but I'm not going back there. An infantile habit."

Exactly, Nettie thought, but did not say.

Mars continued to stand at the window. When he turned around, he had a troubled expression on his face.

"What?" Nettie said.

"I think I've missed something important."

"And the important thing you missed was?"

"The cartridge," Mars said. "By my theory, the Green Man was reloading when he dropped the cartridge in the field. That means he'd already fired without hitting his target. And he was reloading because he was still trying to find his target . . ."

"Meaning . . ."

"Meaning Andrea may have gotten away."

"Okay," Nettie said, not sure where Mars was going with his point. "And you're thinking this now because . . ."

Mars rubbed his head hard with both hands. He wasn't sure yet why. So he talked it through out loud. Thinking while he talked.

"You said one of the tip sheets was from a woman named DeeDee Kipp, who lived in Vermillion, South Dakota—the same town where a woman was shot who showed up in our first search for convenience-store victims . . ."

"Yeah—when we were looking for people who'd been shooting victims at convenience stores in the five-state region. And we decided that gave us too broad a selection, so we looked at abductions, instead. That's how we got our three cases, one of which was Andrea Bergstad."

"Do you remember the date when the woman was shot at the Vermillion convenience store?"

"Sure," Nettie said. "I just scanned that stuff the other day. Rhonda Billich. She was coming out of a convenience store in Vermillion, South Dakota, in 1987. She was shot in the head when she left the store after her shift . . ."

"Damn," Mars said.

"I'm not following . . ."

"How about this," Mars said. "The reason the Green Man came after Andrea Bergstad in 1984 was because she was pressuring Campbell about their relationship. What she hadn't told Campbell was that she was pregnant. And she had a daughter in 1984 . . ."

"Wait—wait—wait," Nettie said. "How do you know she didn't tell Campbell she was pregnant?"

Mars shook his head. "I'm getting to the part about why I don't think Andrea told Campbell she was pregnant . . ."

Nettie's face went blank, then she said, "You're saying we've been investigating a single victim involved in two different cases? That Andrea Bergstad and the woman shot in Vermillion in 1987—Rhonda Billich—are the same person?"

"Remember what Boyle said about the Green Man having a kind of code of honor about how he did his jobs?"

"What he said was that the Green Man was noble, in his own way."

"Same thing," Mars said. "If Andrea Bergstad did get away, the Green Man is not going to let that outcome stand. He's going to finish the job. He found Andrea and shot her . . ."

Nettie was shaking her head. "How does he do that? Three years after she disappears, he finds her?"

"I'm guessing that shortly before Andrea was shot she made contact with her parents. I'd guess she also told them not to try to find her, that it would be dangerous for her and for them if they did . . ."

"So how did the Green Man find her? Who was she living with? Was DeeDee adopted?"

"I don't know. Not about how he found her. I know enough about him to know he'd do whatever it took to finish what he started. And I don't have a clue about how Andrea got to Vermillion after she ran away."

"DeeDee Kipp said on her tip to *TGL* that the woman who looked like Andrea Bergstad was her babysitter . . ."

Mars shook his head. "DeeDee would have been about three when Andrea was shot. She wouldn't remember that she had another mother. What she'd remember is the pictures she'd seen of herself with a woman she was told was her babysitter. More than that, I'd guess Andrea gave DeeDee up right after she was born. To protect her. She keeps the kid and the Green Man finds Andrea, she and the kid are both dead."

Nettie scribbled on a piece of paper, looked at what she'd written, then said, "It doesn't work, Mars. The dates. If Andrea Bergstad was pregnant in 1984—October of 1984—but not pregnant enough that anyone else knew—she couldn't have had the baby until 1985. DeeDee Kipp said she's nineteen. Meaning she would have been born in 1984."

"I can't answer all the questions, Nettie, but say Andrea was four,

196

five months' pregnant in October of 1984 and had the baby prematurely in December. Not impossible."

Nettie looked like what Mars was saying made sense. Then she said, "You were going to explain why you think Andrea didn't tell Campbell she was pregnant."

"That's the only question you've asked that has an easy answer," Mars said.

"DeeDee Kipp is still alive."

They both thought about that.

"You know what it means, Nettie—if my theory is right, that DeeDee Kipp is Andrea Bergstad's daughter?"

Nettie closed her eyes and shook her head. "I don't think I know anything anymore."

"It means we've got the possibility of a direct link between Campbell and Andrea. A genetic link."

Nettie frowned. "My problem is, I'm not sure where we cross a line to a connection with the Green Man and where we don't. Maybe we can prove that DeeDee Kipp was Andrea and Campbell's daughter, but to make the connection between Campbell and Andrea's death— that takes us right back to the Green Man. And I'm a lot less confident than Boyle is that the Green Man isn't going to get itchy if we get close to Campbell."

She was right. The possibility of a genetic link between Campbell, Andrea, and DeeDee Kipp didn't resolve their basic problem. How to stay clear of the Green Man was still an issue.

"All I know for sure is we've got another reason for not doing anything until we know what we're doing."

"Another reason?" Nettie said.

"DeeDee Kipp," Mars said. "We can't do anything that tips off the Green Man that DeeDee Kipp may be Andrea Bergstad and Alan Campbell's daughter." He looked at his watch. "I should be getting back to the apartment. Why don't you come over to the apartment and have dinner with us. You haven't seen Chris since he got back."

They saw Gunner first. The dog came from the living room into the front hall at a wary trot, a new leather leash trailing from his collar. He gave both of them a close look, acknowledged Mars by being disinterested in him, then approached Nettie.

"Who's this?" Nettie said, smiling and taking the dog's head in her hands. "He's gorgeous. You didn't say Chris got a dog." Then, "You can have a dog this big in the condo? I thought . . ."

Chris came in from the living room. "I went over to the *Star-Tribune* and got last Sunday's paper. There wasn't anything about a lost . . ."

He saw Nettie and grinned. "Hi," he said, walking over to Nettie and giving her a hug. Gunner observed the hug closely. After Chris's demonstration of affection, Gunner looked at Nettie with increased respect.

Chris had become Gunner's true north for determining human worthiness.

"You brought the dog back from Cleveland?" Nettie said.

Mars said, "We found him last night, over on the bluffs. We're not keeping him . . ."

"I talked to Mrs. Dorphy," Chris said. "She said she'd send a message to the board about our trying to find the owner."

There was something tentative in what Chris said. A tentativeness that Mars was coming to recognize as a signal that what was being said was only part of the story.

"And?" Mars said.

Chris's face screwed into a calculated expression of thoughtful seriousness. "It's just that I was wondering *why* the board has the rule about dogs being thirty-five pounds or less. Mrs. Dorphy said she'd talk to the board about that, too." He hesitated, then said, "Dad, I told her I would be doing a second shift of dog walking, so I could walk her dog . . ."

The tentativeness was still in Chris's voice.

"And?" Mars said.

Chris didn't look directly at Mars when he said, "I sort of said that I could do another shift of dog walking—if we didn't have to move." And in a much softer voice, "Because of Gunner."

Mars groaned. "Chris. I warned you. If we can't find the dog's owner . . ."

"*Dad,*" Chris said, "I already walk dogs for two of the board members. With Mrs. Dorphy, it'll be three. And one of the other members is on my waiting list, and that would be a majority. I got the bylaws and . . ."

Mars put his head in his hands. "I knew it," he said. "I walked right into this."

Still in his tentative voice, Chris said, "Dad?"

"What?"

"When I went over to the paper, I left Gunner here."

"And?"

"He doesn't like being left alone."

"So?"

"Well, I sort of put him in my room. I mean, I wasn't sure if he was house-trained or what."

Sort of was also becoming one of Chris's verbal signals, Mars thought.

"And?"

"He tried to get out."

The three of them walked back to Chris's room, Gunner at their heels. Chris's door was shut.

"I know how to open it," Chris said.

Mars and Nettie looked at each other.

"I thought he learned how to turn a doorknob at ten months," Nettie said.

Chris went through a complicated set of motions involving his shoulder, his right foot, and both hands. Gunner waited patiently beside him, unperturbed.

When the door was open, the problem became obvious. Gunner had attempted to dig under the door, ripping the carpet and the carpet pad into shreds. When the door was shut, it pulled pieces of the carpet under the door, causing it to jam.

They all looked at each other.

"I'll pay for it," Chris said.

"Yes," Mars said. "You will."

They talked about going to Restaurant Alma for dinner, but decided leaving Gunner alone in the apartment wasn't a good idea. Chris, eager to be useful, offered to forage on the Skyway, a second-story walkway that connected their condo to other downtown buildings. The Skyway system had a wide selection of restaurants and take-out food.

When Chris left, it became clear that Gunner's problem had less to do with being left alone than being separated from Chris. He paced at the front door, muttering to himself, panting, and drooling.

Nettie and Mars, who'd gone back to a discussion of how to proceed in investigating the connection between DeeDee Kipp and Campbell, tried to get Gunner to stay in the living room with them, but being forced away from the front door only intensified the dog's anxiety.

Eventually Mars and Nettie gave up and moved their chairs into the hall. Gunner didn't stop panting, but he did at last lie down by their feet, his head between his front paws, his eyes darting right and left, his ears lifting with each sound from the hall.

They were there when Danny called to say the office was clean.

"This could be a full-time job, Danny. Can you do the office and the apartments once a week until further notice?"

"Will do. And Mars? This had better be one hell of a story that I'm waiting to hear."

Moments before Mars and Nettie heard Chris in the hall, Gunner was on his feet, his tail swinging with the pleasure of recognition.

"How does he do that?" Nettie said. "Did you hear anything?"

"No," Mars said, "but he's got better hearing and smell senses than both of us put together."

Gunner twisted in circles of joy when Chris came in.

"Bombay Bistro," Chris said, dropping a large brown bag on the kitchen counter, then dropping down on his knees to embrace Gunner. After a lengthy exchange of mutual affection, they both went into the living room, lying down parallel to one another on the carpet, Chris stroking the length of Gunner's body. Gunner's eyes were half-closed.

"He's exhausted," Mars said, bringing plates, silverware, and cartons of Indian food out to the table that sat at one end of the living room.

"You would be too, if you'd spent most of the day trying to dig through two layers of carpet and a concrete floor," Nettie said. "Chris? What did you get?"

"I got pakora and samosa for appetizers and three entrees. Chicken Tikka Masala, Beef Vindaloo, and Daal Makhani."

"It smells wonderful," Nettie said. "Bombay Bistro is on the Skyway?"

"Not *on* the Skyway," Chris said. "It's at street level on Marquette. But you can get there on the Skyway."

Mars looked at Chris lying next to Gunner. Both of them looked like they were ready to tank.

"Chris, c'mon and eat. Then get to bed. You're beat."

"I'm on eastern time," Chris said. "It's an hour later in Cleveland. But I've got to take Gunner out again . . ."

"Eat," Mars said. "I'm going to walk Nettie down to her car after we've eaten, and I'll take Gunner out then."

"He's going to let you leave Chris alone in the apartment?" Nettie said.

Chris said, "I'll tell him it's okay. Then he'll let you."

And he did. Reluctantly, but motivated by the fact he needed to go out, especially after Chris had, without Mars noticing, shared his Beef Vindaloo with Gunner. That this had happened became obvious when the room's air was suddenly filled with a thick, deadly fart.

"Gunner!" Nettie said, putting a paper towel up to her nose.

"Oh, my God," Mars said.

"How do you like having a dog so far?" Nettie said, still grimacing behind the paper towel.

Mars and Gunner walked Nettie to her car, parked at a meter on Washington a half block away.

"See you in the morning," Mars said as he closed the car door behind Nettie.

Nettie gave him a quick wave as she headed out.

Mars turned to head back to the apartment, but Gunner didn't move. His eyes remained firmly fixed on Nettie's car until it was out of sight. Then he turned and followed Mars, stopping every few steps to look back in the direction where Nettie had left.

Mars shook his head.

"You've got one hard life ahead of you, pal. Keeping anyone who comes within Chris's airspace under surveillance."

Gunner rewarded this observation with a quick squat that produced a pile of soft, sloppy poop. A wafting odor of Beef Vindaloo rose from the pile.

Mars looked at the plastic bag Chris had handed him before they'd left.

"Correction. I'm the one that's got the hard life living in your airspace."

CHAPTER

30

Mars stood in the corridor outside the State Bureau of Criminal Apprehension's meeting room, dreading the moment when he had to transform himself into a team player who was carrying his weight as a Cold Case Unit investigator.

Nettie usually covered the CCU's weekly status meeting. But with the active investigation on the Bergstad case stalled, Nettie had more to do at the office than Mars, so they'd agreed that today Mars would carry the torch.

There were a lot of good reasons for Mars to attend the meetings, at least on an occasional basis. It was the only scheduled time that he saw his new colleagues, whose offices were in a different location from Nettie and Mars's office.

Mars liked his fellow investigators. What he knew of them. And it wouldn't hurt for him to get exposed to how experienced cold case investigators worked, to hear firsthand about the cases they were involved in and how they were moving their cases forward.

But the meetings had been uncomfortable because Mars didn't have much to say for himself. Nettie always had plenty to report. But that wouldn't work indefinitely. Eventually, reasonable people would have reasonable questions about what Mars was doing.

Ironically, today he had a lot he could say. Things he could say that would be directly responsive to the principal agenda topic: how to demonstrate in the face of the state's fiscal crisis that the CCU provided value to justify the unit's budget allocation.

Mars had noticed from the first that the tone of these discussions was different from similar discussions at the MPD. There was precious little grandstanding, no implied threats to public safety if budget cuts were threatened. The CCU had no leverage for such actions as their principal constituency was the friends and relatives who suffered the ongoing pain of unresolved death. Compared to the number of voters who'd never suffered such a loss but who felt perpetually vulnerable to violent crime, the CCU's constituency was impotent.

The very nature of the unit's work undercut that kind of strategy. Rarely were they in a position to argue that the work they did would prevent future deaths—even if there were instances when that might have been true. The work they did was perceived as providing justice to those who'd already suffered a failure of public safety. No one would argue against it, but the cause did not carry the same weight as protecting the living.

It was one of the reasons the unit had been enthusiastic in its support for Mars's and Nettie's work on convenience-store crime. That project was seen as a way the CCU could demonstrate that it was not only redressing past wrongs, but that it was also making a contribution to public safety going forward.

As Mars listened to the discussion around the table he considered the effect of saying, "Nettie and I are gathering evidence that Senator Alan Campbell was involved in the 1984 disappearance of a young woman who gave birth to his child and was subsequently murdered. Our investigation suggests that the senator was also involved in the murder of a political opponent and the murder of a potential witness to the disappearance of the mother of the child. In addition, there is evidence to suggest that Senator Campbell was involved in atrocities during his service in Vietnam."

He imagined their faces, slack-jawed with disbelief. Then he imagined the questions they would have, none of which he could answer. Couldn't answer because he didn't have the answers and couldn't answer because he didn't want to risk what he did know about the Green Man leaking out.

So when it was time for him to give his report, he talked about Nettie's concerns about the DOJ's proposed slackening of information quality standards for criminal databases, and the work he and Nettie were doing to review the tip sheets that had come in response to *The Get List* program.

"We had a call from Senator Campbell's office about the status of the investigation," the unit director said. "Anything I can pass on that would make them happy?"

Mars froze. "Campbell's office is asking questions about the investigation?"

"Routine. Given the senator's public interest in the case, they want to make sure he's current. He'll probably try to make political hay out of any progress we do make. That's to be expected."

Mars said, "Nothing to pass on at this point." It had chilled him to be reminded of how close Campbell was to the investigation.

He had just finished his report when his cell phone vibrated. He excused himself and went out to the hall to return Nettie's call.

"Get back to the office," Nettie said. "There's someone here you need to meet."

His first thought when he walked into the office was that his theory about Andrea Bergstad had been all wrong. She couldn't have been shot at a convenience store in Vermillion, South Dakota, in 1987 because she was now sitting in his office next to Nettie.

It took seconds before his brain was able to make sense of what he was seeing. The young woman sitting next to Nettie was an exact replica of the images he'd seen of Andrea Bergstad, but the young woman before him today was maybe twenty years younger than Andrea Bergstad would be if she were still alive.

"DeeDee Kipp?" Mars said.

DeeDee Kipp nodded.

"I didn't expect anybody to contact me after I called into *The Get List*," DeeDee said. "I knew what I said didn't make any sense. But I couldn't think how else to say it. After I called, I sat down and tried to write a letter, and that got all tangled up. So when my roommate said she was coming up to the cities today to find a bridesmaid dress, I got off work . . ."

She looked at her watch. "I've only got, like, another couple hours before she picks me up. I had a hard time finding this place. We went to the BCA's main office first, but the guard at that building gave me this address. My roommate dropped me over here, but she's got to get back to Mankato by six, so we need to leave . . ."

"DeeDee," Nettie said, "I can get you back to Mankato. It's important that we talk this through now that you're here. And there are things you need to know. Things that are important for you to understand . . ."

DeeDee said, "I've got to be back tonight. I work the A.M. shift at a nursing home. So I've got to be in my uniform and ready to leave my apartment by six-thirty tomorrow morning."

"Tonight isn't a problem," Nettie said. "What I want you to do now is to tell Mars what you told me."

There was a disconnect between DeeDee Kipp's soft voice, her pretty, delicate appearance, and the shrewd, observant young woman who emerged from the story she told.

"There were always things about my family that didn't make sense," DeeDee said. "Like, my parents were way older than any of my friends' parents. When I was maybe eleven or twelve, one of my friends said her mom thought I was adopted, because she thought my mother was too old to be my biological parent. I even asked my parents if I was adopted. They said 'no,' but I'd always wondered. Not just because they were older, but I didn't look anything like them.

"The other thing that was weird was that my family was just me and my mom and dad. No grandparents, no aunts and uncles, no cousins. Just the three of us. From what I'd been told, my parents moved to Vermillion right before I was born. But it never made sense to me why they'd moved there. My dad opened an insurance agency in Vermillion, but he retired when I was still in grade school. Why would they move, start a business, then retire? It was like there was another reason they moved to Vermillion—but I couldn't ever figure out what the reason was."

"You remembered your babysitter," Mars said.

DeeDee shook her head. "No. I just said that when I called in the tip. This is the part that's so hard to explain . . ."

"Just talk," Mars said. "We'll figure it out along the way."

DeeDee drew a deep breath. "My dad died when I was a freshman in high school and my mom died my senior year. My dad had been sick, but my mother died suddenly. I mean, she hadn't expected to die, she'd seemed pretty healthy and everything. After she'd died, I was going through all their stuff and I found a photo album with lots of pictures. Family pictures—I'm sure. And there were three pictures of me with this young woman. One picture when I was a baby, one when I started to walk—she was behind me, holding my hands—and one when I was sitting on her lap. I must have been two or three in that picture. The thing is, the way she touched me in those pictures, the way she looked at me—it wasn't like she was a babysitter. It seemed like she was someone closer to me than that.

"The other thing was, she looked just like me. I mean, it was like looking into a mirror or something. I knew when I saw those pictures that there were things about my family my parents hadn't told me. I thought, maybe she was my older sister? I just couldn't figure out *why* they wouldn't tell me.

"The other thing I found was my parents' birth certificates. My mother was sixty-nine when she died, which meant she would have been at least fifty-two when I was born . . ."

DeeDee looked at Mars and Nettie. "Wouldn't that be like a world record or something for a biological birth? My dad was seventy-three when he died. But they'd both told me they were ten years younger than they were."

DeeDee sighed. "I wanted to figure out the whole thing right then. But I couldn't. Like I said, my mother hadn't expected to die, or I think she probably would have destroyed the things I found. After she died I moved in with a friend's family until graduation. But besides school, I had to do all this stuff with lawyers to get my parents' estate settled. I couldn't find a birth certificate for me and there was no record of my birth in Clay County. So I was never able to get social security benefits. What I got was money from selling the house—which wasn't all that much—and a scholarship to attend Mankato State. I've had to work, like thirty hours a week, to support myself while I've been going to school. Summers I work full-time at the nursing home and that keeps me going.

"The point is, I haven't had time to figure out my family's mystery. I'd kind of put it on hold until I finished school. Then, the night *The Get List* program was on TV, I was in the kitchen popping popcorn, and my roommates started yelling for me to come into the living room. They said I was on TV. And there was my picture—I mean, Andrea Bergstad's picture. The same woman in the pictures with me when I was little. What I thought was, maybe calling the program would be a way of figuring out what had happened with my family. The only thing I could think to say was that my babysitter looked just like Andrea Bergstad. I hadn't heard the whole program, so I thought they were saying she'd been murdered in 1984. I didn't know she'd just disappeared."

DeeDee was quiet for a while. Then she said, "She does have something to do with me, doesn't she?"

Mars said, "We'll talk about that, DeeDee. But first I need to know what you think. Like, any reason your parents wouldn't have wanted you to know that you were adopted?"

"What I've thought is that maybe they got me illegally. You know, paid money to get a baby. We hardly ever went anywhere. But when my dad got sick, we'd go up to Sioux Falls to a hospital there. Once, while we were in Sioux Falls, a woman recognized my mother. She came up to her and hugged her and said how much everybody in 'God's Choice' missed her. When she saw me, she said, 'Oh, so you did decide to adopt. I'm so happy for you. I know how much having a child meant to you.' My mother hardly said anything. She just got me away from that woman as fast as she could. Why would she have done that unless there was something to hide?"

DeeDee looked up at Mars. There was an expression on her face somewhere between dread and guilt. "When I heard the TV program about Andrea Bergstad, when I thought she was dead, I even thought maybe my parents had something to do with her death. I mean—I didn't believe that, but I thought about it. Would they have taken her to get me? And they were so protective. Not just about normal things, like being careful crossing streets, but about everything. When I think about it, I wasn't ever left alone. One of them was always with me. It was like they were afraid of something . . ."

Nettie and Mars looked at each other. There was an implicit message that passed between them. It would be Nettie who would tell DeeDee what they knew about her mother.

Nettie sat down close to DeeDee, taking one of DeeDee's hands between her hands.

"We don't begin to know everything about what happened between your parents and Andrea Bergstad, but we think Andrea Bergstad was your mother."

Nettie gave DeeDee time to take in that message. At first DeeDee didn't show much emotion. But then her expression began to contort, her eyes filled with tears, and she buried her face on Nettie's shoulder.

Nettie looked up at Mars, near tears herself. She signaled Mars to bring a box of tissues. Then she put a hand on DeeDee's shoulder.

DeeDee lifted her head, taking a tissue and blowing her nose loudly. "Is she dead—Andrea Bergstad?"

This was the hard part. Telling DeeDee that her biological mother had been murdered and that because Andrea Bergstad *was* her biological mother, DeeDee was also at risk. Telling DeeDee that there had been a good reason why her parents had been so protective.

Slowly, Nettie said, "DeeDee, we think your mother was involved in a relationship with a powerful man. The man who was your father. To keep anyone from finding out about the relationship, this man arranged to have your mother murdered . . ."

DeeDee drew in a sharp breath. It was one thing to suspect that a woman of whom you had no direct memory was dead. It was quite another thing to be told the woman was your biological mother and that the man who was your biological father had arranged to have your mother murdered.

DeeDee shuddered. Mars was suddenly conscious of the fact that DeeDee was dressed in classic teenage style. Low-riding jeans, sandals, and a soft white-cotton sleeveless top that left her midriff bare. In the air-conditioned office, barraged with one brutal fact after another, DeeDee was turning blue before their eyes.

Mars got a sports coat he kept in the closet and draped it around DeeDee's shoulders. She pulled the lapels closer together and said, "Could I have a coffee or something?"

Nettie laughed. "You're in the only office in the civilized world where no one drinks coffee. Mars . . ."

"There's a coffee room on the first floor," Mars said. "I'll get you a coffee down there."

When he came back, Nettie and DeeDee had leaned back on the couch, Nettie still holding DeeDee close to her, DeeDee's head on Nettie's shoulder.

Nettie was the last person Mars would have described as being maternal, but the bond between the two women was just that. An affectionate protectiveness on Nettie's part, a trusting dependence from DeeDee.

Already DeeDee looked calmer. She sat up as Mars handed her a paper cup of coffee. After taking a sip, she said, "Do you think my parents—I mean, the Kipps—knew why Andrea was murdered?" Then she stopped. "Wait. If she was murdered, how was I born? How did the Kipps get me?"

Mars talked DeeDee through what had happened at the Redstone One-Stop in 1984. "As for how the Kipps got you—we haven't had a clue. But what you said before about your mother running into a woman in Sioux Falls who talked about the God's Choice organization—that may be the link. I know from the investigator in Redstone that Andrea Bergstad's mother . . ." Mars paused. "Your grandmother. Ruth Bergstad. Ruth Bergstad had been active in a number of Right to Life organizations all over the Midwest. I'm thinking Ruth Bergstad met your mother through God's Choice. Maybe Andrea met the Kipps, too. And when she ran, she ran to somebody she thought would give her shelter. Somebody she thought would take her baby, give her baby a different name, to protect the baby."

Nettie picked up the story.

"We think Andrea was killed at a convenience store in Vermillion in 1987. By the same person hired by . . ." Nettie stopped. She couldn't bring herself to refer to Alan Campbell as DeeDee's father. Instead she said, ". . . the same person who had been hired to abduct Andrea in 1984."

DeeDee clasped her head between both hands. "*How* did he find her in 1987? And if he found her, why wouldn't he have killed me, too? I would have been proof that my mother had a relationship with the person who hired him . . ."

"We don't know how he found her," Nettie said. "We just know the shooter was a person capable of finding almost anyone, almost anywhere." Then, in a soft voice, a voice meant to comfort DeeDee as she began to confront the most terrifying aspect of her family's mystery, Nettie said, "That he didn't find you, DeeDee, is a tribute to your mother. Both your mothers. A tribute to how much strength and courage they both had to make you safe. How carefully they planned to protect you."

DeeDee stared at Nettie.

"The man who was my father. Is he still alive?"

Mars said, "Yes."

DeeDee didn't ask who he was. Instead she said, "And the man who shot Andrea. Is he still alive?"

Again Mars said, "Yes."

DeeDee said, "So now that you've started this investigation, they could start looking for me?"

Mars said, "There's no reason they should know you exist, any more than they did in 1987. Nettie and I figured out that Andrea may have had a child through pure happenstance. We noticed on your tip sheet that you were from Vermillion and we knew from the database that Nettie had been developing that there'd been a convenience-store murder in Vermillion three years after Andrea disappeared. That got us thinking. Nobody else knows that, DeeDee. Not our colleagues in the Cold Case Unit, nobody at *The Get List*. That you are still alive is solid proof that nobody else has made that connection. And we've put the investigation on hold because we don't want to put you in danger. Not until we're sure there's a way it can be done without creating more risk."

DeeDee looked away from them, quiet, before she said, "So I live the rest of my life not being sure. Not knowing if some night, when I'm alone, the shooter might come after me. Not knowing if my children—who will have a genetic link to the man who was my father—will be in danger."

She looked at each of them. Mars and Nettie looked at each other.

They all sat in silence for a long time. Then Mars said, "Maybe there's a way. Timing would be critical, but maybe there's a way."

"How?" Nettie said.

"We need to inoculate ourselves," Mars said. "We need to go public with what we know."

DeeDee said, "I don't understand . . ."

Mars looked at DeeDee. The stress was showing on her face. She was holding up well considering everything they'd hit her with over the past hour. But she needed a break before she could rationally consider what he was thinking about.

"Let's do this," Mars said. "Your friend is going to be here to pick you up when?"

DeeDee looked up at the wall clock. "Maybe another hour."

"Can you get hold of her to tell her Nettie will be bringing you back to Mankato?"

DeeDee shook her head. "I don't know where she was going shopping . . ."

"No cell phone?"

DeeDee grinned. "She's driving her mother's car. And her mother won't let her have her cell phone in the car because she doesn't want her to drive while she's on the phone."

"A mother after my own heart," Mars said. "Okay. Nettie, you free for dinner tonight?"

"You buying or Chris cooking?"

"Chris said he was going to cook tonight. Then he's going over to Denise's sister's. Why don't we plan on going back to the apartment after DeeDee's friend stops by. We can have dinner, and after Chris leaves, we can talk through what I'm thinking about. It won't take long. I'd like the two of you to be on the road no later than nine, so Nettie can get back here before midnight."

"Sounds good to me," Nettie said.

"Perfect," DeeDee said.

CHAPTER
31

It had been more than a week since the Green Man had seen DeeDee Kipp in Mankato, and during that week, the two cold case investigators he'd been tracking hadn't left Minneapolis.

Campbell's office maintained contacts with *The Get List* production staff. Nothing from that source indicated that the investigation had picked up on DeeDee Kipp. The Green Man told Campbell to have his office contact the director of the BCA's Cold Case Unit to ask how the investigation was going. That query had come up dry as well.

All indications were that there was nothing to worry about. The tip had been too vague to suggest any meaningful connection to Andrea Bergstad. The only real danger, as he saw it, would be if someone made a connection between the death in Vermillion in 1987 and that a tip had come in from Vermillion linking Bergstad and DeeDee Kipp. Nothing suggested that had happened.

The Green Man was getting restless. Patience was essential to a successful sniper, but patience needed to be combined with potential to be justified. He wasn't seeing any potential. More and more it was feeling like things were under control on this assignment. And he had two active assignments with other clients that needed his attention.

It was time to move on. He could wait another six months, a year, and then arrange for DeeDee Kipp to have an accident.

But moving on was hard to do on this assignment. He had a nineteen-year history of things going wrong. He'd be damned before he'd be beaten by another teenager.

That line of thinking, he told himself, was emotional. It was not a rational response to his present situation. Emotions could beat you. Every bit of rationality he possessed told him he could spend the rest of his life waiting for the cold case investigators to connect with DeeDee Kipp without anything happening. He needed to move on. He'd close his Minneapolis operation that night and get a flight out first thing in the morning.

That decision made, he slipped back into the daily routine he'd followed since coming to Minneapolis. Then he drove to the small office building on University Avenue near the Minneapolis-St. Paul border to remove the Global Positioning monitors he'd installed on the two investigators' vehicles.

He turned into the driveway that led to the parking lot at the rear of the building, drove into the lot to make a U-turn—only to find his exit blocked by a car that had come into the lot behind him.

Another goddamn teenage girl, parked by the building's entrance, blocked the driveway to the street. He honked his horn, but the girl was focused on the door. Then, just as he was about to get out of his car and have a word with the girl, three people came out of the building.

He recognized the two adults from *The Get List* program. Marshall Bahr and Jeanette Frisch. The girl with them took his breath away.

DeeDee Kipp.

A simultaneous flash of heat and cold washed over him.

What the hell! And again, the reflexive fear that she would recognize him. In the next instant, he remembered that she didn't know him. None of them knew him. Nonetheless, it violated every principle of his training, every innate instinct within his soul, to be visible to his targets.

Bahr, the only one of the three conscious that they were blocking the driveway, turned toward the Green Man's car to give a signal of apology. The Green Man pulled down the visor to shield Bahr's view of his face. Then he forced himself to concentrate on what he was seeing.

The only thing he was certain of was that something had gone

214

seriously wrong with his information sources. It was difficult to believe that nothing would have come to him through Campbell's office if the Bureau of Criminal Apprehension management and *The Get List* producers knew that DeeDee Kipp was related to the case. If he was right about that, it had to mean that Bahr and Frisch were keeping the details of their investigation quiet. Did that mean they suspected Campbell? If they suspected Campbell, had that prevented them from passing information to Campbell's office?

Was it possible they knew of his involvement—that they knew of his thirty-two-year involvement with Campbell? If they did, they were much, much more dangerous to him than he had anticipated.

He wanted to leave the parking lot, but he didn't want to draw attention to himself by honking again. DeeDee Kipp was taking something out of the backseat of the parked car—a windbreaker and a baseball cap. Still talking to the driver, she dropped the hat on her head, pulling the brim down. She bent over, leaning into the front seat, and embraced the driver, then walked backward, away from the car. She was staying with Bahr and Frisch.

As the car reversed, then pulled forward to leave the parking lot, Bahr turned toward the Green Man, holding his arm up in a casual wave to acknowledge the waiting car's patience.

The Green Man lifted a hand in return, then drove slowly past the three of them and back out onto the street. After a block, he turned onto a side road and parked, keeping his eyes on the GPS monitor.

Within minutes, two blips began to move, heading toward downtown Minneapolis. The Green Man pulled out, following the direction the vehicles were taking on the monitor. He needed to be sure DeeDee Kipp was with them.

When he saw the silhouette of DeeDee Kipp in the car with the Frisch woman, the baseball cap still on Kipp's head, he pulled over again. He watched the monitor for almost fifteen minutes until the blip for Bahr's vehicle stopped moving. Within another five minutes, Frisch's blip was motionless.

He recognized the location where the vehicles had stopped from previous surveillance. Bahr's vehicle had entered the garage at his downtown Minneapolis condominium. Frisch's vehicle was parked on the street, approximately a block from the condo.

Which was where the Green Man headed as soon as he was sure the target vehicles were no longer moving.

Now, it was a waiting game.

CHAPTER
32

"Go on up," Mars said to Nettie and DeeDee, meeting them in the condo lobby. "I'm going to get the mail."

Mars smelled the perfume a fraction of a second after the elevator door closed behind him. In another heartbeat, he heard the evening office manager calling his name.

"Marshall?"

Mars stood still, his eyes closed as he heard Connie Babb's four-inch heels clicking across the tile lobby from the office. One of the condominium's attractions for Mars had been that in addition to the code-controlled entrance, the building's glass-fronted office was located in the lobby and was staffed twenty-four hours a day. It was a significantly more secure living situation than a house, a factor that was important to Mars with Chris on his own more.

But there was this maddening *balance* in human existence. For everything you got that was good, there was a downside trade-off.

In this case, the downside trade-off for having a human being keeping watch over the lobby was that the human being was often Connie Babb.

"I *thought* it was you," Connie Babb said, her brilliant red lips spread in an enormous smile as she approached. "I've been looking out for you. The building manager asked me to remind you to let us know when you have service people coming in . . ."

Mars looked at Connie Babb. "I'm aware of that. It hasn't been necessary, but if we have someone coming in, I'll be sure to . . ."

Connie Babb frowned. "I was sure he said Time-Warner Cable came for your unit the other day. He had your request order, so they let him up—the manager buzzed but didn't get an answer . . ."

"Wrong unit," Mars said. "I didn't schedule anything."

"Maybe I'm not remembering the right unit number," Connie said. "You're in—oh, no. That's right. You're in 802 and now that I think about it, the note the manager gave me was 602. I always confuse even numbers. 802, 602, *all* even numbers. Impossible to remember."

She waited expectantly. Mars edged toward the mailbox. "Not a problem. Have a nice night."

She followed him to the mailboxes. "I know what I'm thinking about. We had a note from Mrs. Dorphy, the association president. She said you had permission to have a dog in your unit that doesn't conform to the bylaws while the board reviews the rules. Your son is home now?"

"Got home a couple days ago," Mars said, relocking the mailbox and moving back toward the elevators.

"He's a darling boy," Connie said, smiling at Mars as if this observation were a shared intimacy between them.

"He's a good kid," Mars said, giving another punch to the elevator up button. The elevator dinged behind him. He gave Connie a little salute with his handful of mail and made his escape.

He *had* to get a handle on Connie Babb's schedule. Chris could do mail pickup the evenings Connie was on.

As he entered the apartment, Gunner approached him in a friendly, if not enthusiastic spirit, accepted a quick head rub, then trotted back to the kitchen, where Chris was making a sandwich. DeeDee Kipp was on a chair, watching Chris and Gunner.

It was then that Mars noticed that Gunner was wearing a wristwatch.

"Am I hallucinating, or is Gunner wearing a watch?"

"I'm training him," Chris said, then changed the subject. "You've gotta see this, Dad. I gave Gunner part of my sandwich. It was sourdough bread with tomatoes, cheese, lettuce, and salami. He chewed and chewed, and when he was done, he spit out the piece of lettuce. It was *perfect,* Dad. I mean, no tooth marks or anything. So now I'm making him a sandwich with all this other stuff, and I've put in this little piece of lettuce. I want to see if . . ."

While addressing Mars, Chris kept glancing over at DeeDee, who was holding Teddy Nelson, a small, white bichon frise. Chris was showing off for the benefit of the lovely DeeDee.

"Teddy staying overnight?" Mars said, walking over and giving Teddy a pat.

Chris shook his head. "I'm going to take him back to Mark and Marcie's when I take Gunner out." He looked over at DeeDee. "You want to come with? We can go down to the river. I'll show you the falls . . ."

DeeDee looked up at Mars. "Can I?" she said.

It was feeling to Mars like he had suddenly become the father of two kids. It made him think that if he'd had a child when he was eighteen, nineteen years old, he would now have a kid DeeDee's age.

Mars looked at his watch. "Sure." Then to Chris, "What's in the oven?"

"I'm making pot roast for dinner . . ."

"I could smell it as soon as I got off the elevator."

"Are you hungry for pot roast?"

"Not a typical hot summer night dinner, but I'm always hungry for pot roast," Mars said.

"Yeah, but it's supposed to cool off tonight and rain."

Mars gave Gunner another look. "I'm still trying to figure out the wristwatch."

"Oh," Chris said. "I got him a watch that's got an alarm. I set the alarm to go off in five minutes, then I told Gunner to stay. I went out, and when the alarm went off, I came back in. Then I set it for ten minutes, then for a half hour. He's already got it, Dad. When I went to get stuff for the sandwich, I was gone an hour. He was fine. Now, watch this . . ."

Chris bent down, giving Gunner a command to sit, which the dog did promptly, never taking his eyes from a hunk of sandwich that would have fed a multitude. Then Chris offered Gunner the sandwich, which Gunner took with the gentle grace only a dog bred for generations to retrieve with a soft mouth could have managed.

219

Just as advertised, Gunner chewed prodigiously, never dropping a morsel. After a final gulping swallow, he hesitated momentarily, then spat out an untouched piece of lettuce.

Chris howled with satisfaction. "You know what? I'm going to videotape this. I'm going to send it in to *Stupid Pet Tricks* . . ."

"*Stupid Human Tricks* might be a better option," Mars said. "Listen. You and DeeDee need to be back by six. The pot roast will be ready when?"

"Six-thirty."

"And Aunt Gwen is picking you up at . . . ?"

"I'm supposed to call her as soon as I'm through with dinner."

"That'll work," Mars said.

After Chris and DeeDee left with the dogs, Mars walked out to the living room. Nettie was on the futon couch, reading a paper. He dropped down next to her.

"I'm thinking I should drive down to Mankato with you. Or you could stay here and I could take DeeDee back."

Nettie drew the pages of the paper together and folded it on her lap. "I thought you left a message with *The Get List* producer to call you tonight?"

"Yeah. I did. But I gave him my cell and home number."

Nettie stretched and shook her head. "It doesn't make any sense for both of us to go. It's only what—seventy, eighty miles? No traffic this time of night . . ." She sat up, leaning toward Mars. "Besides. For once, I'm the one who's got a bond with a—what do we call DeeDee—she's not a victim, not just a family member—whatever, there's a real connection between us. She's been through a lot, and I think my support means something to her."

"If you're okay with it, fine. Just feels like breaking the deal we made when you became my partner . . ."

"Our deal?"

"That you'd never have to be a street investigator, dealing with the scum of the earth."

"Whatever DeeDee is, she's *not* the scum of the earth, Mars."

"Agreed."

220

Nettie continued to stare at Mars. "So what you're thinking about is it's time to go public. How are you thinking about doing that."

"It's what I said before," Mars said. "Timing will be everything. We've got to pull off a full court press on a single day, no advance notice, with local and national media coverage, and we've got to have everything we know in place to smoke out Campbell and the Green Man. DNA from DeeDee, Campbell's and the Green Man's connection in Vietnam, the stuff about what happened to Campbell's political opponent . . ."

"We're going to have proof of that anytime soon?"

"No. It's going to be a bluff. We'll challenge Campbell to take a DNA test. That's our ace. Once we're out there, once DeeDee is out there—I think there's a chance the Green Man will back off. The other thing we'll have is Jim Baker. I think he'll be credible. He's got nothing to gain by coming forward at this point other than a clear conscience. That will come across. Who knows what else will come out when Baker tells his story. Baker can't be the only guy who was in Vietnam in 1971 who knows about Campbell."

"And Baker's willing to do it? You're sure about that?"

"I don't have any doubt," Mars said. "I think he's been waiting for thirty-two years to tell this story in public."

"And our soup can and golden oldie?"

"We'll use everything we've got, Nettie. If Campbell doesn't like it, he can sue us."

Nettie thought it over. "And what you want to ask DeeDee tonight is if she's willing to take the risk and go public."

"Exactly."

They heard Chris and DeeDee come in, Gunner panting ahead of them. Chris went straight into the kitchen to check the pot roast.

"It's starting to rain," he announced, coming into the living room. "And the pot roast is ready."

Gunner sat near Chris at the table. Mars caught a glimpse of Chris's hand moving from his plate to below the table. Then Gunner's head would drop down, popping up again in seconds, his gimlet eyes fixed on Chris in some sort of canine mind-control exercise.

"It's good he gets along with other dogs," DeeDee said. "But he sure doesn't much trust strangers."

"He's protective," Chris said. "And it's like he's got a lot of rules about how people should look. He doesn't like hats and umbrellas and he doesn't like people carrying bags."

"My baseball cap didn't bother him," DeeDee said.

"That's because he knows you. He knows your scent. You can wear a hat, open an umbrella, and carry a bag all at the same time if he's met you once. Then he knows your scent. That's all it takes."

"Pot roast on a summer night," Nettie said. "A neglected pleasure."

Nobody had much to say while they ate. By unspoken agreement, Mars and Nettie didn't want to discuss the case while Chris was around.

Chris started to clear the table, but Mars waved him off. "Call Aunt Gwen. She'll be waiting to hear from you. I'll catch the dishes after Nettie and DeeDee leave."

"I should probably take Gunner out again," Chris said. "I gave him a little bit of pot roast."

Gunner looked sideways at Mars, with exactly the same expression Mars had seen on the faces of partners in crime when one of the partners admits to something the other wanted to keep quiet.

"I'll take him when I walk you down to meet Aunt Gwen. And he can go out again with me when I go out with Nettie and DeeDee."

Gunner had a sixth sense that Chris was leaving. He started worrying about the prospect as soon as Gwen's car pulled up. It took all of Mars's strength to drag Gunner back into the apartment. Once upstairs, Gunner stayed by the front door, pacing and occasionally letting loose a low whine. From time to time he'd walk back into the living room, staring plaintively at Mars.

"Ignore him," Mars said. Then he turned to DeeDee.

"We have two options. Which option we choose is totally up to you."

DeeDee looked taken aback. "Why just me?"

Mars fixed DeeDee with a hard look. "Let me explain the choices. Then I think you'll understand why 'just you.'

"The first choice is that we do nothing. That we walk away from the investigation of your mother's death and that we let people know that's what we've decided to do. That might be the safest option. The person who killed your mother is, for the most part, rational and efficient. He doesn't kill unless he has to. At this point, there's no evidence he even knows you exist . . ."

"*How* can you be sure?"

"This is going to be hard to hear, DeeDee. But you need to hear it, so when you make a choice, you understand the risks . . ."

Mars waited before he went on, wanting to be sure he had DeeDee's attention. When her eyes met his, and held his gaze, he said, "We're pretty sure he doesn't know about you because you've stayed alive for nineteen years."

DeeDee didn't flinch. Then she made a statement that contained a question. "*You* found me."

"Only when we were looking for something else."

DeeDee thought about what Mars had said. "I'll never know for sure, will I? I'll never be sure that if *he's* looking for something else, he won't find me."

Nettie said, "No. You'll never be sure. But how much certainty do we get about anything? Not being sure has a name, DeeDee. It's called life." Nettie let DeeDee think about what she had said before she added, "We can't tell you for sure you'll be safe if this is the choice you make. We can only tell you we think it is the choice that has the least risk. Mars? Do you agree?"

Mars nodded.

DeeDee said, "Okay. Tell me about the second choice."

Mars said, "It's what I started to say at the office. That we protect ourselves by announcing publicly everything we know and everything we suspect about your father and about the man he hired to kill your mother. That we put you front stage and center as your father's daughter. And we hope that by doing that, they'll decide that coming after you will only prove the point that they're guilty. It is kind of like getting a vaccination. You expose yourself to risk and that makes you immune to the risk."

DeeDee looked between Mars and Nettie. "Why is that riskier than doing nothing?"

"Because," Mars said, "there's one thing about the man who killed your mother that worries me. I've said he's rational and efficient and he only kills when he has to. But there's something else about him. The *way* he killed your mother worries me. He didn't attempt to make it look like an accident. He shot her in a public place. That tells me that he's a man who is vengeful and does not tolerate being beaten."

"But why can't you catch him? Then I *could* be sure I'd be safe—" She stopped herself, acknowledging what Nettie had said before. "Not safe from everything. But safe from this man . . ."

"Maybe the best thing about the second choice, DeeDee, is that it would allow us a chance to do just that. But I have to tell you. This is a man with extraordinary resources that could prevent his being caught. I can't promise you that he would be caught. I guess what I'm saying is, I think there's a smaller chance that he will find out about you than there is a chance he could find you if we don't catch him."

DeeDee sat silent for a long time after Mars stopped talking. Finally, she asked the question Mars had been expecting.

"Who are they? My father, and the man he hired. Who are they?"

Nettie and Mars exchanged a glance.

Nettie said, "Your father is Alan Campbell, DeeDee. Minnesota's junior senator."

If DeeDee had any reaction to that news, she kept it to herself. "And the man he hired. The man who killed my mother. Who is that?"

Mars thought about how to answer the question. To this point he hadn't told DeeDee that the Green Man had killed anyone other than her mother. Maybe, he thought, she needs to know the whole story before she makes a choice.

"He's a man of many names," Mars said. "The name we've known him by isn't a name at all. He's called the Green Man."

After Mars had told DeeDee everything he knew about the Green Man, DeeDee said, "I don't understand—all these things he's done—

224

why can't you say you're dropping the investigation about my mother and still find him because of the other things he's done?"

It was a good question, a question to which Mars knew the answer in an implicit way. He wasn't sure he could make a nineteen-year-old girl understand the answer.

"The Green Man, DeeDee, operates in a world most of us can live our lives without knowing it exists. He has connections in government, in the intelligence community, with the military, with foreign drug cartels—I don't begin to know or understand all his connections. There are a lot of things that have made him invincible: powerful people who have a stake in making sure the Green Man is never held accountable for what he's done, his own intelligence and skill, the fact that he's had so many identities . . ."

DeeDee had folded her arms across her middle as Mars talked, hunching her shoulders forward as if preparing to withstand an unseen blow. She said, "That's what I really hate. That he doesn't have a name. He doesn't even seem human without a real name."

She was right. There was a mystique that attached to an unknown malevolent force. Mars expected that the Green Man knew that, too.

"I hadn't thought about it before, but you're right," Nettie said. "He *is* scarier because he doesn't have a real name."

DeeDee said, "I guess I understand why you're saying he's dangerous and that it will be hard to find him. But I still don't understand why that's easier to do if you make this big public announcement about my mother's case."

"Only because I think what we can reveal about your father's and the Green Man's connection is so bad that people who protect him now will disassociate themselves from him. I think going public with what we know, what we suspect, will isolate him. And it will create political pressure to bring in other resources to find him and hold him accountable. We don't begin to have the resources to do this without public support. When people know what he's done, I think that support will come."

Mars didn't say it, but what he also knew was that DeeDee was important to the case not just because she provided a genetic link to Campbell. Almost more important, she put a real face to the Green Man's victims. You can tell people about atrocities that affect millions, but what gives people the gumption to take action is usually a single sympathetic face. If it was a sympathetic face you were looking for, you couldn't do better than this lovely, gentle, but ultimately tough-as-nails, brown-eyed girl.

DeeDee sat perfectly still, avoiding looking at Mars and Nettie. Then she said, "It's just so weird to think that all this is connected to my mother. A teenager working at a convenience store." Another long pause, then she straightened up. "I don't want to live my life not knowing if the Green Man knows about me or not. You know what else? I don't want to live my life knowing that he's still doing this stuff. I'd rather go for it than let him get away.

"And I want to know his real name," DeeDee said, her chin setting, her eyes looking straight on at Mars and Nettie.

It was just after eight-thirty when Mars walked Nettie and DeeDee out to Nettie's car. There was a slow, gentle rain. Nothing that would make driving difficult, just enough to lower the temperature and make the summer night darker, sooner.

Gunner disapproved of Nettie and DeeDee leaving. His hackles raised and he kept up a low, grumbling growl of displeasure. Nettie opened the trunk to take out a jacket, dropping her big leather duffel purse into the trunk. DeeDee put on her jacket, then dropped down, butt on her heels, to give Gunner a hug.

Gunner whined plaintively, trying to convince her to stay.

"He'd want everybody he loves to live in one room, with him, for the rest of our lives," Mars said. Then he was surprised by DeeDee, rising to give Mars a hug. The brim of her baseball cap brushed against Mars's cheek, and she lifted one hand to keep it in place.

"Thank you," DeeDee said. "I can't tell you how much it means to me to finally know something about my family. Both my families. And to know that I've got both of you to help keep me safe."

Mars returned the hug, thinking at that moment he'd like to have a daughter. Provided she could be a clone of DeeDee Kipp.

"I'll be in touch with you as soon as I have a schedule for the press conference," Mars said. "Then we'll bring you down here a couple days ahead of that and put you under protection."

DeeDee nodded without saying anything. She got into Nettie's car, giving Mars a final wave.

Mars did something he'd never done before. He gave Nettie a hug before she got in the car.

"Call me as soon as you're back," he said.

CHAPTER
33

The Green Man was considering what to do if nobody came out of Bahr's condo in the next hour or two.

The kid and dog coming out with DeeDee Kipp earlier had confused him. This wasn't looking like an investigation. It was looking like a family reunion. He'd considered whether to follow them, deciding to stay put. This wasn't the time or place. It was rush hour in downtown Minneapolis. There was no way he'd have a chance to get DeeDee Kipp.

Then there was the dog to be considered. As the kid and Kipp passed near his car, the dog had erupted into a violent display of barking and lunging. In his direction.

There was only one explanation for that. He'd turned the car off when he'd parked, killing the air-conditioning. Instead he had all the windows down. The dog had picked up his scent, recognizing it from the Green Man's foiled attempt to get into Bahr's condo when the Green Man had first come to Minneapolis. As soon as he'd inserted his tool into the lock, he had heard the dog. It would have only been moments before the dog drew others' attention to the Green Man's presence. He could have gone in and dealt with the dog, but doing that would have been evidence someone had been in the apartment. That would have defeated his purpose.

In the end, he had given up on the idea of needing audio surveillance in the condo. It was a labor-intensive way of keeping track of someone. In this case, keeping track of two people in three separate places. Not practical. The GPS vehicle-monitoring system would work and he could manage it working alone.

But this current situation was difficult. He would have given anything to have had audio surveillance in Bahr's apartment now. He had waited anxiously until Kipp came back with the kid, relieved that he'd once again have all three targets in one location. But he still couldn't figure out what was going on with the three of them, and an audio surveillance system would have given him that.

Then Bahr had come down with the kid and the kid had gotten in a car with a woman and left. The dog was with Bahr and picked up the Green Man's scent again. The Green Man broke into a light sweat as he watched the dog struggle against the lead. If Bahr dropped the lead, the Green Man had no doubt the dog would have come straight at him.

The dog didn't get away, and Bahr and the dog went back into the condo.

What now? What if Kipp was going to spend the night in the condo with Bahr and Frisch? Should he spend the night on the street in the car? Should he go back to his base and wait for the GPS monitor to beep?

There was no clear answer. He decided to wait until dark, then reevaluate his choices.

It wasn't quite dark when Bahr, Frisch, and Kipp came out of the condo together. They walked to Frisch's car and after farewells, the two women drove off, leaving Bahr and the damn dog heading back to the condo.

The dog struggled against the lead, pulling himself toward the Green Man's car, even though the Green Man had rolled up the windows when it had started to rain. Whether the dog could still pick up his scent was questionable, but there was no doubt the dog remembered the car.

The Green Man watched until they reentered the condo. Then he turned the ignition in the car and switched on the GPS monitor.

He needed luck. If Frisch and Kipp went back to her apartment, he'd have to get into the apartment and take care of both of them there. Then find a way of getting into Bahr's apartment.

Messy. Very messy.

What would be *close* to ideal would be if Frisch and Kipp were headed back to Mankato. The Green Man had paid close attention to the road between the Twin Cities and Mankato. There was no end of opportunities on that road for him to deal with the two women. *Ideal* would have been if Bahr had been with them and he could have taken care of all three at once. But Bahr didn't worry him much. The women were a priority. DeeDee Kipp and her genetic link to Campbell were a priority. Once the women were taken care of, he could call Bahr, tell him there'd been an accident, and draw him to a location where Bahr would be an easy target.

He had no expectation of disguising the fact that all or any of the three had been murdered. That possibility was long lost. The most he could hope for now was to eliminate all three before what they knew was shared with anyone else. He would leave Frisch and Bahr's bodies, but would remove Kipp's body. And he'd make sure there was nothing left of Kipp's body and its genetic link to Campbell. The most he could hope for now was to get himself out of this situation with as little exposure as possible. If Bahr and Frisch had not disclosed what they knew about DeeDee Kipp, it would be a better outcome than he could have hoped for.

He drove slowly, checking the GPS monitor frequently. Frisch's car was near the intersection of Washington and Fourth Avenue. If Frisch was taking Kipp back to her apartment, she'd cross Fourth Avenue and proceed east. If they were headed to Mankato, she'd turn right on Fourth and follow it to the Interstate 35 south ramp entrance.

He was stopped at a light several blocks behind Frisch when the blip on the monitor turned right and headed south.

He was overdue good luck on this assignment, and he'd just gotten it.

Gunner lunged after the car as Nettie pulled out.

It took physical force and shouting for Mars to get him redirected toward the apartment. Even after they'd gotten into the lobby, Gunner continued to strain against the lead, making low, unhappy noises.

He saw Connie Babb watching him through the glass wall of the office. Mercifully, she looked sullen rather than friendly. It occurred to him that she'd seen him leave with Nettie and had assumed that Mars and Nettie were a couple.

Seeing Connie Babb while he struggled with Gunner ticked something in Mars's brain. Nothing he could hold on to, but something.

Once back upstairs, inside the apartment, Gunner failed to settle down. He stayed by the front door, pacing and drooling.

Mars walked into the hall. "Gunner! Enough." Gunner stared at him with a beseeching expression.

It was then that Mars put two facts together. What Connie Babb had said about a cable service guy coming in with a work order for their apartment. Was that the day Gunner had torn up the carpet in Chris's room?

Mars shook his head. Connie'd been pretty clear about having the wrong unit number. And even if it had been someone trying to get into their apartment, there was no way they were going to get by Gunner.

Except Gunner had been shut in Chris's room. Was it possible someone—hell, not someone—was it possible the Green Man had gotten into the apartment after Danny had done the sweep?

Mars walked into the kitchen and took the phone apart. He wasn't an electronics surveillance expert, but he couldn't find anything that looked out of the ordinary. He walked through the apartment to check the two smoke detectors. He knew from professional experience that listening devices were often positioned near home detection equipment.

Nothing.

He went back into the living room, the sound of Gunner's restless, plaintiff grumbling following him. He shook his head. All their talk about the Green Man, Nettie and DeeDee out on the road alone, and Gunner acting like a maniac had spooked him.

He looked into the kitchen. The dishes he'd promised Chris he'd take care of awaited him.

Mars was halfway through the cleanup when the phone rang. Drying his hands, he looked at the Caller ID screen. At first he didn't recognize the area code. Then he realized it had to be *The Get List*'s producer calling him back.

Without telling the producer why, Mars asked how long it would take *The Get List* to send a production crew to Minneapolis if they had a major break on the case.

"If the story's big enough," the producer said, "we'd charter a plane and have someone there within a matter of hours. Why? You've got something big coming up?"

"Too soon to say," Mars said. "It may be nothing. Just want to be prepared. I'll keep you posted."

"Do me a favor, will you? Keep Campbell's office posted. They've been driving us crazy asking for updates on the investigation. We keep telling them to call you, but they seem to think using us instead of calling you saves taxpayer dollars . . ."

Mars was too stunned to speak. Then he said, "You've been giving them information on the case?"

"Just what we've given you—which wasn't much. The tip sheets. That's been it."

"The tip sheets?" Mars said. "You gave them all the tip sheets you sent us—or just the hot tips."

"They asked for everything we gave you. I don't know exactly, but if we sent you all the tip sheets, I'd guess that's what we sent them . . ."

Mars didn't take time to put Gunner on the leash. He made a quick stop at the hall closet to pick up his service revolver, fumbling at the combination lock on the box in which it was kept. Then the two of them left the apartment at a run.

As he ran, Mars dialed the state patrol on his cell phone. When he reached the duty officer, he identified himself, gave the officer the tag numbers and vehicle description for Nettie's car, and said she was en route between the Twin Cities and Mankato.

"I need a patrol car to pick her up as soon as possible," he said, "and hold her until I arrive. She has a young woman with her. Deandra Kipp. They're being stalked, and I have reason to believe her stalker may be armed."

The officer hesitated for a moment. Mars could hear computer keys clicking. Then the officer said, "She taking Interstate 35 to County 62 to 169 to Mankato? Or is she going Interstate 35 to state road 60 and going west to Mankato that way?"

Mars broke into a sweat. He didn't know. "One-sixty-nine is shorter, right?"

"Definitely. And it's four-lane all the way. State 60 is a two-lane between the freeway and Mankato."

"Look," Mars said. "This is important. Can you get patrols out on both routes?"

"Will do," the officer said. "What can you tell me about the stalker."

"Nothing," Mars said. "I can't tell you anything about the stalker."

CHAPTER
34

The Green Man liked to drive.

He liked the feel of the steering wheel under his large, strong hands. Liked the time the drive gave him to think, to focus—a process enhanced by the clear, intricate sounds of Bach's Goldberg Variations, transcribed for strings, on the car's CD player. He liked the intimacy and solitude of the dark world through which he drove. He even liked the gentle slap of the windshield wipers as they swiped soft rain off the glass.

He liked the sense of perfect control driving gave him. Liked that everything he needed was safely locked in the car's trunk. He liked that, at long last, this mission was back on track.

When things begin to go wrong, there is no end to problems.

That was something experience and observation had taught him. It had taken almost three years after that October night, nineteen years ago, to find Andrea Bergstad. He'd thought then, with considerable satisfaction, that the mission had been accomplished. The furthest thing from his mind had been the possibility that sixteen years later he'd still be trying to tie up loose ends. All because of two teenage girls. As much as anything, that's what bothered him. To have this much trouble—all because of two teenage girls.

And this teenage girl—DeeDee Kipp—potentially more damaging than Andrea Bergstad had been.

He looked at the lighted clock on the dash. He was maybe six or seven cars behind Frisch's car. He'd know when they came to the junction between County 62 and Interstate 35 which route Frisch would take to Mankato. He was guessing 169 rather than staying on 35. He'd stay behind them until they were out of the metropolitan area. Then he'd pass and gain time.

He needed to be five minutes ahead of Frisch's car to carry out his plan. It wouldn't be easy. No matter. Harder was what he liked. Harder required more imagination, more precision, more control. Harder tested the skills he'd been honing all his life.

Frisch passed the cutoff to Interstate 35, continuing west on County 62, just as the Green Man guessed she would. He stayed well behind her, headlights from other cars silhouetting the two women's heads from time to time.

He'd memorized the car's license tag number, knew its color and make. Even without that, the occasional glimpse of Kipp's head in profile, illuminated by passing cars' headlights, the brim of her baseball cap clearly visible, would have been enough.

They drove for another twenty miles before they were well out of the metropolitan area and there were fields on either side of the road. Traffic was sparse. If there was a moon, the rain clouds obscured it.

Damn near perfect conditions. He accelerated, closing the distance between his car and Frisch's. As he passed, he glanced over at them. Neither noticed him. They seemed to be engaged in a deep conversation. At this moment, it pleased him to consider that their conversation might have been about him.

He sped ahead, keeping track on the monitor how much distance was between them. When he judged it to be adequate, he pulled well off the road. Once parked, he got out of the car and walked back to the trunk, from which he lifted a long, narrow, wooden case.

It wasn't possible in the dark to appreciate the craftsmanship of the case—the polished wood, the hand-cut brass fittings—but he knew and loved the case, could feel in its smoothness, its weight, what a fine thing it was.

It had to be fine to be worthy of its contents. With the case open next to him on the car seat, he indulged himself. He allowed himself a moment's light from the flashlight to consider the perfection of the Heckler & Koch PSG-1.

To his mind, the finest sniper rifle ever assembled.

And this particular weapon the finest of the fine. Custom-made for him by a specialist in Frankfurt. A man who loved diamonds and guns the way some men loved—what? He could think of nothing other men loved as much as that man in Frankfurt loved diamonds and guns.

It was perfect for what he needed to do this night. And he would not make the mistake he had made before. Tonight his weapon would be ready, at his side. Tonight the scope would be mounted and in place.

He glanced at the monitor. Frisch's car was now approximately three minutes behind him . . .

His glance froze on the monitor screen: a blip was moving across the screen, coming down Interstate 35, maybe thirty minutes away. Bahr was on the move. His first reaction was panic. His second reaction was that having Bahr show up wasn't bad. He could take care of Frisch and Kipp before Bahr showed up, then wait for Bahr. Not only wasn't that bad, it was good. He just needed to be sure he was ready when Bahr showed up.

He lifted the weapon from the soft felt of its case. He fitted the Hensoldt 6 × 42 infrared scope, complete with an LED-enhanced manual reticle, onto the barrel in complete darkness, using his hands like a blind man. The scope-mounted activator would produce a red dot on his target for thirty seconds.

A cheat, in his terms, but tonight was not the night for bravado. Tonight he needed certainty.

The last thing he did was to load the five hard-point .308 cartridges into the box magazine.

Then he checked his watch and the GPS monitor.

Frisch was ninety seconds away. Bahr was now on County 62. He was taking their same route.

The Green Man got out of the car and moved into position. Just in front of the right front headlight. The late hour and the rain were a godsend. No one would stop to offer aid at this time, in this weather.

He'd kneel for the first shot, then stand for the next two shots.

As other cars passed, he lifted the H&K to his shoulder, fitting the reticle into his eye socket. He checked the license tag numbers through the scope. Two cars passed before the scope picked up the numbers he was waiting for.

He dropped his sights down.

Then, holding his breath, he touched the trigger. A small red dot appeared on the left rear tire. He squeezed the trigger.

The report of the shot was simultaneous with the swerve of Nettie Frisch's car. It had sounded as he knew it would: like a tire blowout.

He waited, crouched down, waiting for them to come out of the car.

He waited.

They didn't get out.

The two things happened almost simultaneously.

The steering wheel froze in Nettie's hands at the same time she heard the loud, cracking sound.

"Oh, my God," Nettie said as she struggled to pull the car over to the side of the road. "A blowout on a night like this—after the day we've had."

With the car idling, listing slightly to the left, telling her it was one of the driver's side tires that had blown, she considered what to do next. She had just released her seat belt, telling DeeDee to stay in the car, when the image came into her mind.

A scene from *The Godfather II*. Michael Corleone standing at his bedroom window. His wife lying in bed, watching him.

"Michael? Why are the drapes open?"

Nettie dropped down on her side, pulling DeeDee down with her, at the same moment in her memory of *The Godfather II* that Michael Corleone had fallen to the bedroom floor, bullets shattering the windows above him, exploding through the room.

"Nettie! What?" DeeDee said.

"This might be crazy," Nettie said, "but do you remember when Mars told you about the other woman the Green Man killed? Your mother's friend?"

DeeDee didn't answer, but Nettie felt her nod.

"She was driving at night and had a flat tire. When she got out of the car, he shot her. Then he threw her body in front of a passing car. Everybody thought it was an accident . . ."

"And you think the Green Man shot out our tire?"

Hearing DeeDee say it made Nettie realize how crazy the idea was.

"Probably not," Nettie said. "I'm probably just spooked because we spent so much time talking about him tonight." Still, she hesitated.

"Stay down. I'm going to try to look back through the side-view mirror and see if anything's behind us."

She twisted on the seat, raising herself high enough to glimpse the side-view mirror, but keeping her head below the seat back. At first she couldn't see anything. Then a passing car's headlights illuminated the mirror, backlighting a silhouetted figure standing next to a car parked maybe a hundred feet behind.

She dropped again. Was it her imagination?

Or had the figure been moving toward her?

"I'm going to call Mars," Nettie said, wondering where her purse was, then remembering she'd dropped it in the trunk.

"Shit!"

"What?" DeeDee said.

"You don't have a cell phone, right?"

DeeDee shook her head. "Can't afford one. You don't have yours?"

"It's in my purse," Nettie said. "In the trunk."

"You want me to go back and get it?"

"No!" Nettie said, raising her voice for the first time. "Stay down."

"You still think somebody may be back there?"

"Maybe," Nettie said, wondering if it was possible that their lives could now be at risk for as trivial a reason as that she had put her purse in the trunk instead of next to her. She knew it was. You didn't work homicide investigations for as long as she had without knowing how haphazard death could be.

She realized something else. That the other car parked behind them would make passing cars think that they were helping each other. No one else would stop. Not at night, not when it was raining.

She raised her head again, waiting for headlights to brighten the side-view mirror.

238

This time she was sure. The figure was closer. And it was carrying something that looked like a rifle.

He'd waited long enough. He'd only used this strategy twice before. But both times the driver had gotten out of the car to check the tire within seconds of coming to a stop. Then something occurred to him. It had been years since he'd used this tactic, long before cell phones. Frisch could be on her cell phone, calling for help.

He shook his head in frustration. Frustration with himself. He was getting too old for fieldwork. How could he have been so stupid as not to consider that Frisch would use a cell phone?

He needed to know what was going on in the car before he did anything.

"DeeDee," Nettie said, whispering now. "Don't say anything, don't ask anything. Just do what I tell you. Give me your hat, then we've got to change places. As soon as you're on the driver's seat—stay down as much as you can—turn the car on, but not the lights. Then, accelerate—I mean, *floor it!* Drive through that fence, into the cornfield. As soon as we're into the cornfield, get out of the car and run parallel to the road, staying in the cornrows. Don't stop running until you get to the end of the field, then try to get back to the road as soon as you see a car coming that has more than one person in it . . ."

DeeDee started to cry. "He's back there, isn't he? The Green Man . . ."

"He might be. We can't take a chance it's not him—DeeDee—did you hear what I told you to do?"

DeeDee shook her head. "I can't. I don't want to leave you. I don't want to be out there in the dark, alone, with him . . ."

Nettie grabbed DeeDee's head between her hands and pulled DeeDee's face next to hers. "Damn it, DeeDee. Nineteen years ago your mother ran from this guy. It was cold, she was pregnant, she had no place to go, but she ran. She ran for you, DeeDee. And she made it. You owe it to her to make it now . . ."

DeeDee drew a deep breath, stifling her sobs. "But you . . ." she said.

239

Nettie pushed DeeDee away from her. "Do it, DeeDee. Now!"

DeeDee did it. The car roared off the shoulder, lurching on its flat tire, crashing through a wire fence, then landing five or six rows into the cornfield.

Nettie looked over at DeeDee and screamed at her.

"Run, DeeDee. *Run!*"

Nettie waited until DeeDee was out of the car and had disappeared into the cornfield. She waited until she heard the sound of someone coming through the field.

Then Nettie got out of the car. She pulled the brim of DeeDee's baseball cap down firmly. She ran in the opposite direction from DeeDee.

If the Green Man had any doubts about what Frisch knew about him, the doubts were dispelled when he saw her car career off the road into the cornfield. In that moment he knew that the hex that had plagued him over the past nineteen years was still in place.

"Damn!" he said under his breath as he ran after the car, into the field. "I will *not* be beaten by another teenage girl."

He followed the swath the car had cut through the rows of corn to where it sat, the driver side door open, the driver's seat empty.

But on the other side of the car, he saw a figure moving away from the car, deeper into the field.

The figure wore a baseball cap.

"I will not *be beaten by another goddamn teenage girl,"* he said as if chanting a mantra.

He tracked her through the field, but she was darting sideways, dropping down, then rising again, moving in another direction. She had an advantage in that all she had to do was run. He had to stop repeatedly to search for her through the infrared scope. Meanwhile, Frisch was God knew where. It was almost a half hour since he'd left the car to take his position. Bahr could show up at any moment.

He was beginning to think Frisch should have been his first target. Following Kipp was an emotional choice.

I will not be beaten by another goddamn teenager.

He heard a crash ahead of him. She had fallen. He had to move fast to make up the distance between them before she lost him again.

He lifted his rifle to his shoulder, fitted the scope into his right eye, then swung the rifle back and forth in the direction of the noise. He saw the figure rise from the ground, off balance, before it moved again. When the sight fixed on the back of the figure's head, just below the cap, he gave a light squeeze on the trigger.

The red dot lit.

CHAPTER

35

Mars slapped the magnetic flasher on the dash. Once on Interstate 35, his speedometer registered eighty-five miles per hour. He held his cell phone in one hand, punching Nettie's cell phone number as he drove. There was no answer. That worried him until he remembered that Nettie had tossed her purse into the trunk.

Gunner sat in the backseat, oddly calm. It was pretty obvious that in Gunner's mind, Mars was finally doing what needed to be done.

Mars had just turned onto Highway 169 when his cell phone rang. A state patrol dispatcher said, "Just wanted you to know we've completed a patrol on Interstate 35 to State 60. No vehicle matching your description there. We're going to go north from Mankato on 169 and see what turns up . . ."

Mars struggled to keep his voice level. "It would have been better if you'd covered 169 first, driving south—I'm pretty sure that's the route they'd be taking. Don't you have two patrols you can get out on this?"

"Sorry. We're doing the best we can. We're down three patrol cars in this district since the budget cuts. I had to assign a vehicle based on where we had a patrol available . . ."

"Thanks," Mars said. "I appreciate the help. But the sooner you can have a patrol on 169 South, the better."

Mars calculated that based on his speed, he'd be catching Nettie within the next ten miles. When he came within range of where he expected to see her car, he slowed, not wanting to miss anything, and tracking milepost signings in case he needed to call for help.

He noticed the empty car pulled well over on the shoulder just beyond milepost 74. It wasn't Nettie's car, but Mars slowed, pushing the remote to open the rain-streaked window on the passenger side to get a good look.

As soon as the window went down, Gunner went wild. He threw himself against the door, then leapt over the seat and tried to go out the open window. Mars grabbed him just in time. He struggled to hold on to the dog while getting the window back up. Gunner pawed against the window, looking back at Mars in desperation.

"Gunner! No!" Mars said. But he wasn't prepared to ignore the dog's anxiety. Gunner had been right more times than Mars on this case. Mars looked at the car again. The memory came back to him immediately. Standing in the parking lot behind the office. The car waiting for DeeDee's friend, the driver pulling the visor down when Mars looked back at him—even though the sun was behind the driver.

"Gunner. Stay," Mars said, reaching over to the glove compartment to take out his service revolver. Gunner let out a howl as Mars squeezed out the car door, using the door as a shield against Gunner's pressure. Mars went to the trunk, got out a flashlight, then approached the abandoned car. He held the flash against the car's windows, first flashing over the front seat, then the backseat.

On the floor in the back was a wooden gun case.

Behind him, he could hear Gunner tearing at the inside of the car. He went back and let the dog out. Before he could get hold of Gunner, the dog was gone, racing in leaps toward the cornfield.

It was as Gunner disappeared into the field that Mars heard the sound of the rifle firing. Instinctively he yelled.

"Nettie!"

There was no answer. But at the far end of the field, near the road, a figure scrambled out from under the fence. Mars's flashlight wasn't strong enough to illuminate the figure, but he heard the heavy, emotional breathing as the figure ran toward him. Whoever it was, they were trying to gather breath to call out.

"DeeDee?" He recognized her at the same moment another figure emerged from the field, coming between Mars and DeeDee. The figure carried a rifle, raised to his shoulder. Mars released the safety on his revolver, meeting the rifle's aim.

He couldn't have fired if he'd wanted to. DeeDee was in a direct line behind the Green Man. If Mars's shot missed the Green Man, it could hit DeeDee. Even if he hit the Green Man, the shot could pass through the first target and hit DeeDee.

The best thing he could do was to warn DeeDee to drop, then try to draw the Green Man's fire away from her, hoping he'd have time to get off a shot.

He didn't have time to do that. Before either of them could get off a shot, Gunner came at the Green Man with a force that knocked him off his feet, the rifle flying in the air in DeeDee's direction.

"The rifle, DeeDee, get the rifle," Mars shouted as he ran toward the Green Man. The Green Man had struggled to his feet, trying to get back to the road, Gunner's teeth gripped on a leg.

"Halt!" Mars shouted, taking a firing position. "Halt, police!" Mars shouted again.

The Green Man turned toward him for a fraction of a second. Irrationally, Mars thought how ordinary he looked. Then he pulled the revolver trigger.

It was the first shot he'd fired with his revolver since he'd been a patrolman in uniform. It went home to its target with deadly precision.

It was enough to make you believe in God.

The state patrol car showed up within moments after the Green Man dropped. Mars had already called in for backup and a search helicopter. All DeeDee could tell him was that Nettie had left the car after her.

It was, of course, Gunner who led Mars to where Nettie was lying. She was facedown, DeeDee's baseball cap pushed back, half off her head. The brutal wound at the base of her skull had bled down her back, around the side of her neck, staining her white shirt.

Mars had seen more dead bodies than he cared to count. He always knew on sight if a victim was alive or dead. This time his sixth sense failed him. It wasn't possible Nettie was dead. He dropped down beside her, saying her name over and over, his hand searching along her neck for a pulse. He pulled her over, looking away as soon as he saw her expressionless eyes.

Gunner was lying on the ground beside Nettie, his head between his paws, his eyes darting back and forth. Guilt and grief behind his eyes. He had failed someone he loved. Anyone who doubted that dogs shared human emotions had only to see Gunner at this moment to know how wrong they were.

A state patrolman came up behind him, putting a hand on Mars's shoulder. "We've got an ambulance on the way," he said softly. No urgency in his voice. He knew without touching the body that there was no hurry. "They'll bring a gurney out here to take her in."

Mars shook his head, sliding his arms under Nettie's body. He lifted her from the ground, shifting her once to bring her head onto his shoulder.

"No," he said. "I need to do this."

She was dead weight in his arms.

DeeDee Kipp stood on the shoulder of Highway 169, held back by a state trooper, staring out at the cornfield that was all but invisible in the dark.

"It would just complicate things to have you out there," the officer said.

There were now a half dozen state patrol troopers at what their crackling two-way radios—audible from open car doors, their voices speaking into cell phones that never left their ears—described as "the scene." Four officers had gone into the field, guns drawn, huge-headed flashlights following the swath cut through the field where DeeDee had driven Nettie's car through the fence. An ambulance was parked near the patrol cars, its back doors open, the bright interior lights shining out.

The Green Man was already in the ambulance, encased in a black body bag.

Two paramedics stood next to the truck, a wheeled gurney between them, waiting for a signal from the troopers that they were needed in the field.

At first distant, then suddenly directly overhead, came the *thunk-whack-whack-putter* sound of a helicopter.

DeeDee Kipp had been raised in a fundamentalist Christian home. To her, the searchlight shining down from the copter had a sanctifying, spiritual impact on the scene. The light, blurred at the edges by the soft rain, confirmed her hopes. Her hopes that at any minute, Mars and Nettie would walk out of the field. Her hopes that the crack of the rifle she had heard did not mean what it might mean.

The copter swung back and forth over the field, then circled and held position. After what could have been seconds or minutes, it rotated its position and headed slowly back to the road, as if lighting a path between the field and the highway.

The trooper's grip on DeeDee's shoulder tightened, confirming what they both expected next. DeeDee could see the corn stalks moving under the copter's searchlight. Then she saw Mars, carrying Nettie, her head on his shoulder.

She closed her eyes in relief. When she opened them again, a hard slap of fear swept over her. One of the troopers had raised his hand toward the waiting paramedics.

The raised hand was a signal. The hand's thumb was turned down.

CHAPTER
36

Mars waited in his car outside Nettie's sister's house.

He had to do this now for all kinds of reasons. Because Val had to be the first to know. Because it was possible the media would show up. Because Mars needed to tell Val himself, now, while he was still numb. He had to tell Val about Nettie before he believed what he was saying was real.

He watched the house for over three hours until, just after four o'clock in the morning, a light went on in an upstairs window. It was a high, small, shuttered window. Probably a bathroom window.

Mars could see motion behind the partially closed shutter slats. Then, improbably, one side of the shutter opened, and Val looked out.

Maybe to check the weather. Maybe because the emotion that had filled the night had reached her. She was looking out the window to try to understand why she felt the way she did. Why she'd wakened at four feeling worried.

She started to close the shutter again, then stopped. Mars saw her see his car, saw her peer more closely. Then she closed the shutter and turned out the bathroom light. He tracked her progress by lights being lit as she left the bathroom, came downstairs, turned on the hall light, then turned on the porch light.

When the porch light came on, Mars got out of the car and started toward the house.

Val opened the front door, holding the door with one hand, clutching her robe closed over her chest with the other. She squinted at him, still not sure she was seeing what she thought she was seeing.

"*Mars?* What in heaven's name . . ."

Then she pulled back, suddenly knowing what it meant that he was there, alone at night.

Her words were soft at first—"*Oh, my God, no. No. Oh, God, no*"—then she came at Mars, screaming, her fists pounding against his chest.

"It's your fault," she screamed. "It's your fault. Why did you get her into this . . ."

Val's husband Roy came down the stairs, barefooted, in his shorts, grabbing his wife, trying to understand, looking at Mars, then at Val.

"It's Nettie," Mars said. "She was killed last night . . ."

Tears filled Roy's eyes, and he pulled Val closer. He nodded at Mars. "Maybe you should go right now. I'll call you in an hour or so . . ."

"It's his fault," Val wailed. "It's his fault."

Roy shook his head looking at Mars. "She doesn't mean it," he said, "it's just such a shock."

But Val hadn't said anything Mars didn't believe himself.

When Chris came back at eight-thirty, Gunner wasn't at the door to greet him.

He walked into the living room where his dad was on the couch. Awake, but silent. Gunner was lying at Mars's feet. He didn't move.

"Dad?" Chris said. "What's happened? What's wrong? Why isn't Gunner . . ."

Chris dropped down to his knees and took Gunner's head between his arms. He looked up at Mars.

"Is it Nettie?"

Roy and Val came over shortly before noon.

By then Val was subdued, contrite when she looked at Mars.

"I'm sorry," she said. "About what I said before . . ."

Mars said, "It was nothing more than the truth, Val. Nothing that I haven't been saying to myself."

Val got angry. "No! I won't have you say that. It wasn't wrong for me to say it because it was rude. It was wrong for me to say it because it wasn't—it isn't—true. It was disrespectful of Nettie for me to say it. Nettie didn't do what she did because of you, Mars. She did what she did because she loved her work, because she was good at it, because she wanted to do it. To say anything else is to disrespect who she was.

"And something else," Val said, starting to cry again. "She was grateful to you, Mars. Grateful you gave her the chance to do what she did."

Val had meant telling Mars that last bit to comfort him. It didn't. It made him feel worse. He turned away from her.

Roy said, "We want to talk to you about the funeral."

His back to them, Mars closed his eyes. *Funeral.*

"I don't want one of those processions with police cars lined up for miles, with flashers going," Val said. "It will just make me think about how she died . . ."

Mars still couldn't face them, still couldn't open his eyes. Everything they said, every image their words conjured up, caused so much pain he couldn't draw a breath.

"And we're wondering if there's someone who can help us with the media," Roy said. "We're already getting calls. From all over, not just local . . ."

Mars forced himself to draw a deep breath, then turned toward them. "Of course," he said. "I'll take care of that. And the funeral, if you want me to do that . . ."

Val shook her head. "No. If you could let us know who should be invited. Her colleagues. We'll take care of family. We want the service to be private, otherwise we'll be overrun with media."

"I'll get you a list," Mars said.

The morning of the funeral, Mars looked out an apartment window toward City Hall. As he stood there, he saw the flag on the Hall's tower being lowered. He turned from the window, lowering the blinds. Then he moved the metal shelving from the living room, standing the shelves in front of the window. There would be snow on the ground before he opened the blinds again.

* * *

Everybody that mattered came.

John Turner came from San Diego. His wife was ill, so he wasn't able to stay. But Turner being there was the first balm on Mars's soul since Nettie had died.

The mayor came, the Hennepin County medical examiner, representatives from the local FBI office, Danny Borg, and their colleagues from the BCA's Cold Case Unit. Each of the five states Nettie had worked with on the Integrated Information project sent staff. The governor's office had requested details regarding the funeral and had been told the service was private.

"He just wants to get attention," Val said.

Mars, Chris, DeeDee Kipp, Boyle Keegan, and Karen Pogue went together. Mars had hesitated about inviting Karen, but not to have invited her would have been cruel. Nettie had never been cruel—not with anybody, not about anything. And whatever her personal feelings had been about Karen, Nettie had respected Karen professionally.

There was one other presence at the funeral. Gunner attended. Gunner's coming had been Chris's idea, and it had felt right to everybody.

"There were two heroes in that field that night," Mars said. "Nettie and Gunner. He deserves to be there."

And because the story of Nettie's death was the story of two heroes—a beautiful young woman and a courageous dog—that involved decades of wrongdoing by people in high places and people who operated behind the wizard's screen, media coverage was beyond anything Mars had seen before. Nettie was profiled in the local press, on cable television, on the BBC World News—there was seemingly no end to it.

Mars thought that he'd gotten it across to local law enforcement that Val didn't want a police presence at the funeral. But as they drove from the church to the cemetery where Nettie's ashes would be interred, police squad cars lined either side of the road. They were there from all five states, their flashers off, but they were there.

Mars hoped Val didn't mind. Somehow it felt right to him. The motionless cars, flashers dark. It just felt right.

As they left the interment ceremony, Val stopped Mars. She put a small glass vial in his hands, closed her hands around his, stood on tiptoes to kiss his cheek, then returned to her family.

Mars didn't have to look at what she'd put in his hands to know what it was.

Who it was.

Boyle and Karen went back to the apartment with Mars, Chris, and Gunner.

Karen was quiet, Boyle was bereft. "I should have locked you both up," he said. "I should have arranged for federal protection . . ."

"Don't," Mars said. "I can't think about all the things *I* should have done to keep this from happening."

"Give me something to do," Boyle said. "Something that Nettie would have wanted. Anything."

Mars thought about DeeDee Kipp. About the one thing she had asked him for before Nettie had died. That she had asked him about again at the church.

"Nettie put her life on the line to save DeeDee Kipp," Mars said. "Something that would mean a lot to DeeDee Kipp would be knowing the Green Man's real name."

Karen said, "What an odd thing to ask. Why would she care?"

Mars—the foster child in Mars—understood perfectly why DeeDee Kipp cared about the Green Man's real name.

"DeeDee Kipp's life has been a mystery. Now she knows everything except the name of the person who killed her mother. Knowing that would give her a word I've never liked. Giving DeeDee the Green Man's name would give her closure."

CHAPTER

37

At the end of the day, it was a single piece of paper that made the link between Alan Campbell, the Green Man, and the deaths of Campbell's political opponent, Andrea Bergstad, and Erin Moser.

It was the tip sheet found in a briefcase in the Green Man's car.

One of 1,133 tips sent in.

A tip sheet that included Alan Campbell's and the Green Man's fingerprints.

All the evidence in the case came to bear when Alan Campbell was charged. Even the Campbell's soup can and the golden oldie.

For Mars, the moment at which something like real justice came about was the day Alan Campbell was in court to be charged. Mars and DeeDee Kipp were sitting one row away from the rail that separated the spectators from the defense table. As Campbell was led into the courtroom from a side door, he saw DeeDee. He balked, changed color, his jaw loose.

The photo on the front page of the two local papers the next morning had been shot from behind DeeDee's profile, Campbell's stunned face behind her profile. At that moment, Campbell had to have believed that what he was seeing was Andrea Bergstad, risen from the grave.

And as is often the case when things start to go wrong, things only got worse for Alan Campbell.

Jim Baker went public and told his story of what had happened in the Khe Ranh Valley in 1971. He was backed up by the Marine he'd left for dead. A Marine who had followed Baker's, Godfrey's, and Campbell's path, and who had witnessed, from the opposite side of the village, what Jim Baker had seen. He had, in fact, seen more than Baker, because he had not left the protection of the jungle until Campbell and the Green Man had left. He had seen Alan Campbell shoot Vietnamese women and children without provocation. He had stayed there, hidden in the jungle, for almost twelve hours before he'd gotten up his courage to return to base camp. When Jim Baker had seen him, this witness had remained silent—not out of anger at being left behind for dead—but out of shame for what he'd seen.

Mars and Chris lived in a hollow, unreal world in the days that followed Nettie's funeral. They didn't leave the apartment except to walk dogs. Mars sent in all his case reports from Chris's computer. Colleagues from the CCU came to the apartment to talk through what needed to be done. They asked as little of Mars as was possible. And they all cried as they tried to tell Mars how much they cared about Nettie. About how much they respected her professionally. About how hard she would be to replace.

The director of the CCU came after the others.

"Take the time you need. You've got almost enough leave banked to take you to retirement, anyway," he said, trying to make a joke.

"I can't go back to the office," Mars said.

"I can understand that. You don't have to. We're moving into our new building next week. There's space for you there. I'll send people over to close out the office. You don't need to go back there. Think about it. Don't decide anything right now."

That was where they left it.

Chris didn't cry during the day. But Mars could hear his sobs at night. What bothered Mars as much as anything was that in the space of less than a year, Chris had lost the three most significant women in his life. Evelyn had left, his mother had moved to Cleveland, and now Nettie. Mars hadn't thought much about how big a part of Chris's life Nettie had been, he'd taken that for granted, just like he'd taken for granted how big a part of *his* life Nettie had been. Now it was impossible to ignore the fact of how important Nettie had been to each of them.

One night, when Chris's crying had gone on longer than usual, Mars opened the door to look in. Chris was completely under the covers, his head under a pillow. Gunner's head was on the pillow, his eyes open wide with worry. He looked at Mars for only a moment before he looked away. Still guilty, still grieving.

None of them were anything like they'd been before.

The only person who didn't cry was Mars. He was still numb. He was too afraid of what would happen to him if he were to let his emotions break through. The pain was on his brain like a vise. Every time Mars saw something, thought of something, heard something that reminded him of Nettie, the vise tightened and the pain became unbearable.

All he could do was stay with Chris and Gunner. And hold on to he knew not what, he knew not how.

Almost two weeks after Boyle had returned to Washington, he called Mars.

"I know it's late," he said, "but I'm guessing you're not sleeping much, anyway."

"Spot on," Mars said.

"Virgil Musch," Boyle said.

"What?"

"Virgil Musch. The Green Man's name was Virgil Musch."

"Jesus."

"I've had two people working full-time since I got back. They started with his records when he joined the service in 1967, then traced backward. Turned up more than eleven aliases before they got to Virgil Musch. Virgil grew up in a small town in the Texas Panhandle, only child of an unwed mother. I've even got his high school records. A school counselor's report describes him as a social isolate—listen to this. *'In a school district survey that asked high school students in four schools to name their three best friends, only five of the seven hundred fifty-seven students participating in the survey failed to be identified as a "best friend." Virgil Musch is the only one of the five who exhibits no anxiety regarding his lack of normal social relationships.' "*

Boyle made a guffawing noise. "Is that our man, or what?"

Mars stood silent after he hung up. Then he walked over to the table where the vial containing Nettie's ashes had been since the funeral.

He picked it up, holding it tight in his hand.

Behind him, he heard Nettie's voice, in bell-clear tones.

"Virgil Musch! A name like that, what else are you going to be but a nut?"

Mars spun around. There was nothing there. A chill ran through him. It wasn't that he'd *thought* about what Nettie would say on hearing the Green Man's name and then imagined those words. It *had been* Nettie saying the words.

He didn't turn the light off when he left the living room to go to bed.

The next morning, Gunner bounded from Chris's room as Chris got up. It was the first time since the night in the cornfield that Gunner had been anything like his old self.

But Chris was even quieter than usual at breakfast. He barely touched his food.

Mars said, "You okay?"

Chris nodded. Then he said, "Dad—something weird happened last night."

The chill Mars had felt on hearing Nettie's voice the night before ran down his spine again.

"I woke up, because it felt like someone was on the bed. And then I saw Nettie. She was sitting on the edge of the bed." Chris stopped, anticipating that Mars wasn't going to believe him. "I mean, really, Dad. I wasn't dreaming. I know I wasn't. And then she took Gunner's head in her hands—you know, the way she always did—and she kissed the top of his head. She said, 'Such a brave dog.' I mean it, Dad. I heard her, I really did, and it wasn't a dream or anything."

He stopped. "It was real, I mean it, she was there."

255

CHAPTER
38

It was the last week before Chris went back to school. They'd twice delayed Chris's planned visit to his maternal grandparents' farm because neither of them was ready to be separated.

Now, after Nettie's nighttime visit, Mars, Chris, and Gunner were all doing better. So Mars arranged to drive Chris and Gunner down to the farm. Denise's sister Gwen would bring Chris back a couple days before school started.

For Mars, the trip meant he could no longer avoid going back to Redstone Township. He should have gone down immediately after Nettie had been killed and the media started carrying stories about the Green Man's involvement in Andrea Bergstad's and Erin Moser's deaths. He hadn't wanted Sig Sampson to find out about Erin Moser's death by reading a newspaper, but that's what had happened.

Mars didn't completely understand why it was so hard for him to go back to Redstone until after he'd dropped Chris and Gunner at the farm. As soon as he was on the route he'd taken on his first drive to Redstone, the agonizing sense of opportunities missed, of mistakes made, engulfed him.

"I should have come right away," Mars said as he climbed the front steps to Sig's house, Sig holding the screen door open for him. "I didn't want you to find out about Erin Moser in the newspaper. But after what happened—I was crazy . . ."

He looked at Sig. "I'm still crazy."

They went back to Sig's den. It was, as ever, dim, and the air conditioner was still dripping into the coffee can. More than anything, Mars wanted this to be the day he'd first sat in this room, hearing the soft plinks of the dripping air conditioner. He wanted to be able to start the case over, avoiding all the mistakes he'd made.

Or, at least, avoid one of the mistakes he had made. Was that asking so much? To be able to go back over a case where hundreds of decisions had been made and undo one?

Sig said, "I told you the first time you came. I wasn't up to this case. It was me being incompetent that caused all this trouble in the first place."

Mars said, "Believe me, Sig, any mistake you made, it pales next to the mistakes I made on this case. Starting with my holy crusade to prove there was a sexual predator out there taking advantage of lax security at convenience stores."

Sig shook his head. "You've got to remember, Mars. DeeDee Kipp is alive because of what you did. Everyone else—hard-hearted as it is to say it—everyone else who died made a choice that took them where they went. Andrea got involved with Campbell. Erin chose not to tell us what she knew. Nettie was doing a job—from what you've said, a job she loved doing.

"DeeDee was the innocent one. And she's still alive."

Mars looked over at Sig. "You're a lot tougher character than I've given you credit for. But you're wrong about DeeDee."

"Wrong how?" Sig said.

"What I did put DeeDee at risk. If we'd never started this investigation, Nettie would still be alive and DeeDee wouldn't have been at risk."

Sig shook his head again. "From everything you've told me about that young lady, as soon as she was able, she would have set off on her own to find out about her family. And she would have walked right into the Green Man's maw. Without ever knowing what had hit her or why."

Mars knew Sig was right, but he wasn't ready to let go of his guilt on that point. He changed the subject.

"There's something else I want you to know. Something that hasn't been in the media since we got the Green Man. There were things I didn't tell you because I didn't think you needed to know them. Things that may never be known. About what he did when he wasn't working for Alan Campbell. Things I thought might put you at risk to know . . ."

Sig said, looking at Mars straight on, "Like what?"

Mars told Sig the story Boyle Keegan had told him. The story of the three hunts.

When he stopped talking, Sig stared.

Then he said, "Have you ever heard that business about a butterfly's wings that move in one place setting off a hurricane someplace a thousand miles away?"

Mars nodded, understanding Sig's point before he made it.

"Chaos theory," he said softly, more to himself than to Sig.

Then, turning toward Sig, he said, "Funny you should say that. When my friend first told me the story of the three hunts, he said chaos—chaos in the intelligence community—was what gave rise to this whole thing."

"That's what this feels like to me," Sig said. "The smallest thing having connections no one in their right mind could anticipate."

He shook his head slowly. "So how do we know what happens?"

"What happens?" Mars said.

"Say next month, the administration announces it's captured Osama. That means your friend was wrong? There was only the one hunt? The official hunt?"

Mars said, "I can tell you what my friend told me. If the capture is announced anytime before the summer of 2004, the hunt to prevent using the capture for political purposes succeeded. And that they traded their capture prize for something big. Something more important to them than embarrassing the administration."

"And if Osama's capture is announced right before the election, say, next summer, into the fall, the Green Man got his job done before he died in that cornfield?"

"That would be my friend's best guess."

"And if the election comes and goes, with no capture . . ."

"As much as it would pain you and me to hear it, my friend would say the Green Man died too soon."

"You don't feel that way, do you?" Sig said.

Mars shook his head. "That's an impossible question for me to answer. I can't separate the Green Man's death from Nettie's death."

They were quiet for a while, both of them thinking about those possibilities.

"So you're saying people like the Green Man should be left to do whatever? That finding justice for the dead isn't important?"

Mars didn't answer for a long time.

"Let's just say justice is less clear to me now than it was when I started on this case. Ask me if finding Andrea Bergstad's killer was more important than Nettie's life. The answer is no. I don't even have to think about it. The answer is no."

"You're saying you want to be God, Mars. You're saying you want to be in charge of the questions and answers. We don't get that. Not in this life."

"That's the same thing you want, Sig."

Sig rocked a little on his recliner. His lower lip protruding slightly as he thought about what Mars had said.

"Well, maybe that's something we both need to work on. It's not going to happen right off, but maybe sometime."

Then he said, "But you were right, you know. About what happened to Andrea in the first place. She might still be alive—they might all still be alive—Andrea, Erin, your partner Nettie—if Andrea hadn't been working alone at the One-Stop in 1984.

"You weren't wrong about that."

It was just before midnight when Mars drove into the condominium's parking garage. His slamming car door boomed in the deserted, high-ceilinged space, his footsteps echoed as he walked across the concrete floor. Then, sound and space closed in around him as he entered the hallway off the garage and took the elevator up to the apartment.

It was the first time since Nettie had died that he'd been alone in the apartment.

"I should have left a light on," he said into the dark emptiness. In the next moment, he was just as glad he hadn't. Seeing the walls around him would have brought on a fresh wave of the claustrophobia that had plagued him since Nettie died.

Instead, he felt his way through the shapeless dark, found the latch on the sliding door to the terrace.

He stood on the terrace for more than an hour, comforted by the muffled sounds of the city at night, the occasional car passing on the street below.

To the north, he saw a light on in the window of a condominium near the river. Light surrounded by a darkness that reminds you of how isolated you are.

Probably like the One-Stop had looked that night nineteen years ago.